...e watcher on the Cliff

From the reviewers:

Mary Tant carries the narrative forward almost entirely in dialogue and the style suited this country-house murder mystery perfectly. There were plenty of red herrings among the clues as to who had carried out a brutal attack... and plenty of motives too. Of course, it's up to the family to sort it all out...

Strong distinct characters, a delightful setting and further books to follow make this a winner...   *Stow Times*

...an intriguing tale about familial relationships and friendships with an idyllic pastoral setting and skilfully drawn characters.   *Miriam Reeves*

Mary Tant in her first Christie-style classic murder mystery gathers a small group of polite characters in a rundown Tudor mansion and ruined Cistercian priory in the West Country. It has been owned by the Rossington family for generations ... in the Christie tradition, murder ensues, followed by a tense denouement   *Oxford Times*

✶✶✶✶✶ rating – One to watch. This is very reminiscent of Agatha Christie with its West-of-England country house setting. A good plot, very good dialogue and the first of a series. I can envisage it adapting well to the small screen...

...o.uk

First published 2011 by
Threshold Press Ltd, Norfolk House
75 Bartholomew Street, Newbury
Berks RG14 5DU
Phone 01635-230272 and fax 01635-44804
email: publish@threshold-press.co.uk
www.threshold-press.co.uk

British Library Cataloguing in Publication Data
A catalogue record for this book is available from the British Library

ISBN 978-1-903152-27-0

Designed by Jim Weaver Design
Printed in Great Britain by the MPG Biddles, King's Lynn

MARY TANT

The Watcher on the Cliff

Threshold Press

FOR TIRN,
WHO HAS SAT BESIDE ME
ON MANY CORNISH CLIFFS
LOOKING OUT TO SEA

ONE

Lucy Rossington squeezed past a natural pillar of granite and through the gap in the rocky face of the cliffside, following the distorted sound of voices with Ben, her young collie, pressing closely on her heels. Behind her, the wind from the sea below was reverberating in the narrow gully. It shook the stunted gorse and hawthorn bushes, blowing a few more crisp autumn leaves off the willow trees beside the stream to whirl madly along with it.

The noise was cut off abruptly as Lucy rounded the outcrop of rock that screened the outer world, wincing as a jagged finger of granite poked her knee through her jeans. She stopped suddenly, Ben bumping into her legs, surprised to find herself in a small cave, dimly lit by dull late morning light filtering through tiny holes and cracks in the walls. Looking quickly around, she realised that it was not actually a cave, only a wide crevice in the gully. It widened at its furthest end and was partly roofed by another slab of granite which had fallen over the top of it, wedging itself against the sides.

As she brushed a strand of chestnut hair away from her small pointed face Lucy's eyes were drawn to the two men at the far end of the crevice. They were quite unaware of her presence as they stood motionless, their own gaze riveted on the figure between them. The torches they held shone directly onto it; creating a blaze of light, but the men stood in deeper gloom, unrecognisable, their backs to the entrance. They said nothing, but one man moved his torch abruptly, running it downwards, stopping the beam again quite suddenly.

Lucy stared disbelievingly at the bony fingers pointing towards her from the centre of the torchlight. She drew in her breath sharply and the light flickered, so that the skeletal hand seemed to move. She threw up an arm to protect her eyes from the torch beam that had swung onto her face, and Ben slipped past her, rushing forwards.

'No, Ben,' she called anxiously, taking an uncertain step after him.

A louder voice overrode hers, 'You damned dog, get down.'

At the sound of it Lucy lowered her arm, peering through the gloom. The collie was squirming excitedly beside the man, whose torch had fallen to the ground, its light bouncing off the rough walls as it rolled. 'Mike,' she exclaimed in relief, recognising the square face under tousled red hair. 'What on earth are you doing here?'

'That's what I should be asking you,' he said crossly, stroking Ben absentmindedly as he stared at her. 'Why on earth do you always take risks, Lucy? You come poking around without any idea of who might be down here. You could have got into serious trouble again.'

Lucy ignored this, moving forward to stand next to the other person, who had swung their torch back to the still figure before them. Lucy's eyes widened as she looked at it, noting how it was seated on a rough throne of piled boulders. This loomed above a sea of dried bracken within a line of jagged rocks that formed a rough oval.

The browned bones of both hands were attached to a skeleton, patchily visible beneath a covering of disintegrating rusty chain mail. One of those hands hung over the arm of its rude seat, and beneath the other, the one that rested on its lap pointing accusingly outward, lay a sword. Her awed gaze moved briefly upwards to where the dark shadows of eye sockets lay behind the narrow nosepiece of a rounded helmet, but it was drawn back to the yellowed teeth that grinned at her threateningly from the skull.

She turned aside to Mike, who had retrieved his torch and was also staring at the figure again. Lucy gestured towards it wordlessly, and he glanced at her, his face expressionless as he shrugged.

'Will there be gold with it?' another voice asked breathlessly. Lucy peered beyond the other torch beam as Ben came back to press against her legs, but could only make out a slight figure that she guessed to be young and male.

'I shouldn't think so,' Mike replied curtly. 'Let's get outside, up into the field. I don't want any more disturbance in here or anywhere nearby.'

Lucy led the way, the collie close behind her, as they squeezed through the narrow entrance, Mike cursing volubly as he barked his ankle. They emerged onto a ledge halfway down the gully in a small isolated world. Burning russet bracken billowed around ranks of gorse bushes, all rimmed by dark clumps of heather with sere brown flowers tipping the wiry branches.

A sky filled with scudding grey clouds pressed down as they wordlessly began picking their way over the springy heather and through the stands of damp bracken towards the field above. Startled rabbits scuttled away into cover and a thwarted kestrel hovering above sheered off. Ben pushed by Lucy, obeying her firm command to leave them although his nose was twitching excitedly as he sniffed around the roots of the nearest gorse bush.

Rather than walk back to the coastal path at the sea end of the gully where a stile gave access to the field, Lucy bent to slip carefully between the slack strands of a barbed wire fence that filled a gap in the drystone wall. Most of the field surface had been carefully cut back and piled in strips beyond the yellow digger that stood motionless above a shallow quarry carved into ledges and pits. A cold wind from the sea blew in their faces, splattering them with drops of rain and whirling Lucy's hair into her eyes. She tucked loose strands under her woollen beret and pushed her hands into the pockets of her jeans, hunching her shoulders beneath the thick grey fleece jacket she wore as she stepped into the shelter of the machine and stopped. Ben pottered happily over the edge of the field, glad to be outside again, carefully inspecting the tussocks of grass in the rough turf, while overhead rooks screeched in delight as they rode the gusting air currents.

The men joined her, Mike Shannon's wild red curls standing up untidily around his head as he turned to glower back down the gully. The younger man leaned against the digger, lighting a cigarette as he stared at Mike. He was young, as Lucy had guessed, surely still in his late teens, wiry and dark, his sharp-featured face drawn tight with excitement above his waterproof jacket. And perhaps with the cold, Lucy thought, pulling her beret more firmly over her ears.

'Tell me again,' Mike said, turning round abruptly, 'just how you found it.'

The young man dragged deeply on his cigarette before he spoke. 'We have the rights to dig here,' he said in the soft local burr. 'My family and a few others.' He glanced at Lucy. 'For serpentine, like.' His eyes turned back to Mike, who was shifting impatiently. 'This old pit hasn't been opened since it was worked by hand, and with the JCB we can get further in, between the layers like.' He drew on the cigarette, blowing the smoke out slowly. 'We haven't worked here for a while ...'

'How long?' Mike demanded sharply.

The young man shrugged. 'Two weeks, maybe three. I'm not sure. Since the weather was bad. Anyway, I've been busy with my Da in the workshop, and I wanted some air, so soon as the weather was clearing I came on up here.' He looked along the gully. 'I've been working since first light,' he flushed unaccountably, 'and I wanted a break, like, so I went for a stroll and found that gap. I was curious, no more than that, and it was a real shock to find him there.'

'So what did you do then?' Mike asked, a frown growing blackly on his face. 'How many people did you call?'

'None but my Da,' the young man said indignantly. 'I scrambled up to top, to get reception, like, and he said he'd sort it out. Get an archaeologist. Called you, didn't he?' he demanded.

Mike nodded. 'If he's Peter Teague.'

'He is,' the young man asserted. 'And I'm Kevin.'

'Where's your dad, then?' Mike asked. 'Why isn't he here?'

'Why should he be?' Kevin demanded. 'He'll come later. Right now, he'll be having his meal.' Mike snorted disbelievingly and the young man said defensively, 'He was out right early at the oyster fishery. I expect you were still sleeping when he was working. He's on the haul-tow punt and weather's been right bad lately with the wind, like, so he wanted to make the most of today.' He scowled at Mike. 'What's this all about? I've not done nothing wrong. I could've said nothing and left him to lie.'

Mike's expression lightened and he clapped the young man on the shoulder. 'So you could, Kevin. I appreciate the call. It's just odd, though,' he added in a lower voice.

Lucy glanced at him quickly, but Mike went on, 'I'll write down all you've told me, and bring it round for you to sign. We have to keep a full account of how things are found.'

Kevin nodded. 'Fine. D'you want my address then?'

Mike was already searching the pockets of his thick donkey jacket, then of his mud-stained trousers. Lucy tucked a hand into the pocket of her fleece and pulled out a pad and pen. 'Here, use these.'

Mike took them gratefully. 'Thanks, Lucy. Right then, Kevin.'

The young man gave an address in Portharrock, the nearby village, as he pulled off his waterproof. He turned to throw it into the cab of his digger and put his foot on the step, ready to climb in.

'Hang on,' Mike said. 'Where are you going to work with that thing?'

Kevin gestured at the quarry, his face darkening. 'Here, you're not going to stop me, are you?' he demanded belligerently.

Mike chewed at his lip thoughtfully, staring around the landscape, as Lucy called Ben back to her side. 'I'm afraid so,' he said briskly. 'But I don't think it'll be for very long. Is there anywhere else you can work for a couple of days?'

Kevin scowled in disgust. 'Wish I'd said nothing,' he muttered, pulling himself up into the cab.

'Where are you going with that?' Mike shouted.

'I'm not leaving it here,' Kevin yelled. 'My Da would kill me.'

Before Mike could say another word, the young man started the engine and the digger lurched, so that Mike leaped back out of the way. He stood, arms akimbo, watching it jerk across the field into the one beyond, sending a flock of crows whirling into the air with raucous scolding.

'Damn!' Mike exclaimed suddenly. 'I should have asked him where to find the landowner. I was up at the abbey excavation at Ravenstow when the message about this reached me. It's a hell of a drive down, but I didn't want to hang around.' He began to search his pockets again. 'I made a note of the name, but I think I've left the damned paper behind. Some bloke called Rasmussen. I suppose somebody'll know how to get hold of him. It can't be that common a name down here.'

'That's easy,' Lucy said. 'We're staying with him. We got here yesterday and I've just come from his house now.'

Mike stared at her. 'Well, I'll be damned. I wondered why you were here. I assumed you were doing more work on the botanical cliff survey.' His eyes narrowed. 'Who's with you?'

'Hugh,' Lucy replied. 'Why?'

Mike's expression relaxed. 'I wasn't sure whether to expect

that brother of yours to come bounding over to explore.'

A gamine smile flashed across Lucy's face. 'Well, Eric Rasmussen is Will's godfather, so my dear brother should be turning up over the weekend, and Gran too, if she has time before she goes off to Italy. We were all invited to stay here for a few days.' As Mike groaned she added, 'Think yourself lucky. It's half term, so Will could have been here already. As it is, he's gone up to Cumbria with David.'

Mike looked at her blankly and she carried on with a touch of impatience, 'Really, Mike. Once you get on to archaeology everything else seems to go out of your mind. David,' she enunciated clearly, 'Will's estate manager at Rossington Manor. They've gone to a big ploughing match. Horse ploughing, of course. They're actively looking for a pair of Shires now. Although Clydesdales have been mentioned too.'

'Why,' Mike demanded explosively, 'are we wasting time talking about horses? Where's Hugh?'

'He's down at the coastal watch station. I was on my way to meet him.'

'Where and what is it?' Mike asked shortly.

'It's the concrete blockhouse above the coastal path, just before you get to the village. I think it was something to do with the lighthouse when that was first built, and now it's where the volunteer coast watchers are based. Why don't you come with me?' She glanced at her watch. 'Ben and I were going to have a long walk on the far side of the village before joining Hugh, so if we go straight to the station instead we should be just in time to meet him. Then we can all go back to the house together,' she said firmly. 'Eric won't be there before lunch anyway. He had to go into town this morning.'

As she began to move Ben sped off enthusiastically towards the hedge that screened the wall of the field by the cliffs and Mike fell into step with her as they walked along beside it. 'What are they looking for, these coast watchers?' he asked curiously. 'Dolphins and whales? Or I suppose, as Hugh's interested, it's birds.'

'Well, no doubt they keep a note of those,' Lucy said, climbing up the wooden steps of a stile in the far corner and lowering herself down on the other side. She paused, back on the cliffside again, looking out over the sea, heaving and rolling under a grey sky that drained the brightness from the gulls that wove speeding patterns across it. 'But their main role is to keep a log of boats and people passing by, so they can be traced in case of accidents.'

Mike jumped heavily down beside her. 'Looks like rain,' he said abruptly.

'Not yet,' Lucy said with the authority of a born coastal dweller. 'See how clear the cliffs are.' She pointed along the coastline. 'You can see the huer's hut at Polkenan.'

Mike stared eastwards. 'I don't really know this stretch at all,' he muttered crossly, focusing on a small building on the distant headland. 'What is a huer, for God's sake? Something else to do with this coastal watch?'

'No, it's where Polkenan villagers used to post a look-out to spot the pilchards in the autumn, giving the local fishing fleet plenty of chance to put out in time for a good catch. It's quite a spot,' she said, setting off along the narrow path over the cliff top. 'Fantastic sea views, of course. As it's well tucked away from the village I guess the look-out must have had a bell or a chain of watchers back down to the harbour to give the alert. I believe he directed the fleet with semaphore signals once they were at sea.'

'It sounds worth a visit,' Mike conceded behind her, his voice vanishing as she rounded a huge boulder. 'But,' he said furiously as he caught up with her, 'we're digressing again. What's Hugh doing with this coastal watch operation?'

'He's just interested,' Lucy said. She paused to watch Ben try to follow a scent under the thick ranks of spiky sloe bushes, studded with tiny purplish fruit, that covered the slope below her. 'You know Hugh, he's interested in most things. But he's got the chance to visit it because he has a new author in the area who's involved with it and offered to take Hugh along on his shift.'

'Hmmph,' Mike grunted. 'What's this bloke writing?'

'Well, he's the local vicar, covering Polkenan and a couple of other parishes. He's written about West Country holy sites and churches, a scholarly work that Hugh thinks will do well, even in the general market.'

'Oh,' Mike said reluctantly, 'I might find it worth a look myself.'

'He sounds an unusual bloke,' Lucy said, her lips twitching as Ben backed out of the bushes, thwarted in his endeavour. 'A contemporary of Eric's.' They followed the dog on along the path, which dipped down to a narrow valley. Ben rushed ahead to lie in the brook, lapping up water, his golden eyes gleaming up at them as they reached him.

Lucy's brows drew together as she picked her way across the water on a zigzag route of large stones. 'They were at university together, but I'm not sure you'd say they were friends. There seems to be a bit of an atmosphere when his name is mentioned at Pennance, Eric's house.' Her expression lightened. 'Hugh thinks I'm imagining it. Anyway, Alastair, the vicar, has worked with a regional journalist to put together a pageant to celebrate local life from the past to the present, and he's brought Anna in to help with it.'

'What!' Mike exclaimed in heartfelt horror. 'You don't mean she's down here too, do you?' he asked, almost pleadingly.

'Really, Mike,' Lucy said crossly as she came out of the valley onto the cliff top. Ahead of her were the roofs of Portharrock, fringed with tamarisks bent landwards from the force of the wind, and fronted by the coastal watch building that perched a few yards above the path. 'I thought you and Anna were getting on better these days.'

'Hah!' he snorted, jerking aside as Ben pushed past him, adding damp patches to the marks already on Mike's trousers.

'Why on earth can't the woman decide what she's doing and stick to it. From all I've heard,' he sounded disbelieving, 'she was doing well as an actress. Then she gives it up for writing and directing a trivial production at your family place. And now,' he snarled, 'up she pops again with some bizarre local festival.'

'Well,' Lucy said, stepping sideways to let the collie get ahead of her, 'you won't have to see anything of her. She's very busy, and when he's free Rob Elliot comes down to go walking with her, so there's not much chance of her crossing your path for long. That's how they met Alastair, when they were walking here last month. They got talking about his plans for the pageant and Anna was interested. She's only got a short time free, of course, before she has rehearsals for her next play in London.'

Mike looked puzzled. 'Who did you say she was with?'

'Rob Elliot. You know, *Inspector* Elliot.'

He frowned. 'So what's this then? Are they an item now? Why does nobody ever tell me anything?'

Lucy shrugged. 'She hasn't said. And you could see for yourself how things are, if you only looked.'

He stared at her uncomprehendingly. 'Why should I? I've better things to do with my time.'

She stopped and turned away from the village outskirts to look at him. 'Yes, digs all over the West Country. Mike, what's bothering you about this discovery?'

His face darkened. 'What makes you think it's bothering me?'

'Well, normally you'd be talking about nothing else,' Lucy pointed out as the collie returned to hover nearby. 'By this time I expected to know masses about Viking burials. Although I thought they were buried in ships,' she finished.

Mike scowled. 'A common misapprehension, but you should know better. What,' he demanded abruptly, 'makes you think of Vikings?'

'Well, the helmet, I suppose,' she said slowly. 'Isn't it?'

'Oh yes,' Mike said furiously. 'It's a Viking helmet, and Viking mail too, in strikingly good condition. If I'm not mistaken, and that's not likely, the sword is very fine as well – and extremely rare.'

'Well, isn't that good?'

'No, it bloody well isn't,' he snarled. 'The whole thing's wrong. Genuine fittings, yes, and I'd guess a genuine skeleton too, although how old is anybody's guess. But a Viking burial ... hah!'

Lucy looked blankly at his angry face. 'Isn't it then?' she asked, puzzled.

'Hell, Lucy, don't you understand? It's a plant! And that bloke seemed damned fishy to me. Why was he so shifty about how he found it?'

'Oh Mike,' Lucy said, 'he went for a pee, and didn't want to say in front of me. That's all. Are you sure it's a plant?'

'Of course I am! A damn good one,' he conceded bitterly. 'It would fool the general public. But it's obvious that little scene has been set recently. For God's sake,' he exploded, 'there was no debris anywhere, for a start. That crevice is open to the weather, and there the skeleton sits, unencumbered by sand or leaves or animal remains. And no sign of rotted material on or around the bones. No grave goods either. There should have been traces of clothes, of wood and leather. After all, there are amazing patches of chain mail left, and that rarely ever survives.' The expression on his face was thunderous, and he ran his hands roughly through his hair. 'If I thought that somebody was trying to make a fool of me ...' The words disappeared in a low growl.

'Look,' Lucy said quickly, 'the watch station is just here. Let's leave it until we've got Hugh on his own.'

He jerked his head curtly and she turned away. Ben raced joyfully ahead of her, past a rock cluster where the wind and rain had worn the upper segment into an arch, framing a small section of the sea. A wren perched within, tail cocked as it watched her for a second before bursting into a strident alarm call and flitting into the shelter of the bushes.

Lucy called Ben back as she walked under the wide glass windows of the utilitarian building a few yards above her head, Mike stomping behind her. Lucy walked up the zigzag path to the building and pushed open the door, releasing a fug of hot air. 'Phew,' she said, quickly pulling off her beret and unzipping her fleece. 'It's roasting in here.'

She looked round with quick interest, noting the white-painted walls on three sides were hung with maps and charts, with postcards of sunny and faraway places covering the gaps. Hugh was leaning back against the long counter that ran beneath the windows, a man of medium height in brown tweed trousers and a thick tan jumper, which matched his own colouring, causing him at first glance to seem bland and innocuous. Lucy's gaze was drawn beyond him, her eyes widening appreciatively at the sweeping view over the cliffs and the bay.

Ben, though, leaped over to greet him and Hugh stroked the dog as his glance went past his wife's slight boyish figure, one of his eyebrows quirking upwards. 'Well, well,' he drawled. 'And where did you find Mike?'

Lucy opened her mouth, but before she could speak Mike said forbiddingly, 'Just some work in the area. Lucy pretty much fell over me, so I thought I might as well come along to see what you're up to.'

Hugh's gaze had sharpened. 'I guess you're joining us for lunch then,' he said casually. 'Meanwhile, let me introduce you. Lucy, this is Alastair Drewe. You'll have to forgive him if he keeps his attention outside. It wouldn't do to miss anything.'

The man next to him rose, turning a smiling face to Lucy as he held out his hand. She shook it politely, taking in his great height and extreme darkness, thick coal-black hair and eyes, finely drawn features and an expression of strained intentness. Fascinated, Lucy struggled momentarily to place him, finding his appearance strangely familiar.

'Hello,' Alastair said in a pleasant baritone. 'I don't need to excuse Hugh's humour to you, of all people. But you must excuse me for not chatting right now. I believe we'll have a better opportunity later, thanks to Eric's invitation.'

'You remember,' Hugh said, glancing at Lucy, 'Eric has asked Alastair and Anna to lunch with us at Pennance tomorrow, so you'll have chance to talk then.' As he introduced Mike, forbearing to describe his occupation, he added, 'If you're in the area, no doubt the invitation will be extended to you too.'

Mike grunted as he grasped the vicar's hand and said, to Hugh's astonishment, 'Fine. I'm likely to be here for a bit. You'll have to tell me of somewhere decent to stay.'

Alastair had seated himself at the counter again, one hand resting on the powerful binoculars that lay near the fixed scope. He looked round quickly at Mike, saying 'I have a spare room at Polkenan. It's nothing fancy, but you're welcome to use it for a week or so.'

'Thanks,' Mike said, rather taken aback. 'That would be a help.' He frowned. 'Polkenan's the next place along the coast, isn't it?' He looked at Lucy enquiringly. 'With the pilchard look-out.' He searched his memory quickly for the right term. 'The huer's hut, that is.'

'More or less,' Alastair replied, fondling the collie's silken head as Ben pressed against him. 'The next village, at any rate. There are a few houses, and a little hamlet before you get there. Tamsyn lives in the wildest spot of the lot, right out on the cliffs.' He gestured to the woman at the far end of the counter, who had shown no interest at all in the visitors. She kept her back turned on them, her neatly braided hair coiled around her bent head, concentrating on the radar screen in front of her. 'We usually share the same shifts,' Alastair added.

'I'm sorry, I should have introduced you,' Hugh said, 'Tamsyn, I'd like you to meet my wife Lucy and an old friend of ours, Mike Shannon.'

The woman turned her head slightly, exposing a weather-beaten face, lips tightly clamped together and hooded eyes impenetrable. She ignored Ben who had come over to her side and nodded in a restrained fashion, before turning back to her vigil.

'Well,' Hugh said as he picked up a thick corduroy jacket, 'we mustn't disturb you any longer. Thank you both for showing me what you do here. See you this evening then, Alastair.' He glanced at Lucy. 'I'm joining Alastair for a couple of hours, while you're out with Anna tonight. He's doing extra shifts in the evening to cover his time off with the pageant.'

'We don't always do evening shifts,' Alastair said, 'but we do try to fit them in during the school holidays, and of course it's half term at the moment. It should be very pleasant tonight; there'll be a full moon, so if the sky is clear we'll see it framed in that rocky arch below the watch station, just as if it was a painting.'

Lucy pulled on her beret and zipped up her fleece, as Alastair scribbled some directions on a piece of paper, which he handed to Mike. 'Here, this will help you find my cottage. If you leave your car in the upper car park you'll just need to follow the path down to the village. I'll be in or somewhere around there from two this afternoon. Ask about if I'm not at the cottage, someone will know where I am.'

Mike tucked the note away, mumbling his thanks, and with general farewells the trio left. Ben pushed past them and headed confidently back along the cliff path.

'It was nice to be warm for a bit,' Lucy muttered, leading the way eastward. The wind was blowing hard against them so speech was unanimously discarded, and they strode on, heads bent against the blast. Ahead of them, Ben's white-tipped tail streamed behind him, floating before the walkers like a guiding marker as he moved between the sloe thickets and gorse bushes. At the stile he hesitated, looking back towards Lucy. She gave him the word of command and he scrambled quickly over, hovering on the far side to make sure she came too.

As soon as she reached him, he moved off along the line of the hedge beside the wall. Now more sheltered from the wind, Lucy followed the collie slowly, waiting for the men to join her. As soon as they had, she demanded of Mike, 'Well? Are we going to show Hugh?' She glanced at her watch. 'There's just time before we have to be back for lunch.'

'No,' Mike said abruptly. 'I don't want anybody else messing around in there.'

Hugh stopped as they reached the stile above the gully, and leaned against it, his eyes on his friend. 'Well, what's it all about? Something has clearly rattled your cage.'

Mike scowled as he came to a halt, and Lucy explained quickly, 'Mike was called in to an archaeological site on Eric's land.' Mike grunted irritably, but she ignored him, waving a hand towards the shallow excavations on their left. 'A young bloke had just started digging for serpentine, and wandered off into the gully down there for a pee break.' Hugh was watching her face closely, reading every expression that chased across it. 'He came across a small cave, more a sheltered crevice really, and the most amazing thing in it.' She paused, drawing breath for her revelation. 'A seated Viking in chain mail with a sword, all ready to defend the shore.'

Mike bared his teeth in a furious snarl. 'Grrrr, that's exactly what the bloody papers will say, if they ever get hold of this.'

'So?' Hugh asked curiously. 'If it's that stunning a find, you must expect a lot of publicity.'

'It's a plant,' Mike snapped shortly. 'And I don't want publicity as well. I hate bloody reporters at the best of times, and they'll have a field day here.'

'Aaah,' Hugh said thoughtfully, rubbing his earlobe absently. 'Just as well you kept quiet about it at the watch station.'

'Why?' Mike demanded.

'Tamsyn is a journalist on the local paper. I imagine that usually means covering the minutiae of life here, fêtes, concerts, and whatever the seamier side consists of. But no doubt this will be a bit of a coup for her.'

Mike ground his teeth audibly, and Hugh suppressed a smile, his gaze on a small bird that was flitting along the drystone wall behind the hedge, picking off insects. 'Look,' he said, dragging his attention back to his friend, 'let's get to Rasmussen's and see what we can do to limit the damage. You'll need to talk to him and he'll be back for lunch, so I'm sure you'll be asked to join us.' He levered himself away from the stile and the collie looked up expectantly from the gingery hairs he was sniffing on the lower strand of the wire fence that filled the gap in the wall above the gully.

'How far away is this bloody place?' Mike demanded. 'I've left the car on the lane up there.' He pointed inland. 'A few fields away.'

'Then why don't you fetch it and go on to Eric's? You only have to follow the lane, go down a dip, cross a stream and go up the other side, where there's a drive to the right. There's no special marker, only high green banks that shield the house just below the peak of the hill. That's where you'll find Pennance.' He glanced interrogatively at Lucy, who nodded in agreement. 'We'll walk back with Ben, and we should all arrive at about the same time.'

Mike strode off without a word, watched anxiously by Ben. Hugh glanced at his wife, a glimmer of amusement in his eyes as he stood back to let her scramble over the stile. He followed, almost tangled with the dog who was keen to join his mistress, and found Lucy waiting for him above the gully.

'I believe he really does think it's a plot to discredit him,' she said thoughtfully.

'Mike can be big on conspiracy theory,' Hugh commented, scanning the gully. He noted the hawthorn and sloe bushes that grew up against the rocky sides, behind the head-high band of gorse and bracken that covered each steeply sloping bank of the stream below, where an occasional stunted willow gestured stiffly inland. 'Whereabouts is this grisly guardian of the shore?'

Lucy gestured down to her left. 'Along there, on this ridge. I'd come across the stream with Ben, when I heard these weird sounds. After a bit I realised they were voices, louder than normal and distorted.'

'So you went to look for the source,' Hugh said resignedly. 'Lucy, will you never learn to be careful?'

She ignored this remonstrance. 'They were in this large crevice, roofed by a fallen slab, Mike talking to Kevin, the young bloke who found the place. And between them was this figure, a skeleton in chain mail and a helmet shining under the light of their torches.' She glanced at Hugh. 'I suppose you shouldn't take a tiny peek? There's a faint track towards it, more of an animal route than a human one, I think.'

He shook his head. 'No. It sounds as though Mike's got enough problems on his hands without my meddling with his site. Come on, let's get going or else he'll arrive before us.'

His face was thoughtful as he began to walk down the narrow path that led through the gully, Ben edging past him to get to the stream. By the time they reached it, the collie had just levered himself up from the water, and shook himself vigorously as they joined him on the far bank.

Hugh's expression grew pained as muddy droplets spattered his trousers, but Lucy wrinkled her nose scornfully. 'It won't show,' she said. He glanced at her jeans, noting that she had avoided the shower, but before he could comment she added, 'Alastair's quite something. I thought I knew him at first, but it's just that he reminds me of one of those early Renaissance pictures of the saints, rather otherworldly. What do you think about Mike staying with him at Polkenan?'

'Not a lot,' Hugh replied, rather bewildered. 'Why should I?'

'Oh Hugh,' Lucy said exasperatedly. 'You know very well that Anna is staying in the village too. And Mike does as well, because I told him so myself. At least,' she amended judiciously, 'I said she was working with Alastair on the centenary pageant.'

'Does it matter?' Hugh demanded, bending forward against the wind again as he emerged from the gully.

Lucy pursed her lips as Ben wriggled by her. 'I suppose not,' she said reluctantly, almost to herself, as she rounded the rocky outcrop that shielded the headland. 'I thought they'd been getting on better, but Mike was his old awkward self when I told him Anna was here. Still, if he's chosen to overlook it that's his problem.'

'Too right,' Hugh said, catching the tail end of this as he stopped to open a gate into a field for Lucy. He glimpsed a fleeting startled expression on her face as he swung the gate shut behind her and the dog. 'What is it?' he demanded.

Ben was racing ahead as Lucy walked lithely across the rough turf, a slight smile on her lips. 'Well,' she cast a sideways look at Hugh as he fell into step beside her, 'he did seem rather put out at the thought of Anna and Rob Elliot as an item. You don't think ...'

'I don't,' Hugh cut in forcefully. 'The thought of Mike and Anna ...' He broke off, lifting his shoulders in an exaggerated shudder, before asking a second later, 'She and Elliot aren't that serious, are they?'

'I don't think so,' Lucy said slowly. 'Anna hasn't said. We'll just have to wait and see. If she hasn't met up with Mike by the time I see her at the pub this evening I'll have to warn her he's around.'

Ben was hovering as they reached a high stone wall, screened here and there by the feathery branches of tamarisk trees that were whipping about in the wind. A wide gate made of inter-twining wooden curves swung open at a touch, and they passed beyond it onto a flat granite bridge spanning a large rectangular pool. The wind had blustered over the wall and through the trees to ripple the water and rustle the reeds and rushes around the edges, filling the air with a continuous dry whispering.

The collie raced ahead again and Lucy tucked her arm through Hugh's as they reached the far side of the pool, where the granite continued as paths up the sloping garden, one on either side of a long water stairway. The paths were edged with wide beds where swathes of long golden and russet grasses waved gently in the breeze. Lucy looked at them appreciatively as she asked, 'Are you trying to avoid a tête-à-tête with Eric?'

His lips twitched as he glanced at her while they slowed their pace, a faint scent of lavender rising around them as Lucy brushed against the neatly clipped low hedge that fringed the water. 'Is it that obvious?'

'Well, probably only to me,' she said. 'Don't you like him?'

'It's not so much that I don't like him,' Hugh replied slowly, 'just that I find his earnestness rather hard work. I am concerned with environmental issues, but not as exclusively as Eric is.'

'I know what you mean,' Lucy admitted as they reached the head of the canal, stepping onto a patio where naturally coloured stone fragments swirled in mosaic loops. 'It is difficult to maintain that level of dedication. And actually I thought, with this new role coming up at the Wronham Trust, I'd slip away for a couple of hours to look at the heath beyond Pennance. If I'm to take on responsibility for moorland conservation and regeneration I really do need to know more about the smaller patches.'

Hugh's eyes gleamed with laughter as they climbed shallow steps past thick drifts of frothy pale grass that looked like a silver river rippling along. Lucy absentmindedly ran her fingers through it, watching Ben as he stood on the terrace above, his tongue lolling out of his grinning mouth as he stared at them.

'Of course, it's a good opportunity,' Hugh agreed. 'Although I'm still not sure how you're going to fit all this new work in, if you're carrying on with the coastal survey too.'

'It won't be a problem,' Lucy said confidently as they reached the terrace, where Ben was now sniffing at the paving. 'We'll have moved into Withern before the new job starts, so we'll both have a lot more time without the renovations to supervise.'

'Hmm,' Hugh murmured, his eyes on Mike Shannon. The archaeologist stood beyond one of the granite obelisks that dominated each corner of the terrace, his feet firmly planted on the stone terrace, his arms akimbo as he stared at the house in front of him while the collie nudged his leg hopefully.

Hugh grinned to himself as they walked to the front of the building to join him. From the angle at which Mike had first approached Pennance in his car, he would have received the full element of surprise because the rising banks of earth beside the road had screened the sloping sedum-covered roofs and glass-panelled walls of a very modern eco house.

'Stunning, isn't it?' Hugh commented, coming to stand beside him to enjoy his view of the entrance courtyard. He admired once again the slender steel columns supporting a glass roof that was edged at the front with opaque troughs filled with ivy, trimmed into decorative swags to break the sharp edge of the steel supporting bar. In the centre of them, casually draped with strands of the ivy, was a bust of Neptune, trident raised as he gazed across the cliff fields towards the village. Below the roof a path ran between narrow rectangular pools where water flowed downwards over sloping ridges of pebbles, creating a constant gentle murmur.

'This leads to the central pavilion, the living area,' Hugh explained, 'and the private areas lead off it as separate units, all at different levels. It's a clever idea.'

Mike was absentmindedly stroking the collie and stared up blankly at Hugh, so Lucy explained, 'Eric's daughter, Rosen, has her quarters some distance away, and Hugh approves of that. It lets her do what she wants without disturbing anyone else.' She went on quickly, 'All this is very much Eric's own design, and incorporates a lot of his ideas.'

'Like what?' Mike asked.

'Well, power used in the house comes from renewable sources, for a start,' Hugh said. 'It's as well our house can't be rebuilt. Lucy's already comparing the warmth of the underfloor heating here with ours at home. Rasmussen's is much better, and considerably cheaper too. Most of his own domestic energy comes from a heat recovery system, but he has created a field of solar panels too, out of sight over there.' Hugh waved a hand towards the east, at a cluster of sea holly that almost hid a small outbuilding against the stone boundary wall. 'They're electronically operated by a control system which minutely adjusts their positions to maximise exposure to sunlight. They actually create more energy than Rasmussen needs for his own purposes, so he sells it on to an energy bank.'

'That's a field of mirrors, isn't it?' Mike demanded. 'How popular is that locally?'

'Your guess is as good as mine,' Hugh replied.

'And what about planning permission?' Mike's tone was growing belligerent. 'How much did he have to disturb the ground to put these mirrors in?'

Hugh shrugged, and Lucy intervened quickly. 'He incorporates his beliefs outside too,' she said, gesturing further down the garden. 'Over there is a reed bed system to rival Prince Charles's.'

Mike was distracted as he glanced at her, bewildered. 'Read bed?' he queried.

'Reeds, water plants,' Lucy explained patiently, 'for filtration. All the grey water from the house passes through them. You know, bath water, washing water, that sort of stuff. The water that comes out the other end is recycled for flushing the loos and irrigating the garden.'

'What does this bloke do for a living?' Mike asked brusquely. 'Not archaeology, that's for sure.'

'Nor publishing either,' Hugh said. 'I guess he made his money in his early years, as a chemist working for a major petroleum company. I believe he was earmarked for great things. But in his thirties he had a Damascene conversion and changed sides.' Hugh raised a questioning eyebrow. 'You might have heard of him in his later role as an environmentalist. Eric

Rasmussen's a very high profile campaigner, much in demand for sound bites and headline pieces on green issues.'

'He's very well informed,' Lucy said. 'That's how my father came to know him. You know Daddy was a professional explorer. Well, Eric funded a few of his expeditions.' Her lips twitched. 'Of course, Daddy was just fascinated by how other people lived. But Eric always had a purpose – finding out how they used their natural resources. Daddy said he was the most driven person he knew.'

Mike grunted. 'Well,' he said grudgingly, 'he's got himself an idyllic spot just here. No near neighbours either.'

'I believe,' Hugh commented dryly, 'that he owns a lot of the land around here. Although I gather he hasn't got as much as he'd like to have. The quarry field is his, but he's had to honour the old digging contract against his own wishes.'

Mike snorted derisively. 'Locals holding out, are they?'

'I get that impression,' Hugh agreed. 'Although Rasmussen's not prone to discuss anything beyond environmental issues.'

'No, he was always very reticent,' Lucy said, 'but Daddy said he had a surprisingly puerile sense of humour.' She glanced at Hugh. 'I don't think Daddy really approved of his jokes. In fact, I gather they nearly got Eric into trouble in his younger days.'

Mike turned round slowly, his heels grinding on the stone terrace. His eyes narrowed as he stared at Lucy. 'He likes jokes, does he? I suppose he likes to get his name in the paper too. People like him thrive on publicity.'

'Hold on, Mike.' Hugh raised a warning hand. 'Don't get carried away. I rather imagine his sense of humour is typified by the name he's given his house.'

Mike stared at him in angry perplexity. 'What the devil do you mean?' he demanded.

'Pennance,' Hugh elaborated, 'a wonderful local name, and a pun, perhaps implying his eco house may atone for his earlier career.' He continued more seriously, 'You've no reason to think

Rasmussen is behind this ...' he hesitated, searching for the right words, 'this mystery Viking.'

Lucy drew in her breath sharply. 'Really, Mike,' she expostulated. 'First you thought it was professional rivals, now you think it's Eric. I suppose,' she added as an afterthought, 'we should be grateful we aren't on the list of suspects ourselves.'

Mike glowered at her. 'Well, you were right on the spot, so ...'

Before Lucy could reply they heard a car turn into the drive and swung round to see an odd-looking car, rather like a space-age racing mini in ice blue, coming down the drive to pull over beside Mike's muddy estate.

'Electric,' Hugh said in Mike's ear. 'A Renault, Eric's local run-about.'

Mike ignored him, staring at the man getting out of the car, who peeled off string-backed leather driving gauntlets and tossed them onto the driver's seat. Slight, almost emaciated, with a lined face, and deeply sunken eyes, he seemed nonetheless to radiate energy. 'Well,' he said immediately, in the clearly articulated tones of a public speaker, 'you've chosen a good time to visit. I've just heard there's been an amazing discovery down on the cliffs, a Viking chieftain guarding the shore.' Mike choked on an expletive as Eric Rasmussen hefted his briefcase out of the car. 'I'll just drop this indoors and we can go down to have a look.'

'Now just a minute,' Mike said forcefully. 'That site needs to be kept uncontaminated. Hell's teeth,' he clenched his fists, turning away, 'I bet the whole damned village is down there. I must go back.'

Eric eyed him curiously. 'I don't know what business it is of yours, but there's no need for you to be concerned.' He met Mike's glare without batting an eyelid, and forestalled a blistering comment. 'I've sent a couple of chaps from the village to patrol the gully where it was found. No one's getting in until I know what's there. The mention of gold always gets interest going.'

Mike groaned, clutching his forehead. 'That bloody bloke,' he muttered. 'I should have known he wouldn't keep his mouth shut.'

'Eric,' Hugh intervened smoothly, 'this is a very old friend of ours, Professor Mike Shannon, who is also the head of the regional archaeology unit. He was called out to this discovery. Mike,' his voice sharpened and his friend looked up, visibly gathering his forces, 'this is Eric Rasmussen, who owns the land where the discovery was made.'

The two men shook hands as Eric said, 'Well met, Mike. You must stay for lunch and we can talk over the situation. But meanwhile we'll go down together. I can't wait to see this.' He saw the expression on Mike's face, and added, 'Don't worry, we won't go and poke around, but I want to see this figure before the press get here.'

Mike's jaw dropped. 'The press,' he exclaimed, disbelievingly. 'You've notified the press?'

'No need, my friend,' Eric said over his shoulder as he moved towards the front door, which opened automatically at his approach. He stepped inside to drop his briefcase, then came back out, the door sliding shut noiselessly behind him. 'The local reporter, that, what's her name …' He snapped his fingers. 'Warne. Tamsyn Warne. She's already on to the story, and I'll bet my bottom dollar she'll notify the nationals. It's big news, and I want to make sure I get my facts right when the press come calling.'

'Two facts you'd better get straight then,' Mike said loudly, standing his ground as Eric strode past him. 'No gold, and we've got a joker on our hands.' Eric stopped abruptly, turning to face him. 'Somebody,' Mike said, 'has set this up, and done it damned well. I'm sure the artefacts are genuinely old, and an amazing find in themselves, but the rest stinks.'

Eric was very still, staring intently at him, his expression quite unreadable. 'I suppose you're sure,' he said softly.

'I am,' Mike growled, 'and I'm not putting my reputation

on the line alone here. I'm bringing in an expert on the period, and an osteoarchaeologist. I want to know how old those bones are. But I can tell you they've only been on that site for a few weeks at the most, certainly not months, not years, and bloody definitely not centuries.'

TWO

The group was silent as they emerged from the gully on their way back from viewing the Viking. He had been a stunning figure, even seen at a distance from the entrance, the closest they could go without causing Mike to erupt into fury. As it was, they had passed the outer pillar of rock, edged round the projecting finger of granite and stopped to peer round his bulky frame, positioned to bar any further approach into the crevice. And there beyond him the warrior had sat motionless in the strange absence of sound that lay heavily, staring warningly at them, one hand still hovering above his sword.

The wind from the sea battered them as they walked towards Pennance across the field, only the collie relishing this extra outing as he rechecked the scents he had noticed earlier. Each of the people was sunk in their own thoughts, oblivious to their surroundings. As they entered the garden, Hugh glanced at the faces of the others. Eric looked inscrutable, the collar of his waterproof turned up round his neck, his eyes fixed on a picture other than the granite bridge he was crossing. Mike's shoulders were hunched and he wore a familiar scowl as he stalked behind his host, unaware of the stark beauty of the water stairway. Lucy walked lightly beside Hugh, her chestnut hair blowing forward around her face.

'Let's have a drink,' Eric said, as they climbed the shallow steps up to the terrace that ran around the house. He led them through the front courtyard, where the blustering of the wind faded, allowing the gentle murmur of flowing water to make itself heard. The sliding door opened noiselessly at his approach and they followed him into the central pavilion.

Lucy glanced at Mike, amused to see how visibly taken aback he was. She saw that Eric had marked this too as he hung his jacket on a rack beside the door, a faint smile touching his compressed lips. His expression was tightly controlled again as he walked through the sitting area past a bookcase to a wooden sideboard, saying over his shoulder, 'Hang your coats up and sit down while I get the drinks, then we can get on with a discussion.'

To their right a wall of glass panels gave them a view down the garden, where the water effect seemed to lead them straight into the distant sea. It's as if we're still outside, Lucy thought as she pulled her fleece off, just warmer, like being in a transparent cave but with a better prospect than the Viking has in his crevice.

The white oiled oak on the floor added to the overall impression of light and space, which was barely affected by the sparse furniture. Half a dozen wood-frame chairs were carefully placed around a wide coffee table so that their occupants could look outside. The overall creamy white tone of the room was only alleviated by the vibrant colour of the tall vase in swirling shades of greeny-blue that stood beyond the chairs, unofficially demarcating the sitting area from the dining area that ran at right angles to it. The kitchen area was at the back of the pavilion, partially screened by waist-high glass panels and Lucy was still surprised that the smell of cooking never pervaded the open spaces.

Lucy had tried all of the chairs and made a beeline for her favourite, the one covered in white hessian near the glass panels, where she was not distracted by the flickering of the small CCTV screen fitted into the corner of the room. She was mildly uncomfortable with the starkness of the sitting area, where there were no walls on which to hang paintings, nothing littered the table and only a slender serpentine column stood on the nearby sideboard. Accustomed to the clutter of generations at her family home, the lack of books lying around or treasured ornaments on many surfaces made the place seem very bare.

So she settled herself down in her preferred position where she could enjoy the exterior view best, while still listening to the room's occupants. Ben flopped down at her feet as she wriggled into a more comfortable position and accepted the glass Eric proffered.

'I don't favour sherry, but this is a rather good local white wine,' he said. 'From a vineyard a little way from here. I do like to encourage rural enterprise when I can.'

Hugh seated himself too and took a glass of wine, placing it untouched on the table beside his linen-covered chair. He watched Mike impatiently wave away the glass Eric offered him, wondering if the archaeologist was about to demand a hearty red, which he would certainly prefer if beer was not on offer. No, he mused, Mike's only thinking of one thing right now, and that's what's seated down in the gully.

Mike stood before the glass wall, hands thrust into the pockets of his trousers as he glared at them, clearly bursting with anger and the effort to contain it. His face was growing steadily redder, and Lucy could not decide if this was due to rage or overheating as he had not yet removed his donkey jacket.

'So,' Eric said, neatly pulling up his trouser legs a little as he sat down, 'we need to plan what to do.' He sipped his wine, looking enquiringly over the rim of his glass at Mike. 'I suppose there's no doubt this is a fake job? That armour looked pretty authentic to me, but then,' he admitted fairly, 'I'm not an expert.'

Mike's jaw moved, as if he was silently grinding his teeth. His lips parted, exposing clenched teeth. 'Neither am I,' he growled. 'That's why I'm contacting people who are. It's not a question of whether the armour is authentic or not. There's a damned good chance that it is. But neither it nor its wearer have been there for more than a couple of weeks.'

'The area's too clean?' Hugh asked quietly.

Mike nodded in a jerky movement. 'That for a start,' he agreed. 'There was no material residue anywhere, no tunic rags, no decayed wood, no pottery fragments. The skeleton and his armour are virtually dust free.' Mike glowered. 'And none of it has been exposed to the weather for any length of time, neither the bones nor the metal. That crevice is sheltered, but not completely protected from the outside, and I'll swear the chain mail wouldn't have survived for any time there.' He groaned, clenching his fists. 'And if it's genuine I'm leaving it down there for all and sundry to pinch if your blokes aren't competent.'

'I see,' Eric said softly. 'So what's the purpose of this little charade?' A movement near the front door caught his attention, and the collie lifted his head curiously as Eric added, 'Ah Mike, my daughter Rosen is giving us the pleasure of her company. You should feel honoured.'

The others all turned to the doorway as the girl entered the living area. Ben showed no further interest in her, but her spiky black hair and dead white face were an incongruous sight in the minimalist surroundings. The long black skirt she wore flapped around her legs, but her tight jumper outlined every rib in her skinny body. She stopped, staring at Mike, who stared back at her without any change of expression, too used to student fashion to even notice her appearance.

'Rosen, this is Professor Mike Shannon,' Eric said. 'He's lunching with us too. Are you joining us?'

The girl's eyes ran up and down Mike quite openly. 'Oh yes,' she said. She sank down into one of the chairs and gazed up at him.

Ignoring her completely, Mike gave a grudging reply to Eric's question. 'That's what I'd like to know.' He ran his hands through his hair, making the tousled curls stand out even more wildly.

'Did you notice anything interesting about the rocks around the Viking?' Lucy asked suddenly.

Mike shot her an irritated look. 'We don't know it's a Viking,' he snapped. His expression lightened fractionally as he added grudgingly, 'But yes, that's well spotted.'

Eric said softly, 'Do tell the less observant among us.'

Ignoring his tone, Mike said curtly, 'The rocky outline resembles a ship, and it's stuffed with dried bracken, presumably to indicate a pyre.'

'I see,' Hugh said. 'Another indication of a Viking burial.' He ignored Mike's deepening scowl, asking, 'But any professional would know at once that it's a set-up, wouldn't they?'

Mike grunted. 'They ought to,' he agreed morosely.

'But Eric's already found that the general public are excited about the prospect. I wonder how the journalist got to know about it.'

'That bloke, Kevin,' Mike said crossly, 'couldn't keep his mouth shut.'

'Oh no,' Rosen said idly, dangling her arms over the sides of the chair, 'it wasn't Kevin. I was with him when somebody told him about it. He wasn't at all pleased. He seemed to think it was his own little secret.'

Eric's lips tightened. 'You were out with that crowd again, Rosen?'

She turned a blank gaze on him. 'I met him in the village when I got off the bus.'

'So who the hell's spreading the news?' Mike demanded, oblivious to side issues.

'It will be interesting to find out,' Hugh said.

'Tamsyn got an anonymous call,' Rosen said. 'That's what I heard.'

'Then we must expect the national press to be buzzing around soon,' Eric commented, 'if we've got a practical joker with a desire for publicity.'

Mike shot him a glowering look. Eric studied him for a moment, before saying, 'My practical joking days are long gone, Mike, if that's what's on your mind. Although I occasionally like to mildly amuse my guests, there are more serious things occupying my thoughts these days.'

Mike did not look totally convinced, but Eric carried on, 'In fact, I wonder if that's at the root of this. There are plenty of people out there who have a vested interest in opposing my views.' His gaze went to the wall of glass, staring out through it into the distance. 'Anything that devalues my contributions or makes me seem eccentric might appeal to them.'

He brought his attention round to Hugh. 'What do you think we should do?'

Hugh was leaning back in his chair, his fingers steepled across his stomach. 'Put out a stalling statement. Something along the lines of "Yes, there's been an interesting discovery, which is being investigated now". Tell them that when there's more accurate information you'll pass it on to them, but make sure they know that it might not be for a while.'

'That won't hold them,' Eric said.

'No, but a good guard on the site will stop them getting a view, and after a few wild stories the news will die down without either you or Mike making any immediate commitment.'

A loud snort made Hugh turn to Mike. 'How long will it take to get your experts down?'

He shrugged. 'Lynette Mellors, the osteoarchaeologist, is on her way. I sent her a text while I was hanging around waiting for you and Lucy. The Viking expert I want is a bit of a recluse these days, and I haven't been able to get hold of him yet.' He looked down at his watch. 'I'll have another go in a bit.'

Eric was looking at him alertly. 'Your Viking expert, who is it?'

'Roger Bland,' Mike replied shortly. 'Why?'

Eric was nodding, his lined face brightening. 'I thought it might be. Roger and I are old friends, although we haven't seen much of each other for a long time. We used to go sailing together as students. He only had a small boat, but it's amazing what trips we made in it.'

'Hmmph,' Mike said, at last jerking off his jacket and flinging it onto the nearest chair. Eric's fingers twitched, but Mike carried on, 'Nobody's seen much of him for years.' He frowned. 'He's the best there is in the field, but if I can't reach him by the end of the day I'll get hold of Eloise Ryan.' He added reluctantly, 'Bland is the best, but she's not bad.'

Rosen stretched her back, lazily raising her arms above her head before pushing herself to her feet. 'I'm hungry,' she announced, strolling purposefully towards the kitchen area, where one of the screening panels slid aside at her approach.

Eric watched her, obviously annoyed, then said, 'Rosen's right; it is time we had lunch.' He stood up and led the way into the dining area. Low-backed wooden chairs edged a long table, whose shining surface was patterned with gaily-coloured woven mats. Jugs of water sparkled and bowls of apples shone in the soft glow of the lamps concealed in the ceiling, brightening the dull midday light that came through the glass wall.

Rosen came through another sliding panel at the back of the dining area, clutching a tray. This bore a basket of bread, a bowl of roasted vegetables and a large casserole from which wisps of steam and a delicious smell drifted out towards the others as they approached. Rosen put the tray down carefully on the table and unloaded it, then propped it carelessly against the partition behind her. She ladled out a minuscule portion onto a plate, before sitting down with it in front of her.

'Do sit down, Lucy here beside me, Hugh and Mike where you like, and help yourselves,' Eric said tightly, staring irritably at the tray. 'As you can see, that's what we do in this house.'

'It's nothing exciting, just fish stew,' Rosen said, pushing the casserole across towards Lucy, ignoring Ben as he lay down under the table. 'It's nearly always vegetable or fish something or other while Maria is away. So healthy, and of course,' she added maliciously, 'it probably counters the air miles she uses up to go shopping in Rome.'

'My wife is Italian,' Eric said, almost rising to the jibe. 'Maria's visiting her family at the moment. She is the meat-eater of the family. But at least it means we can offer greater support to the locals.'

'They should keep angora goats. Maria would support mohair producers even more.' Rosen put down her knife and fork, leaned across the table for an apple and pushed back her chair, leaving the table without another word.

Eric watched her cross the sitting area, her long skirt flapping. As she disappeared through an opening panel into a dimly glimpsed vestibule that led to her own quarters, he turned apologetically to the others. 'She's going through an awkward spell at the moment, I'm afraid.'

'How old is she?' Lucy asked. 'Fourteen or fifteen? It can be a difficult age.'

'Sixteen,' Eric said shortly. 'And she's been difficult ever since she hit her teens.' He frowned. 'She's in with a crowd of young locals I'm not keen on, but Maria says not to fuss, otherwise Rosen will be even more determined to see them.'

'I'm sure she's right,' Lucy said. 'This is delicious,' she added appreciatively as she used a piece of bread to mop up the juice from her plate.

Beside her Mike was eating his huge serving with great speed, totally disinterested in the conversation, his mind obviously on his own problem. He swallowed the last mouthful and asked, 'What's the weather been like here recently?'

'Very windy, squalls of rain now and again, not great weather for walking the cliffs,' Eric replied after a moment's consideration. 'Is that good?'

Mike shrugged. 'There's less chance of footprints, or marks to show how he got it there. Not,' he added morosely, 'that we'd be likely to find any on that surface, it's too rocky, inside and out. But,' his eyes glittered with fury as he reached out for the fruit bowl, 'it would be a good time for the bastard who did this. Less people about.' He bit hard into the apple he had chosen.

'How on earth,' Lucy asked, 'would he get the skeleton there?'

'Folded up in a large rucksack,' Mike said shortly.

'Dressed in trousers and jacket, with the hood up, he could have been carried, or even walked a short distance across the fields between two people,' Hugh suggested. 'What's the chance of running into anybody? Especially in the early morning or after dusk has fallen.'

Lucy was staring at him, half-horrified, half-disbelieving. 'But what if they had? Somebody passing would surely have seen the skeleton's face.' She shuddered at the thought.

'Then it would be passed off as a joke, a fundraising lark,' Hugh suggested. 'And the skeleton wouldn't have been found here in his den, or at least not just yet.'

Eric was watching him intently. 'Yes, of course, that's probably how it happened. You think then that there was more than one person involved?'

Hugh lifted a quizzical eyebrow. 'Who knows?'

Eric pursued the topic, thinking aloud. 'The helmet and the mail wouldn't be difficult to carry, or the sword. It's the skeleton that would have needed two people to transport it. I'm inclined to think you've hit on the most likely way of getting it here.' He turned to Mike, who was slouching awkwardly in his low-backed chair, glowering as he listened to them. 'Was there anything else with him, other than the sword?'

'The treasure hadn't arrived when we saw him,' Mike replied sardonically. 'Perhaps it will materialise by our next visit.'

'His other hand is hanging over the edge,' Lucy said quickly. 'Perhaps something fell from it, I couldn't see.'

'There was nothing there,' Mike said. 'I looked.' Hugh was staring at him. 'What?' the archaeologist demanded roughly.

'You've got a point, you know,' Hugh said. 'How do we

know we were meant to find him now? Maybe there could have been more treasures to accompany him, and their delivery has been pre-empted.'

'Yes,' Lucy said, her eyes widening. 'Mike, didn't Kevin say they hadn't been working in the serpentine quarry for a bit?'

'Yes,' Mike agreed reluctantly.

'And,' she hurried on, 'I got the impression that he only came on the spur of the moment today.'

Mike grunted, his eyes narrowing. 'Do you realise what you're suggesting?' he demanded, scowling at Hugh. 'That this bastard's got more artefacts to put on the scene.'

'Surely it's a possibility?' Hugh asked reasonably. 'Isn't it?'

'But where the hell's he getting them all from?' Mike burst out.

'An undiscovered tomb,' Lucy offered doubtfully.

'But why move the things?' Hugh asked.

Eric's eyes had swung from one to the other as they spoke. Now he intervened. 'And are they local? Did the Vikings get this far?'

Mike bared his teeth. 'The armour may be Viking, we don't know about the skeleton. We don't even know if it's a male. And the Vikings got pretty much anywhere their ships would take them.' He pulled irritably at the neck of his jumper. 'It's not my period, but I reckon there was a party of Danes in the area, fighting with the locals against Wessex in the eighth or ninth centuries.'

'Really,' Eric exclaimed in surprise. 'Were the Danes Vikings then?'

'Norsemen came from Scandinavia generally,' Mike replied. 'Most people think of them as Vikings, raiders, but they were often explorers, merchants and farmers, just as much as warriors and pirates.'

'So is the provenance of the armour from that period a possibility?' Hugh asked.

Before Mike could reply, Rosen spoke laconically from the

sitting area, where she stood just in front of the open panel that led to her own quarters. 'Perhaps it's an ancestor of ours, brought home to watch over us.'

'My ancestors are Norwegian,' Eric said sharply. 'And this has only been my home for twenty years.'

Rosen looked at him impassively. 'I expect it won't make much difference to most people, because really it's all somewhere in Scandinavia. Still, it'll make a good story for Tamsyn, won't it?' As her father frowned, she added, 'She's just coming up the drive on her bike. I saw her on the CCTV in my room and thought you might like to know.' Without waiting for a response, she turned and drifted off, the panel sliding shut behind her.

'Bloody hell,' Mike snarled, pushing himself to his feet. 'That's the reporter woman, isn't it? I'm damned if I'll talk to her about this.' He looked round the room for shelter, wincing as he heard the sound of an approaching motorbike.

'Take it easy,' Eric said, standing up too. 'I'll speak to the woman. Somebody has to, and it'll be easier for me to plead ignorance about the details.' He walked into the sitting area, pausing beside the chairs to look back at them. 'You stay here. I'll take her into my study, she can't expect to disturb my visitors,' he added seriously.

He moved towards the front door as Mike sank down into his chair again. 'All this bloody glass,' he growled, 'it's like living in a goldfish bowl. And sliding panels everywhere, you never know who's listening in or where they're going to pop up next.'

'Hush, Mike,' Lucy warned. 'You don't want her to notice you.'

'She didn't know I was coming here, even if she knows now who I am,' he countered, although he lowered his voice as a precaution.

'I shouldn't count on that,' Hugh murmured. 'We don't know what her mystery informant has told her.'

Mike shot up again in his chair. 'Will Rasmussen ask her about that? I'd better go ...'

'No,' Hugh said sharply. 'Eric hasn't got where he is without knowing what questions to ask.'

'I guess you're right,' Mike muttered, subsiding. 'Let's hope he uses his wits then.'

A silvery note of music quivered in the air just before the front door slid open. They saw Eric step through it into the courtyard as voices rang across the pavilion.

'Tamsyn, I've been expecting you,' Eric said.

'You've heard the news then,' the reporter said, her soft local accent at variance with the determination of her tone.

'Naturally. I was sure you'd be up to ask me about it, but I'm afraid there's very little I can tell you. No, not the pavilion, Tamsyn, come into the study. The others are still lunching, so this will give us some privacy.'

The front door slid shut noiselessly and silence fell over the dining area as they watched Eric lead the journalist across a narrow strip of stone over one of the pools into the neighbouring unit. She seemed reluctant to follow him, her hooded eyes looking over her shoulder into the main house.

It was only when she was out of sight that Mike pushed himself up in his chair at the dining table. 'I hope they don't stay blathering in there for hours,' he muttered irritably. 'I've got more calls to make.' He drummed his fingers impatiently on the table for some minutes, glancing with growing irritation at Hugh, who was leaning forwards, resting on his arms as he watched the birds on the lawn outside. Mike looked at his watch and shifted again in his chair, gathering his legs to stand up when a nearby noise made him start.

Rosen came out of her quarters, walking past the sitting area without paying them any attention as she hefted a large bag deftly over her shoulder. She had added a thin jacket to her ensemble, and a series of silver studs glittered in her nose and ears as she reached the front door, going out without a word.

The door stayed open as she brushed past her father, who was ushering Tamsyn back into the courtyard.

Lucy met Hugh's amused gaze, her own lips twitching, but Mike grunted, tucking his feet noisily back under his chair. He froze as they heard Tamsyn Warne's voice saying, 'Well, thanks for that, Mr Rasmussen. You haven't given me anything I didn't already know, but I have to cover all avenues. The archaeologist Kevin spoke to is the most obvious, of course, so I'll need to track him down next.'

Mike's expression contorted with fury, but he did not need Lucy's restraining hand to remind him to keep quiet as Tamsyn continued, 'A difficult bloke by all accounts. I thought so when I saw him at the watch station. It's a shame I didn't know about all this then.'

'I'm sure you'll be up to the challenge, Tamsyn,' Eric said. 'I'll be in touch when there's any news.'

'And I hear you may have a personal celebration soon,' the journalist slipped in. 'Are you to be Sir Eric or Lord Rasmussen?'

'What a pleasant fantasy,' Eric replied smoothly. 'I do wonder where you pick up your gossip, Tamsyn.'

'You'd be surprised,' she said. 'I generally get to hear most of what's happening around here.'

Hugh caught Lucy's gaze, one of his eyebrows raised, as the journalist walked away through the courtyard. Eric came back into the pavilion, the front door sliding shut behind him as he crossed the bare floor towards them.

Mike shot to his feet. 'What the hell do you mean, you'll be in touch when there's news?'

Eric regarded him curiously, as the revving of Tamsyn's motorbike heralded her departure. 'But of course I will. It's much better to have the press on side, and give them suitable information when possible.'

Mike spluttered with rage as Eric continued, 'That doesn't mean telling them everything we know, Mike. But if you make a mystery out of the business they'll be even hotter on the scent of a good story.'

Mike glowered, but nodded reluctantly. 'I suppose so. Bloody parasites.'

'Are you going to try tracing Bland again, or just go for the other Viking specialist?' Eric asked.

'I'm not giving up on Bland yet,' Mike said. 'He's an awkward devil, I studied under him at Oxford, so I ought to know, but there's nobody with his degree of knowledge. He has a real feel for the period.' He moved forward, raising a casual hand to Lucy and Hugh. 'Thanks for the lunch, Rasmussen. I'll be getting on now.'

'Well, everyone's out and about tonight, but you must join us for lunch tomorrow and we'll exchange news then,' Eric said briskly. 'Will one o'clock suit you?'

Mike nodded and headed for the door, but Lucy got quickly to her feet and said lightly, 'I'll come out to the car with you, Mike.'

She followed him out of the house and walked beside him towards the red Passat estate that was parked a little down the drive. 'Alright, Mike, don't keep it bottled up,' she advised gently.

He glared at her, his teeth clenched. They parted slightly as he hissed, 'Do you expect me to be rude about a friend of yours?'

Lucy suppressed a spurt of laughter. 'Of course,' she said calmly. 'You're always rude about Anna.'

Mike swung round on her as they reached the car. 'Why the hell do you have such awful friends? I thought she was bad enough, but now ... Who the hell,' he burst out, 'does he think he is? He was virtually giving me orders in there.'

'It's only that he's used to organising things,' Lucy said. 'And he's not really a friend of ours, but of my father's, and I'm not sure,' she added reflectively, 'how much Daddy really liked him.'

'Enough to make him Will's godfather,' Mike said shortly as he jerked the driver's door open.

'Daddy respected his energy and commitment,' Lucy said, 'and he was a generous patron. Anyhow, I think we're here to be useful.'

'What does he want?' Mike demanded, sliding into the car.

'Well, he heard Hugh was coming down to see Alastair Drewe.' She saw Mike's blank look and added, 'You know, the vicar who's written about holy sites around here, the one who's putting you up.'

Mike grunted and she continued, 'Well, Eric made the connection with me and got in touch, asking us to stay for a few days while Hugh and Alastair have discussions. I reckon he wants to sound Hugh out about some work of his own; he's already mentioned an autobiographical book.'

'Occupational hazard,' Mike said, not really interested. 'Hugh must be used to it.'

'And,' Lucy said, her eyes sparkling with amusement, 'I think the sub-plot might concern Will and Rosen. I suspect Eric wants to divert her attention away from these friends in the village he doesn't approve of.'

A glimmer of humour crossed Mike's face. 'Does Rasmussen know your brother well?'

Lucy shook her head. 'The presents usually come on his birthdays and at Christmas, but they've only met a couple of times, when Daddy was still alive.'

Mike was looking much happier. 'Then I hope they'll have a good time together. Will may even develop a strong interest in environmentalism.'

'He already has, really,' Lucy said, aware of her brother's tendency to become absorbed in his latest passion. 'I think he's beginning to combine the things that matter to him, the land, animal welfare, sustainability.'

'I shouldn't think he'd have much in common with Rasmussen's daughter then, although he may dive into the

Gothic with her,' Mike said, switching on the engine. 'I must go, Lucy; I can't stay here all afternoon gossiping about Will. I'd better find this bloke Drewe's place soon.'

She bit her lip as she stepped back, saying lightly, 'Give my love to Anna if you see her.'

Mike's head jerked round. 'What?'

'Mike, I told you she was helping Alastair Drewe with his pageant.'

'Bloody hell,' Mike said desperately, grinding the gears, 'that's all I need right now.' He slammed the door shut and swung the car around, driving off without another word, narrowly missing Eric's immaculate Renault.

Mike stood in front of the faded blue door, waiting impatiently. He used the tarnished brass dolphin knocker to pound out another thunderous tattoo, and stepped back to glare up at the small whitewashed cottage, which was almost hidden by the spreading walnut tree in its front garden.

An elderly man emerged from an outhouse in the neighbouring garden, briefly visible in his thick trousers and guernsey as he stood staring over the boundary hedge of fuchsias. He turned, disappearing from sight, although the bobble on his knitted hat bounced in and out of view as he walked along a path behind the towering bushes. He opened the gate and came out onto the sheltered path that ran along the valley. 'Looking for vicar?' he asked, his words running softly together, so that it took Mike a moment to understand them.

'Yes,' he said shortly.

The man considered him. 'Come about a wedding, have you?'

'No,' Mike growled. 'And not a funeral either,' he added hastily, seeing the question forming on the man's lips.

'Ah,' the man's eyes lit up, 'a baptism, is it then?' Without waiting for an answer, he continued, 'One of them incomers, are you?'

'No,' Mike said, keen to forestall the growing fable, 'I've only come to stay for a few nights.'

'Oh,' the man said, moving a little to his left to see the bag Mike had dumped on Alastair's doorstep. 'A friend of his, are you then?'

'Will it be alright to leave the bag, do you think?' Mike asked.

'Aye, put it round back, it'll lie safe enough, there'll be no rain 'til evening,' the man said to Mike's back as the archaeologist picked up his bag. 'We've a visitor too, my Janet and me. Sent by vicar, she was. Nice young lady she be,' he added with a spark in his eyes. 'Happen he'll introduce you. Especially if you're here for his pageant.'

Mike's brisk footsteps faltered as he rounded the corner of the cottage and the words sank into his mind. He dropped the bag and came back to stand, arms akimbo, in front of the elderly man. 'Who did you say is staying with you?' he demanded.

'The young lady doing pageant with vicar,' the man replied, a grin spreading across his face. 'They'll be down on shore now, with the boats. You'll find them there.'

Mike scowled and strode past him, unaware of the stare that followed his progress along the path towards the village. The small cottages, bulging granite walls cleanly painted in white, had occasional late roses flowering in the greenery that festooned them, while the red and purple bells of fuchsia bushes dangled ubiquitously in all the gardens. A turquoise building stood, conspicuously different, behind a screen of trees whose leaves were drifting down in lazy spirals. As Mike passed he realised that it was a low wooden-walled church.

The path emerged into the single-track village street that ran steeply downhill and then sharply up again round a wide curve. Mike looked down on the sloping slate roofs that covered the squat cottages lining the street. A teashop on the left was doing a roaring trade in spite of the overcast sky and blustering wind. The tables in its small front garden were crammed with walkers, their backpacks resting against the low wall that shielded them from the street, while more visitors crowded the cottage rooms, their breath misting the leaded lights.

Mike walked purposefully down the centre of the street, brushing past the women peering into the windows of the craft shop. He narrowly avoided a collision with a woman emerging from a low doorway on the right, head turned away as she spoke to somebody over her shoulder. Her basket, laden with brown paper parcels, brushed Mike's thigh and she looked round.

'Sorry,' she said amiably. 'If you're after the fish, you'd better get your skates on. It's going fast. Especially the oysters, even though Mark has only just brought them in. And they're the native ones, too, always the best.'

As she swung herself up into a Range Rover and drove away Mike saw the wooden shack the vehicle had screened. The narrow window was laden with stainless-steel trays, mostly empty now, but a few forlorn prawns still lay in a huddle in a bowl. He hesitated, wondering if he should provide something for dinner, then thought he'd better see what his host was planning.

Mike had reached the bottom of the hill and as he passed the shack he noticed the buildings beyond were generally bigger, more solid and utilitarian, with their unpainted granite walls framing a small cove, a natural harbour within sheltering headlands. One of the wide doorways stood open onto the rocky beach and Mike skirted the heaps of lobster pots and faded buoys to peer inside. He recognised the place as a pilchard cellar as soon as he saw the central cobbled courtyard with gutters in the floor leading to a pit where the pressed oil had collected. He was on the verge of stepping inside for a closer look when the sound of voices impinged on his thoughts.

He glanced to where a crowd of people were clustering, almost concealing the boats stranded on the pebbles beyond, their attention focused on three people in their midst. Mike immediately spotted Alastair, his height making him tower over the others, as he talked to a shorter stockier man in an oilskin coat. As Mike watched the two men turned to the woman beside them. Mike groaned inwardly as he recognised the black curling hair falling over the shoulders of a bright red duffle coat that concealed her shapely figure.

Bloody hell, he thought dismally, this is just what I don't need. Damned woman. Why does she always crop up?

The grace of Anna's gesturing hands left him untouched, but the sound of her gurgling laughter spurred him on. Looking round urgently for an escape route he spotted the path leading round the headland above the beach. He strode on purposefully up the street, which rose steeply now to the bend that curved around the rambling bunch of buildings that formed the local pub. As he reached it he was relieved to see the sign for the coastal path pointing to the right. He turned onto it, emerging above the layers of roofs to a stunning view of the sea beyond its protective headlands and of the beach below where the tide was gently encroaching, lapping at the hulls of the furthest boats.

For an instant he thought Anna looked up at him, but he was sure she would not recognise him. After all, she was not expecting him to be here, and she was quite some way off. Nonetheless, Mike set off purposefully along the path, rounding the corner to find the wide expanse of the sea spread out in front of him, a grey mass under a dull sky, only breaking into flashes of sparkling greens and blue where the occasional ray of sunshine touched it.

A low wooden roof on the edge of the headland caught Mike's eye and he turned onto the narrow path that led down to it. As it emerged more fully in front of him he recognised the huer's hut that Lucy had pointed out to him that morning. Standing here beside it, looking out over the wide stretch of the Channel, he understood how well positioned it was to catch the mass movement of the migrating shoals.

Just as he approached the door it opened and a stooping

figure appeared, its bizarre appearance making Mike stop abruptly. The figure stopped too, straightening to loom over Mike. It pulled its billowing dark cloak more tightly round itself, standing so that its face was almost totally shaded by its broad-brimmed hat.

The two stared at each other, Mike feeling a niggling sense of recognition that grew into amazed certainty. 'You!' he exclaimed disbelievingly. 'What the devil are you doing here?'

As the group on the beach broke up, some people walking purposefully away over the pebbles, some drifting into groups to chat, Anna Evesleigh stared up along the cliff path. Now I wonder where Mike's off to, she thought. After musing for a minute or two she glanced at Alastair, who was engrossed in conversation with a couple of women. Anna grimaced. I bet I know what that's all about, she thought. Which of them should play the lady of the manor, the closest any of them will come to pairing off with Mark.

Beyond the women she caught sight of Mark striding off to his dinghy, his oilskins flapping around his long legs. It's a shame he won't play the royalist Cavalier squire, she thought, her mind still absorbed with the pageant, but perhaps the role of Elizabethan privateer is more his style. I'm sure the Queen would have approved of him. He's not exactly good looking, but he has a powerful personality and that impenetrable air of his is quite challenging. I could really see him fighting off the Spaniards. She watched as he clambered into the dinghy and began to row with powerful strokes out to the boat that bobbed gently in deeper water. I wonder, her mind took a more prosaic turn as she swung round, whether Lucy and I will get some of his oysters in the pub tonight.

Anna scanned the cliff path again before she lifted a hand to Alastair, who was quite oblivious to her movement, and began to casually weave her way through the knots of gossipers, exchanging a brief word here and there, but refusing to stop.

Once she was in the street there were fewer people about. The two ahead of her turned purposefully into the pub and as Anna passed it a wave of noise rolled out through the opening door. She smiled to herself, sure the talk had already turned away from the pageant to matters of more immediate concern. Fish, parking and tourists, she suspected.

Turning onto the cliff path she was relieved she was well wrapped up as she met the wind full in the face. It was rising again, she realised, wondering if they were in for another bout of rough weather. She set off briskly, swinging her arms, glad to be moving after so long standing on the beach. Glancing down, she saw Alastair was gradually shifting his two companions towards the street. They were the last people there, slowly leaving the beach to a quiet stillness as the tide crept inexorably upwards.

Anna paused for a moment, enjoying the sight of the boats in weather-bleached blues and reds, melding into the darker colours of the stones. She could quite see why so many artists liked to paint the view. I wonder, she mused, if the person stationed in the huer's hut ever had chance to stand like this, because they must have looked down on almost exactly the same scene, although no doubt there were more boats then. Not, she thought practically, if they were on duty. Once the heaving silver shoals of pilchards were sighted, the huer must have alerted the fishermen at once. Then it would be all action down there.

Her imagination was busy picturing the activity when the sound of raised voices reached her ears. Good heavens, she thought ruefully, Mike has already found somebody to shout at.

Anna hurried on round the corner of the headland and the voices became more audible, coming, she realised from the hut below. She walked down the little path and came upon Mike glaring belligerently up at the strangest figure she had ever seen off a theatrical set. The figure seemed to tower inside its enveloping cloak, its head screened by a broad-brimmed hat.

'I shan't let it rest like this,' Mike said forcefully, shaking his fist at the other person. 'You must be out of your mind.'

The figure shifted awkwardly backwards against the wall of the hut, then darted sideways up another little path to the cliff route, striding away from the village. Mike swung round, taking a furious step after him, but halted as Anna called his name urgently.

'What on earth is going on?' she demanded, taken aback at the black fury on his face as he turned towards her. Used as she was to Mike's rages, she had never seen him like this before.

'What the devil are you doing here?' he shouted. 'Why do you always turn up where you're not wanted?'

Anna's blue eyes hardened, but she kept her voice light as she said, 'It is a public path, Mike. Perhaps you should be glad it's me that came upon this little scene, and not a walker or one of the villagers. You look positively murderous.'

'That's nothing to how I feel,' he growled, turning his shoulder on her and kicking furiously at a stone, sending it spinning away across the path to fall rattling down the cliff face.

'He can't have been doing any harm,' Anna said. 'He's been coming here for years, and the locals are quite happy about him. I've never heard anyone say a bad word about him.'

'What? What the hell are you talking about?' Mike swung back to face her. 'What do you know about him?'

Relieved to see his face had softened into its more normal expression of anger, Anna moved over to the bench placed so thoughtfully against the slope of the cliff and sat down, stretching her long legs out in front of her, elegant even in their jeans and ankle boots.

'Well,' she said, 'he was the hermit, wasn't he?'

'Hermit?' Mike repeated blankly. 'Hermit?'

'Yes,' Anna said. 'I hadn't seen him before, but there can't be many men in black cloaks and hats in the area, can there?' Mike opened his mouth, but Anna gave him no chance to say anything. 'He comes to stay in the hut during October and

November. He shouldn't, of course, but he's been coming for so long that the locals have got used to him. And I've never heard there've been any problems, so I don't think you really need to worry about the building. I didn't realise you would,' she added thoughtfully. 'I didn't think it was old enough to bother you.'

Mike was staring at her, the anger draining from his face, leaving it strangely puzzled. He shoved his hands into his jacket pockets as he said, 'What else do you know about him?'

Anna lifted a shoulder. 'Nothing. I don't think anyone does. I expect the locals were curious at first, but they're used to a lot of outsiders drifting through. There are so many artists who come and go, and there's a strong music group here too, that attracts quite a few itinerant musicians.' She glanced at Mike, surprised that he was paying so much attention to what she said, but pleased that his mood was improving so quickly. 'You should try Friday nights, folk nights; they sing a fantastic selection of local songs. I've incorporated some of them into the pageant. Will you be here for it?'

'I won't be here any longer than I have to,' he snapped.

'Of course, you've got to look into this new discovery, haven't you?' Anna said. 'The Viking Guardian of the Shore. It sounds very exciting.'

Mike scowled. 'How did you hear of it?' he demanded.

'Alastair told me,' she replied. 'You're staying with him, aren't you?' Her eyes sparkled with laughter. 'I didn't know he had a spare bedroom. He palmed me off onto the B&B next door. I suppose,' she added lightly, 'he was worried about giving fodder to the rumour mill. Thomas, my host, is probably the leading gossiper. I should think the only time he isn't on the alert for news is when he's asleep – it's almost impossible for Janet, his wife, to wake him up in the morning. Even though she does a fantastic cooked breakfast, and the first whiff of frying bacon has me out of bed. Maybe you should come and have yours with me. From what she says, Alastair's meals are a bit spartan.'

'Hmmph.' Mike sounded thoughtful.

Anna got to her feet. 'I'm going back to the village for tea with Alastair. I think he's expecting you too,' she said over her shoulder as she set off towards the main cliff path.

Mike fell into step beside her, saying heavily, 'So here we are, all together again. Even Will and his grandmother are going to be with us by the weekend. I wonder what we'll find to do with ourselves this time.'

'Enjoy hearing all about your work, I expect,' she said. She gasped as he seized her arm, pulling her to a halt. 'Don't, Mike,' she said shortly.

'It's a fake, alright,' he growled. 'Keep it to yourself if you can, but the find is a fake. Perhaps not the armour, but the whole scene. Somebody is trying to make a fool out of me.'

'Are you …' she broke off, aware that it would not be sensible to ask if he was sure. 'So maybe it's just as well we are all getting together. We've proved to be rather good at problem solving.'

'Murders, you mean,' he said, his fingers tightening on her arm. 'Well,' he scowled, 'when I find out who's behind this, even if it's …' He pulled himself up with an effort. 'There's no murder yet, unless,' his eyes narrowed, 'the skeleton under the chain mail comes into that category.'

'You'd better fill me in,' Anna said, 'but let go now, Mike, you're hurting me.'

He released her as a young couple appeared round the headland on the main cliff path, looking askance at them as they stood there. 'Come on,' he said gruffly, 'why are you hanging around here?' He stiffened as the couple slipped past them, and turned on the spot, about to go after them.

'For goodness' sake, Mike,' Anna exclaimed, 'where are you going?'

'Nowhere,' he growled. 'That's the bloke who discovered the amazing Viking in his cliff-side tomb, and he's with Rasmussen's daughter.' He frowned as he fell into step beside her. 'I wonder if they're in it together.'

'What?' Anna asked. 'I still don't know what you're talking about.'

Mike began to tell her as they walked back. When they turned into the village street he lowered his voice but kept talking, shooting suspicious glances at passersby, and frequently stopping dead to look over his shoulder. They branched into the pathway that led along the valley, and Mike's monologue deteriorated into conspiracy theory, so it was with relief that Anna saw a distraction through the screen of trees on her right.

'Oh look,' she exclaimed. 'There's Alastair. Hi, Alastair!'

The vicar was on the threshold of his turquoise church and looked round at the sound of her voice. 'Anna,' he said in his pleasant baritone, 'how nicely timed. I'm just on my way home. And Mike too. Thomas told me you'd arrived and left your bag. I'm glad you've found us in time for tea.'

'Why don't we just quickly show Mike the church?' Anna asked, crossing the forecourt. She looked at the archaeologist, who was glowering beside her. 'It's quite lovely, and it's where our pageant is going to start.'

Alastair had turned back and opened the door, leading the way inside. Mike followed Anna reluctantly, hissing into her ear, 'Keep quiet about what I've told you. He doesn't know about it.'

Anna nodded, so that her black curls tickled the tip of his nose, making him sneeze loudly. 'Look,' she said enthusiastically, spreading out her hands.

He lifted his head and looked around at the simple white-washed interior, plain glass windows framing the bare alders that lined the stream in the valley on one side and on the other the oaks that screened the path. Benches were set out neatly on the floor, and every window sill bore a collection of items, carved wooden boats and dolphins, shell-covered boxes, small mosaics of fishes, smooth pebbles and weathered pieces of drift-wood. At the far end of the church stood a stylised life-size wooden figure of a man, his long white beard blending with his turquoise robes.

'The patron of our little church,' Alastair explained. 'It's more than appropriate that it should be St Andrew, the fisher of men, the protector of the fishing community that built this place with their own hands. We're lucky that Mark Teague is such a skilled woodcarver; he made this statue for us a couple of years ago.'

'He's also a very fine singer, and will lead the songs on the beach after the blessing of the boats. We start with a short service here,' Anna explained resolutely in the face of Mike's disinterest as they left the church, 'and then a procession moves through the village, stopping on the way to the bay at a number of spots for recitals. Tamsyn Warne, a local journalist,' Anna refused to be deflected at Mike's spluttering, 'has done some fantastic research for us, so the participants reflect the way people lived in the area from very early times down to the more recent past. We start with a fine group of Phoenician traders, and one chap has grown a beard specially to look authentic. There are Saxons and Normans, no Vikings though,' she added as they approached Alastair's cottage. She hurried on before Mike could retaliate, 'Mark is an Elizabethan privateer.'

Mike muttered something inaudible and Anna ignored him. 'Alastair dons an amazing set of mutton chop whiskers to play a Georgian parson superbly, and we have a John Wesley to match him. Tamsyn plays one of the Victorian women who ran local papers.' Anna stopped in the cottage gateway as Alastair was buttonholed by a passing man, but she carried on speaking, 'Just about everybody's taking part, often as versions of themselves, so the landlord at *The Three Tuns* will be there carrying an appropriate barrel and the doctor is coming as an eighteenth century surgeon in a traditional frock coat. We've a couple of wrestlers and hurlers, some miners and bal maidens. There are preventative officers and sea captains, lifeboatmen, and loads of fishermen, as well as quite a few smugglers – we seem to have a plethora of eye patches, and a couple of crutches, but we've managed to avoid parrots so far.'

Mike was showing faint signs of interest as Alastair rejoined them and they followed him into the garden of his cottage, so she went on, 'We've also got a very good itinerant salesman, complete with donkey laden with packs, and Mark's cousin Peter as a serpentine worker with a genuinely old moleskin waistcoat worn by his great-granddad.'

'Is it an all-male bonding session?' Mike enquired sarcastically.

'No, indeed,' Alastair said hastily, opening the front door and ushering them directly into a small cold living room. 'We've a lot of ladies taking part too.' He briefly glanced at Anna. 'Perhaps rather more ladies than men. A shame they mind so about duplicating roles.'

Anna gurgled with amusement. 'We've got a few fishwives, complete with fake gutting knives, so I hope that competition doesn't get out of hand. In fact,' she tossed back her longs curls as she took off her coat, 'many of the women seem to carry something that could be a lethal weapon. There are a number of spinners, but the most popular roles are the dancers with their belled staves and cymbals.'

'I can't wait,' Mike said with feeling.

'We're all having such a good time,' Alastair said. 'It's even bringing back the happier days of my youth, amateur perform-ances, you know; we were especially fond of Rattigan and Wilde then. Well, Mike,' he added encouragingly, 'we hope that you'll be here long enough to take part in our little production. I'm sure Anna could suggest a suitable role for you.'

Anna suppressed the bubble of laughter that rose in her chest at the sight of Mike's face. Alastair had seen it too, and added quickly, 'No matter, perhaps you'd rather come to the feast on the shore. It's going to be a very fine one – chiefly fish, of course, stewed and barbequed with a variety of sauces and so on. But I hear there'll be stargazy pie too. And there will be singing. Then it will all end with dancing in the old fish cellar.

We're hoping to raise a great deal for the lifeboats. It's never enough though.'

'When is this amazing event?' Mike demanded.

'This Saturday,' Anna said lightly. 'So you timed your visit perfectly. At the very least you can carry one of the oil lanterns that symbolise the pilchard trade.'

Mike opened his mouth to reply, but the words failed to emerge as his eye was caught by the contents of the living room. He stared round, flabbergasted. It was crammed with furniture, old country pieces that Alastair had undoubtedly taken with the place, which only partially concealed the carpet of rampaging red flowers, worn in places, but still vivid in the dark room. Victorian prints smothered the faded wallpaper, with pride of place given to *The Light of the World* over the fireplace, where a pile of cobwebbed ashes sat sadly on the hearth. Every spare surface in the room was dotted with lighthouses, of a variety of shapes and sizes, but each one of serpentine in its wide range of colours.

Alastair laughed, his expression looking more light-hearted and younger than usual. 'It always surprises people,' he commented. 'Peter Teague introduced me to them when I came to the area, and I got rather carried away with the collecting bug.'

'And now,' finished Anna, sitting down on the sagging sofa under the window and tucking her legs up, 'everybody locally brings him one when they find a new version, and he can't turn them down.'

'Teague,' Mike said suddenly. 'I came across a bloke called Teague this morning. Is it a common local name?'

'Oh yes,' Alastair answered readily. 'Mark's one of the Teagues too. Was it him you met?'

Mike shook his head. 'It was a young chap, Kevin, a serpentine worker.'

Alastair brightened. 'Actually, Kevin is Peter Teague's son, and Peter is Mark's cousin. Mark is playing a big part in the pageant, not just with his role and his singing, but by helping us organise the event too. He's a very enterprising man,' Alastair went on approvingly, 'able to turn his hand to almost anything. He started the local oyster beds a few years ago.' The vicar waved a vague hand towards the cliffs. 'You go round the headland beyond the huer's hut and in ten minutes you'll have reached the river where you may see his boats out. I always think the sails going backwards and forwards make it a very timeless scene. And of course Mark has made the fishery a very prosperous enterprise, employing quite a number of people from the neighbourhood now.'

Alastair tapped himself reproachfully on the forehead. 'Tea. I mustn't keep talking or it'll never get made. And I got Janet to bake me some of her scones. Anna's landlady next door, you know. They're very good, very good.' He moved away through a low doorway, stooping to avoid knocking his head on the lintel, and began to bang around in the kitchen. 'Perhaps you'd like to get your bag and take it upstairs, Mike. Come out this way, if you edge past me carefully. There isn't much space, I fear. You're in the room on the right, at the top of the stairs. I'm afraid there's only a view into the tree in the garden, but you do get to hear the sea. The bathroom's at the back.'

Mike got up without a word and went out through the kitchen, returning almost immediately with a bulging canvas bag. He passed Anna, then paused, looking round, rather nonplussed.

'There's a door behind the curtain in the corner,' she said, gesturing towards it. 'It opens directly onto the stairs. Take care,' she added, as he yanked the threadbare velour curtain aside and wrenched the door open, 'they'll be steep and uneven if they're like the ones next door.'

Mike grunted dismissively and Anna listened to him treading heavily up the stairs, smiling a little as she heard him stumble near the top and swear in a muffled tone. She uncurled her legs to stand up and sauntered into the kitchen doorway, surveying

Alastair as he put mismatched cups and saucers onto a tray. Her glance flickered over the narrow work surfaces, where piles of plates were mixed haphazardly with open bags of fruit and vegetables. I wonder, she mused idly, watching him push aside bottles of lemonade, how much he actually eats of this.

Alastair uttered a small exclamation of satisfaction as he grasped a box of teabags. He dropped three into a teapot and looked up suddenly, meeting her gaze. 'Something's bothering you,' he said quietly. 'It isn't the pageant, is it? I'm sure all the squabblers will sort themselves out.'

Anna shook her head. 'It's Mike,' she replied quietly. She hesitated, but heard the bathroom door bang shut upstairs and said quickly, 'He's worried about this new find.'

'This is the Viking in the cave, isn't it?' Alastair smiled as he picked up the steaming kettle and poured boiling water into the teapot. 'I've lost count of the number of times I was told about him, and each recital was subtly different. I don't expect it was even a Viking that was found.'

'It is genuine Viking armour, apparently,' Anna said. Alastair turned with the empty kettle in his hand to stare at her in amazement. She bit her lip, then hurried on, 'Look, I shouldn't say this, but I know you'll keep it to yourself, and you ought to know how jumpy Mike is. He's worried because he's pretty sure the armour is real, but he's just as positive it's been planted there. He's always had a phobia about professional rivals, and this has got him really on edge. I found him on the cliffs at the huer's hut shouting at the poor old hermit, who can hardly have done him any harm.' She stopped as she heard Mike's heavy footsteps crossing the landing.

Alastair had been frozen to the spot, his eyes fixed on Anna as she spoke. Now he seemed to come to himself with a start, and carefully put the kettle down as he said quietly, 'I'm sure it's nothing to worry about. I know the hermit, he's been coming here as long as I've been around.' Alastair paused, and they heard Mike's feet thumping down the stairs. 'Some evenings he drops in for a game of chess, and once in a while I go to watch the sunset with him. I've got an extra shift at the watch station tonight but I'll go down to the huer's hut before I leave and make sure everything's alright. He may even take his evening walk with me. So don't you worry.'

'But surely it'll be dark, he can't go walking then,' Anna said, aware of Mike in the living room behind her, flinging himself heavily into one of the old armchairs.

Alastair pulled open the fridge to take out a bottle of milk. 'Now I wonder where the jug is,' he muttered, looking round rather hopelessly. Anna stepped forward and picked it up from the counter, where it was hidden behind an open cereal packet. 'Ah yes, thank you. I couldn't see it for looking.' He poured milk into the jug, putting it down on the tray and absently leaving the milk bottle on the counter. 'Yes, you were saying, it would be dark, although there's a full moon tonight, you know, and the sky is very clear now. He knows the coastal path and the inland footpaths like the back of his hand, he's walked them almost every autumn night for more than a decade, right across to Portharrock and back. He says,' Alastair murmured as he picked up the tray, 'that he likes to hear the seals sing in the starlight.'

THREE

Lucy pulled the collar of her fleece more tightly round her throat as she strolled down Polkenan's quiet street with Anna and Mike in the darkness of early evening. An owl hooted from inland along the valley, the only sound other than their footsteps and the faint pervasive murmur of the sea on their right. Curtains were still unclosed at the windows of the cottages lining the street, so bright squares shone across their route, lighting the walkers for a brief moment here and there. Smoke drifted upwards from the chimneys, mingling with the opalescent streaks of the Milky Way stretching across the sky in a vast arc.

As they passed the small cove Lucy glanced across it, noticing that the tide was high now. Her attention was caught momentarily by movement in the shadow of the old pilchard cellar, where a cat moved with stealthy confidence over the rim of rocks that was all of the beach left above the sea. A moonlit path led beyond the silent boats rocking on the gently heaving water and out between the headlands.

Lucy drew a deep breath of satisfaction. 'This is just perfect,' she said quietly.

'You should have seen it earlier,' Anna said, her blue eyes sparkling as they approached *The Three Tuns* on the corner. 'It was mayhem.'

'It always is around you,' Mike muttered, turning into the pub courtyard where wooden benches and tables stood deserted under the subdued glow of scattered lanterns. 'You and a peaceful life couldn't possibly go together.'

Anna was about to reply, but Lucy said quickly, 'It's nice enough to sit outside, isn't it?'

'Only if there isn't room indoors,' Mike said firmly. 'Let's see.'

He opened the pub door, releasing a warm fug of air and the roar of many voices. The scent of wood smoke mingled with spiced wine drifted around them as he pushed his way in, followed by the women, and looked about the crowded room, where heads seemed to be just beneath the low blackened beams. Pewter tankards lined the top of the bar, where two women, one in her late teens, the other possibly her mother, were competently serving customers. Just beyond them a bulky man leaned on the wooden counter, chatting to a group of locals. Wall lamps created pools of light and shade over the edges of the room, and Mike's searching eyes spotted a table on the far side, well away from the hearth where logs blazed, the focus of many of the visitors.

He began to work his way past the gossiping clusters of people, straight across the room, clearing a narrow path for Lucy and Anna. There were just three stools lining the little table, whose wooden surface was scratched and pitted with years of use. Mike skirted round it and sat down, leaning precariously against the wall as he unfastened his donkey jacket, revealing a jumper pocked with snags and a couple of small holes. 'Come on,' he instructed. 'Sit down, and then I'll go and get the drinks.'

Lucy and Anna pulled off their coats, tucking them under the stools before they sat down, Lucy with her back to the bar, and Anna next to the neighbouring table.

'Well, what's it to be?' Mike demanded impatiently as Lucy looked round, appreciating the yellowed finish on the bumpy walls, surely imitating the effect of centuries of tobacco smoke, and peering at the collection of framed photographs showing faces and scenes from earlier years in the village.

Anna glanced at Lucy. 'They do a good mulled wine. Do you fancy one?'

Lucy nodded, so Mike straightened himself and got up. 'Right, two mulls then.'

'Please,' Anna said. 'And could you bring us a menu? We want to eat too.'

Mike was already thrusting his way through the crowd and she said crossly, 'I wonder if he heard me.' She stared after him. 'And I don't know why on earth he doesn't get rid of that ancient jumper.' Voices at the nearby table attracted her attention and she turned, her long curls swirling over her shoulders, to meet the eyes of the girl sitting behind her, whose clown-white face and black spiky hair were less conspicuous here than at Pennance.

'Hi,' Anna said happily. 'I didn't see you there. Lucy,' she said, 'this is Rosen, our semi-official photographer. She's keeping a record of the rehearsals as well as the actual pageant, and has done all our publicity shots. Tamsyn Warne recommended her. You know, the reporter who's helped with the research.'

Lucy looked at Rosen, who was staring sullenly at her. 'Hi, Rosen,' she said. 'I didn't know you were interested in photography.' Aware of Anna's curiosity, Lucy added, 'We're staying at Rosen's father's house.'

'I don't mention the pageant there, so don't go telling him what I'm doing,' Rosen said warningly. 'It's not a worthwhile occupation in his view, so Eric doesn't think it's important. He's never heard of photographers like Alixandra Fazzina, and even if he had, he wouldn't think they counted. The only thing that matters is saving the world his way.'

'I haven't heard of her either,' Lucy confessed.

'I guess lots of people haven't,' Rosen said, 'but you'd probably know her pictures. She concentrates on people affected by wars, and what you see in her photos tells you more than masses of words. You should see some of the photos she's done of women in Afghanistan. If I could do something like that ...' She tailed off.

'What about Ansel Adams?' Anna asked. 'Surely he was an environmentalist as well as a photographer?'

'Yeah, sure,' Rosen shrugged, 'but Eric doesn't rate him. And anyhow, I don't want to do environment issues, and not fancy portraits either. I want to get out there in real life and do gritty stuff, stress scenes, conflicts.' Her eyes glittered with determination as she stared defiantly at them.

'She's really good,' the young man with her said defensively in the soft local burr as he turned towards them. 'And so far she's only had chance to do local work, like.'

Lucy realised she knew his sharp-featured face too. 'Hi,' she said. 'You're Kevin, aren't you? I didn't recognise you at first. Anna,' she met her friend's eyes fleetingly, 'Mike and I met Kevin this morning. He found the mystery Viking.'

'Oh Lord,' Anna exclaimed, her eyes widening. She said quickly to Kevin, 'Mike's at the bar, but for heaven's sake, keep your back to the table when he brings the drinks over. We don't want to hear any more about it this evening.'

'Nor do I,' Kevin muttered. Beside him Rosen sipped her lager, her eyes running round the room as he added, 'Fair sick to death of the fuss, I am. Just want to get back to digging the serpentine.' He brightened a little. 'Unless there's a reward, like. Tamsyn said there might be.'

'Don't ask Mike,' Anna warned. The youth glared at her before he swiftly turned his shoulder, shielding his face as Mike bore down on them, two glasses of steaming mull in one hand, a half pint tankard of beer in the other.

'Mike, you didn't bring the menu,' Anna said reproachfully as he put the glasses down on the table. Silently he reached into his coat pocket and pulled out a folded piece of paper. 'Sorry,' she said apologetically, opening it and glancing at it as he sat down. 'Oh great, they've got lasagne again. It was pretty good last time, local beef from the landlord's brother's farm. I'll have that.'

'Me too,' Lucy said, getting to her feet. 'What about you, Mike?'

He swallowed a mouthful of his beer. 'I'm not eating yet. I'm going to walk along the cliff to the coastal watch station and meet up with Hugh and Alastair. Alastair said they'd be walking back after eight, and coming up here to eat. I'll have something then.' He took another gulp of his drink as Lucy went over to the bar, menu in her hand.

'Is that a good idea, Mike?' Anna asked, cradling her warm glass. 'You don't know the cliff path here, do you?'

He grunted dismissively. 'There's plenty of light, and I don't need to hurry.'

'Why not have another drink,' she pressed, peering at her watch. 'It's only just seven, so you've got ages yet.'

He stared at her. 'What's this about, Anna? Short of male company?'

'If I ever were,' she flared, putting down her glass so sharply that the mulled wine slopped over the rim, 'I certainly wouldn't be looking for yours.'

'Just as well,' he answered, draining his tankard, 'because you bloody well wouldn't get it.'

Lucy returned as he got to his feet, forestalling Anna's blistering reply. 'Are you off already?' Lucy asked him in surprise.

'Yes, I've had enough of the company here for one evening,' he growled, shouldering his way through the knots of people to the door.

'What was that all about?' Lucy asked as she sat down again.

'Stubborn pig,' Anna said, her normally equable temper still ruffled as she used a tissue to mop up the spilt wine. 'I tried to persuade him not to walk along the cliff path to meet Hugh and Alastair, and the conceited brute thought I wanted his company.

As if I would.'

'Well, you don't normally try to keep him with us,' Lucy commented.

'It's only that I don't want him to meet the hermit again,' Anna said, 'and Alastair mentioned that he goes walking that way every night.' Lucy was looking completely puzzled as she sipped her mulled wine, and Anna realised that she had not yet heard the story. 'There's an old bloke who comes down here every autumn to stay in the huer's hut on the edge of the headland. Nobody knows who he is, but he's been around for years, and he's just accepted by the locals. Anyway, I found Mike up on the cliff there this afternoon having a furious row with him. Even knowing Mike's temper as I do, I've never seen him like that. He was beside himself with rage.'

'His tempers usually burn themselves out quickly,' Lucy said reassuringly.

'He's quite something, isn't he?' Rosen's voice commented beside them. 'I'd really like to get some pictures of him looking the way he did on the cliff path. Rage personified.'

'Of course,' Anna remembered, 'we passed you near the huer's hut, didn't we?'

'Yeah, I was hoping to get pictures of the old bloke up there, but he went off really quickly in front of us, and disappeared up past the oyster fishery. And I wanted to see what the angles were like for some shots down onto the beach,' Rosen said. 'They'll be okay, give us unexpected views of the pageant.'

'I'd be interested to see what you've got of the hermit. I only got a quick glimpse of him but he must be a fantastic study. Did you get anything much of the rehearsal today?' Anna enquired, keen to keep the talk away from Mike.

A look of mild maliciousness crossed Rosen's white face. 'Yeah, some good pics of the fishwives having a row, and a few others. It always amazes me that people forget I'm there with my camera.'

'Do you mainly take pictures of people?' Lucy asked.

'Not portraits,' Rosen was dismissive. 'Situations are what I like, people doing things, unusual things, real things, not posed ones.'

'She's taken a whole series, like, of serpentine working,' Kevin chipped in, 'from digging to shaping to selling.'

'I'm building up a portfolio,' Rosen said roughly, 'and I reckon there are things done in the industry that most people don't know about. All they see is the finished work sold in the shops.'

'She's got some amazing pictures of the oystermen too,' Kevin persisted. 'That's where we were going this afternoon, like, round to the fishery. Once she's working on a project, like, she never lets up, and the photos she's got already really show what the work is, with the weather and all.'

'She's got a real knack for showing action and mood,' Anna commented. 'You're going to do this professionally, aren't you, Rosen?'

The girl glanced at Lucy. 'Yes,' she said defiantly. 'Eric won't hear of it, though, it's not real work in his book, so I'm funding my own way. I sell a lot of pictures already, especially prints to tourists through the shops. I thought people would just want pretty views, but it's surprising how popular action shots are. And I've had a few photos in the local paper. Tamsyn's been a great help, she often sends me off to take pictures for her articles and her paper prints them without any attribution.'

'Surely your father would be proud of what you're doing, if he knew,' Anna said. 'You really are good at it.'

Rosen's mouth twisted into a sneer. 'You haven't met him yet, have you? And I expect he'll turn on the charm for you when you do. He likes attractive women. If you played your cards right, you might even become wife number four. I reckon number three has had enough. If she's bright she won't come back from Italy, and she'll be well out of it.' Rosen's voice had grown bitter and hard as she talked. 'He drove my mother into a nervous breakdown, and wife number two topped herself, took an overdose with a fraction of the pills she'd accumulated during her marriage. And they were all clever career women when he first met them. But he sucks them dry.'

Anna was staring at her, taken aback by the wild emotions so suddenly exposed. It was Kevin who broke the strained silence. 'He don't care about anything else, I reckon. Not Rosen, not his wives, not the locals, not even natural things, for all he's an environmentalist. He only sees the big picture, like, not the little things that make it up.'

'Let me guess,' a man's voice said from the room behind them. 'You're talking about Rosen's Pa.' A tall man in dark jeans and jumper stood looking down on them. 'Surely there are happier things to spend the evening discussing.'

'Anna hasn't met him, Mark,' Rosen said as the man looped a leg around the stool beside her, drawing it out skilfully so that he could sit down on it. 'We're telling her what he's like.'

'Lucky Anna,' he said, sipping from the tankard he held. 'I'd keep it that way if I were you. But then I'm perhaps biased. We've had nothing but trouble from him in the area, first with this wind farm idea beyond Portharrock, then with encouraging sea sports and increased moorings near my oyster beds, with lectures about integrating all users of the sea.' He gave a bark of laughter. 'But then Rasmussen doesn't like us Teagues much either. I reckon he doesn't like to see us getting above our station. First we bought up fish lofts to convert to holiday flats, so he fussed that we were destroying the chances of local industry.' Mark paused, taking a gulp of his beer. 'As if many of us can live by fishing these days. Then we scuppered both his own little plans. Wind farms on the scale he was talking of would harm bird populations, especially when they're migrating, not to mention put off tourists. And,' his fingers tightened their hold on the tankard, 'I'm not having boating tourists anywhere near my oyster beds, for all his talk about reconciling opposing interests. You can't count on them knowing or caring where they can go and then the harm's done.'

He put down the tankard and smiled, more relaxed than Anna had yet seen him. 'But, as I said, Rasmussen isn't much fun to talk about, and I'm sure Anna and her friend have better things to discuss.'

'I'm sorry,' Anna said apologetically, leaning back to allow her plate to be placed on the table. 'Lucy, this is Mark Teague, who is heavily involved in the pageant, particularly the singing. Mark, Lucy Rossington is my oldest and dearest friend.'

'And she's staying with my Pa,' Rosen said, 'but taking every opportunity to bunk off.' She grinned at Lucy, who smiled back at her and Mark as her own meal was delivered.

'Hi,' she said as she unwrapped her cutlery from a paper napkin. 'Anna's been telling me all about the folk songs she heard here last week. Are you singing tonight?'

'Only on Fridays,' he said. 'Will you be here then?'

Lucy nodded, her mouth full, as Rosen said, 'But sometimes the locals stay on in the evenings, and they all get singing. Especially if Tamsyn's here too. She and Mark sing together.'

'Is she coming tonight?' Kevin asked, leaning back against the wall and kicking a foot against one of the table legs. 'I've got Da's car, like, so I thought she might want a ride, but I couldn't get her on the phone.'

Mark gave his short laugh. 'No way will we see her tonight. She's got a shift at the watch station, but otherwise she's nose down on a scent.'

'This Viking business?' Kevin demanded.

Mark shrugged. 'Probably. But with Tamsyn you never know what she's got up her sleeve.' He fell silent, sipping at his beer as he looked over the crowded room, catching a gaze here and there, lifting a hand in greeting. A plate was laid on the table in front of him and Lucy was amused to see he was eating the lasagne too.

He caught the flash of humour across her face and grinned in response. 'It's the best dish they do, other than my oysters, of course. But I can eat those any day.'

'I don't like them,' Lucy confessed, 'but my husband does, so I expect he'll have them when he gets here. I saw they were on the menu.'

Mark swallowed a mouthful of food. 'Mine,' he said. 'He won't get any better. I supply the local outlets with native oysters when I've got them to spare. Most of them go up to London and across to France, but the shop here had some today and so did the pub. Otherwise they'll be the Pacific oysters, fine, but not such a good taste.'

He returned his attention to his dinner and Lucy glanced at Anna, who was eating her lasagne silently, her thoughts obviously elsewhere. When Lucy spoke, she started and looked up apologetically. 'Sorry, what did you say? I was miles away.'

'I know. I only said you were right about the lasagne, it is very good.' She considered Anna, who had almost drained her glass. 'Are you worrying about Mike?'

'Just a bit,' Anna admitted. 'He's mad to go along the coast path in the dark when he's in such a foul frame of mind about this business. I know it's a clear night and a full moon, but it'll serve him right if he does go over the edge of one of the cliffs.'

'That'll learn him,' Lucy agreed. 'What do you recommend for pudding?'

Anna put down her knife and fork. 'Do you really want one? I don't think I'll bother.'

Lucy swallowed her last mouthful, putting her cutlery neatly back on the plate. She sighed resignedly. 'Are you planning to go after Mike?'

Anna smiled ruefully. 'I might as well, rather than just sit here worrying about what stupid thing he'll do.'

Lucy drank the last of her wine and stood up, picking up her fleece as she pushed the stool back into place. 'Well, you can't go alone, so we may as well get started.'

Rosen had looked up as Lucy moved. 'You won't say anything, will you?' she demanded rather belligerently.

'No,' Lucy said mildly. 'But I would like to see your photos some time, and I'm sure Hugh would too. He's had a number of his wildlife pictures published, so he might be able to give you some useful advice.'

Rosen's tenseness eased. 'Yeah, that would be great. But not when Eric's around.'

Lucy nodded as she moved away, following Anna, who was already at the door. By the time Lucy got there Anna was outside, fastening the toggles of her scarlet duffle coat as bats flitted above her head, chasing the insects caught in the lamplight.

Anna set off briskly down the street as Lucy pulled on her own fleece and raced after her through the patchwork of light from the cottage windows and dark cast by the shadows of the buildings. A light breeze from the sea was cool on her face after the heat inside the pub.

'Do you know the path?' Lucy demanded breathlessly, pulling her green beret out of her pocket and cramming it onto her head. 'It would be stupid if we're the ones to go over the edge and Mike has to rescue us.'

'I've walked it a few times with Rob Elliot,' Anna replied. 'Not at night, of course, but look how clear the sky is.' She gestured extravagantly upwards. 'Once we're away from the house lights we'll be able to see the path quite clearly by moonlight.'

No more was said as they passed the turning leading to Alastair's cottage and continued up the hill until Anna branched suddenly off the street, taking a narrow path beside a low picket fence. This screened the short front gardens of a row of cottages tucked away on the slope that led up to open moorland. A faint bark from inside one of the cottages marked their passing, and a cat slunk into sight behind the fence, stopping to stare curiously at them.

Their path led through a tunnel of overarching trees, and Lucy slipped once on the uneven rocky surface, gripping one of the trunks to keep her balance. She was relieved when they emerged into the open, where the trees gave way to thickets of sloes on each side so that the natural light from the sky was more of an aid as her eyes acclimatised again to its brightness.

Anna was striding on, so Lucy had to increase her pace to catch up with her. 'Do be careful,' she said urgently. 'And please slow down. I don't know this stretch at all.'

'Sorry,' Anna said remorsefully, remembering that Lucy had badly injured her hip earlier in the year. She paused, studying Lucy anxiously. 'I forgot. Look,' she said persuasively, 'I'll go on and you can go back to the village in case I miss Mike and he doubles back.'

'I'm alright,' Lucy said, 'I just don't want to go too fast and slip. And you can't know it that well after just a few days, so let's go more slowly.'

'You're right,' Anna said reluctantly. 'We really don't want to get ourselves into a knot because Mike's an idiot. We'll take it steadily. Anyhow, the path's quite obvious now and for most of the way. The only really tricky bit is just before we get to what I think is the Viking valley.' She grinned at Lucy as they both imagined Mike's furious reaction to the description. 'There's an awkward corner there with a nasty drop down the cliff for the unwary.' She bit her lip, hoping Mike was keeping his wits about him.

It was a beautiful night and more than once Lucy regretted their hasty passage through it. Moonlight lit the scene around them as clearly as if it were day, but with a strange unearthly glow. Below them the sea lay silvered, marked here and there with the blobs of buoys that marked the sites of lobster pots. From time to time she saw other dark blobs and wondered if they were seals, or even dolphins.

Still, we can all take our time coming back, she consoled herself, as they traversed the top of a narrow peninsula. Below a grassy slope, sharply defined shadows at the neck of the headland showed the ditches and mounds that marked the entrance to Iron Age fortifications, mysteriously inviting under the stars,

an ideal spot for sea watching, Lucy realised. As she walked
over the rough turf she saw a fox trotting away across the fields
on her right, moving between the unconcerned cows towards
the dark shape of the farmyard in the distance.

After another ten minutes or so, they passed the gate that led
across to the fields to Pennance, its lit windows clearly visible
in the distance. Lucy thought of Eric, recalling the sunken
eyes glowing in his lined face as they left him that evening, not
disguising his relief at being alone in his house to work away
at his current grand scheme. Her brow furrowed for a second
in an effort of memory. Regenerating desert land, she recalled,
that was it. An interesting and important project, but somehow
Eric had the knack of making it boring when he talked about
it. For an instant Lucy felt a pang of pity, but all thought of her
host disappeared as Anna said warningly, 'Slow down now.'

'Okay,' Lucy replied. 'It's alright, though. I know the bit you
mean, and you're quite right, it is on the edge of Viking valley.
I've walked this stretch in daylight a couple of times since we
came to stay with Eric.' She waved a hand towards Pennance.
'That's his house up there. It was just round the bluff that I heard
the sounds from the Viking's cave this morning and found Mike
there with Kevin.'

The path narrowed as they picked their way with care
round the rocky outcrop, the bushes falling away on their left
to leave a steep drop down to the narrow inlet below, where
the sea-washed rocks glistened in the starlight. The lace-frilled
waves rolled endlessly up the tiny pebbly beach and fell back,
providing a gentle murmuring backdrop to the night.

Anna was on the path down into the gully when she stopped
so abruptly that Lucy bumped into her. 'Listen!' Anna hissed
urgently. 'What's that?'

Lucy regained her balance and cocked her head disbelievingly as she heard the noises. 'They're coming from the crevice,'
she said decisively. 'That's what I heard earlier, some sort of
echo distortion of voices. Mike's Viking's got visitors.'

'God, he'll be furious,' Anna said softly. 'What shall we do?'

'Find out who they are,' Lucy said. 'Move over, I'll lead the way.' She slipped past Anna, walking quickly down the path to jump lightly over the stream and follow an animal track that led up the far slope through the towering bracken. Anna was close on her heels, so near that Lucy was not sure whether it was her friend's heavy breathing she heard or her own. The wiry heather stems caught at their ankles and Anna hissed in pain as she brushed unwarily against a gorse bush.

Lucy held up a restraining hand, slowing down as they approached the granite column that marked the entrance to the crevice. She slid through it, avoiding the projecting finger of granite aimed at her leg, Anna following her every move.

Both women stopped, frozen, staring at the tableau they found inside. The beam of a fallen torch lit the dark mass at the feet of the oblivious Viking, where a man was bent over a body that lay flat and still on the floor. The bending figure moved, the torchlight catching his red hair, and Anna gasped. 'Mike! What's happened?'

Mike tried to stand as he spun round, and fell awkwardly, catching himself with one hand before he hit the ground. 'What the hell,' he growled, getting to his feet, 'are you doing here?'

Lucy had moved to the fallen torch, picking it up to shine towards him. As the powerful beam fell on his face Mike lifted a protective arm to shield his eyes and the light fell on his blood-stained hand.

Lucy directed the beam downwards, to the still figure pinioned to the floor by the Viking's sword, its gilded and jewelled hilt glinting in the torchlight like a monstrous stud sticking out of the fallen man's chest.

Anna drew her breath in sharply as she saw the black cloak and hat that lay near the body. 'Mike,' she said urgently, 'you didn't ...' She broke off as he glared at her.

'Don't be so bloody stupid. I wouldn't damage an artefact.' He stared down at the dead man. 'He wouldn't either, I'd have bet my life on it.'

Anna felt an insane urge to giggle, which quickly subsided as Lucy passed the torch to Mike and fell to her knees next to the still figure. 'Is he dead?' she asked, as Lucy's fingers felt for a pulse in one of the slack wrists. 'He must have done it himself, I suppose.'

'He's dead,' Mike said shortly, holding the torch beam steady on the body as Lucy looked up at him, slowly shaking her head. 'With that through his heart he wouldn't have a hope of surviving. And no,' his tone was sarcastic, 'he didn't lie down there and kill himself. Look at the angle of the sword. Look at how he's lying. Even you must see he's been murdered. And not by me, although God knows I've felt like it.'

Anna steeled herself and looked down at the body stretched out on his back, arms lying limply by his side. She saw a man in his late fifties with striking dark eyebrows that stood out against the greyish pallor of his face, framed in shoulder-length black hair liberally streaked with grey. His chin was stubbly with several days' growth of beard and his lips were slightly parted, as if he wanted to tell them something.

Anna shuddered and turned away, glancing at Mike. 'Should we take the sword out?' she ventured.

'For God's sake,' Mike shouted, shaking the torch so that the light beam wavered wildly around the crevice. 'He's dead. Leave it where it is, you can't help him now.'

'It can only just have happened,' Lucy said, frowning, her curtain of chestnut hair falling away from her face as she rocked back on her heels. 'Feel how warm he is, and look at the state of the blood, it's still flowing from the wound.'

'Of course it's only just happened,' Mike snarled. 'I was right on his heels, but I'm damned if I can see how it did happen. I didn't see another soul around.'

'Why were you following him?' Lucy asked, standing up stiffly. 'Who is he?'

'He's the hermit from Polkenan,' Anna said. 'That's why you

were following him, isn't it, Mike? You saw him on his evening walk.' She seized the torch. 'And for goodness' sake wipe your hand, it's all over blood.'

He stared at her blankly. 'Hermit?' His voice sounded strained as he awkwardly pulled out a grubby handkerchief and began to wipe his hand on it. 'I don't know what the hell you're on about. This is Roger Bland. I've been trying to get hold of him to investigate this bloody Viking business, but I've no idea what the stupid bastard was doing down here in disguise. I didn't know he was until I bumped into him this afternoon. And then I began to wonder whether he was behind this.' He scowled at Anna as he waved an arm at the skeleton that presided over the scene. 'Yes, of course I went to find him. I lurked round that hut for a bit as he seems to be living there, God knows why, but there was no sign of him. I wasn't going to hang around all night so I set off along the cliff path and had barely got to the coastal watch station when I saw him go by, back towards Polkenan, and went straight after him. I can only have been a few minutes behind him, close enough to see him branch off down here.' The grinding of Mike's teeth was audible. 'So close that I couldn't believe he was dying when I got here. I thought he was putting it on, until I bent over him and saw the sword had gone right through his chest. He must have taken his last breath as I squatted there beside him, cursing him, thinking he was making a fool of me.'

'Look,' Lucy intervened, 'we can discuss this later. But in the meantime, we'd better go for the police.'

'I don't expect there's much mobile signal around here, so you can both get to Hugh at the watch station,' Mike said, glancing at his watch. 'He'll ring them, but you'd better get a move on, it's almost eight now, he'll be leaving soon. I'll stay here with Bland.'

'I'll stay too,' Anna said quickly. 'You don't mind going on your own, do you, Lucy?'

Lucy shook her head. 'No, it's only a short distance. And I'll try my mobile from time to time, in case I can pick up a signal.'

'And what about the murderer?' Mike demanded. 'Bland didn't lie down here and stick the sword in his own chest, you know. He could be an awkward devil, but even he didn't manage that. Suppose whoever did it is out there waiting for another victim.'

'They could just as easily get us both then,' Lucy said calmly. 'I'm sure whoever did this is miles away by now, concocting a careful alibi.'

In spite of her brave words, her heart was thudding as she sped away, struggling through the bracken and gorse as she failed to find the easy route along the ledge up to the serpentine quarry. She arrived, chest heaving uncomfortably, beside the fence and squeezed carefully through the barbed wire strands into the field, hurrying across the tussocky grass to the far stile. She scrambled awkwardly over it, almost stumbling as she landed on the path. As she regained her footing and paused to catch her breath, she felt grateful that the path here was wider and more level, then hesitant as the moonlight was partially obliterated by drifting wisps of cloud. She was picking her way forward more cautiously when she heard the sound of a rock falling ahead of her, tumbling noisily down the cliff-side.

Lucy stopped, straining her ears to hear any more movement, then she screamed as something cold nudged her hand. 'Oh,' she gasped, 'Ben, how you scared me.' The collie pushed his head under her hand and she stroked him absently as she peered ahead, her heart pounding. Just as the clouds cleared and the moonlight shone out again, she identified the darker shape of the man approaching her.

'Lucy,' Hugh called anxiously, 'are you alright?'

'Yes ... no ...' She pulled herself together as he reached her and stretched out an arm to draw her closer. 'I'm fine, Ben just startled me, but we've got trouble,' she said succinctly. 'Anna and I were coming along the cliff path after Mike. We heard noises in the crevice.'

Hugh groaned and held her away to shake her slightly. 'Please tell me you didn't go down there.' He shut his eyes. 'No, of course you did. And?'

'And we found Mike at the foot of that awful skeleton, bending over a dead or dying man, his hands red with blood,' Lucy said, pulling away to look at him.

Hugh stared at her. 'For real?' he demanded.

She nodded vigorously. 'For real. The dead man had been stabbed with the Viking's sword.' She shivered suddenly. 'It can only just have happened and, Hugh, Mike said he'd been following this bloke and was right behind him. So why didn't he see the murderer? That doesn't sound good, does it?'

'No,' Hugh said slowly, rummaging in his pocket. 'He did go racing off after a chap who passed the watch station. I couldn't see who it was, he was swathed in a cloak and hidden by a broad-brimmed hat, all very dramatic. And the effect on Mike was equally dramatic. He was off after him without a word, if you discount the immediate cursing. Alastair seemed to know something about it, though, he tried to persuade Mike to stay and was none too happy when he was brushed off.'

'That's him,' Lucy said. 'The dead man. His cloak and hat were on the ground near him.' She frowned. 'Really, it all looked very theatrical. But the blood was real, and the man is dead.'

'Do any of you know who he is?'

'Well, Anna says he's some kind of hermit who lives along the coast at Polkenan. But Mike says he's the archaeologist called Roger Bland that he's been trying to contact.' She shrugged. 'So I don't know for sure. But,' her expression brightened, 'didn't Alastair say? Surely he knows who he was?'

'He was so agitated he wasn't really making sense,' Hugh said slowly. 'He was obviously expecting some kind of trouble. And of course Tamsyn was there, her journalistic ears pricked for news.'

'Is that why you came? To catch up with Mike?' Lucy asked as he found his mobile phone. 'I thought you'd still be at the watch station, so I was going to use the phone there. Mike thought there wouldn't be any signal here.'

Hugh was pressing buttons as he answered, 'Partly, and partly because Ben was getting fidgety after being as good as gold. I thought maybe he needed a pee, but he shot off along the path as soon as we were outside.'

'Good boy, Ben,' Lucy said, stroking the collie's soft fur as he leaned against her legs. 'You knew I needed you, didn't you? Surely there isn't any reception, Hugh?'

'We're in luck, there are odd patches here and there on the cliffs, and quite fortuitously we seem to have struck one. Tamsyn was still at the watch station when I left, so I'll be glad to keep her out of it for a bit.'

'Phew, I'd forgotten that she and Alastair are usually on the same shift,' Lucy exclaimed, breaking off as Hugh began to speak into the phone. 'Didn't she pounce on Mike?'

'There wasn't a chance,' Hugh said. 'Mike had been in full flow from the moment he arrived, then three minutes or so later he'd gone again.' He held up a silencing hand as a voice spoke in his mobile. 'I'd like to report a death,' he said, answering its query. 'A man appears to have been fatally stabbed in a cave near the cliff path just outside Portharrock.'

Hugh was silent, listening, then recited his name, and gave directions to Pennance, promising to meet the ambulance and police there to lead them down to the gully.

He finished the conversation and turned to Lucy, now an indistinct shape beside him as a growing cloud bank obliterated the moonlight. 'Alright, let's get down there. I take it Anna's stayed on the scene with Mike. Why didn't she come with you?' He sounded unusually angry.

'Well,' Lucy said diffidently, 'it was all extremely difficult. I wouldn't say so for the world, but there was just an instant, as soon as I knew it wasn't a spoof, when I thought Mike had done it. And Anna did too. Well,' she added quickly, 'obviously that was nonsense, but I don't think Mike has understood how it's all going to look. I'm sure Anna stayed behind to give him an alibi, or at least to prove he can't have altered or hidden anything.'

'It's rather late in the day for an alibi,' Hugh said shortly. 'There'll certainly be some of his colleagues who will feel their worst fears have been realised. Some of them have been expecting Mike to murder them for years.'

Lucy had started to retrace her footsteps, Ben bounding ahead, but she hesitated, saying over her shoulder, 'Should we contact Rob Elliot, do you think? Or maybe we should leave it to Anna.'

'We definitely won't,' Hugh said firmly, 'and I'm sure Anna won't need to. Elliot heads the regional murder squad. He'll be here promptly.' He gave her a small push. 'And at Pennance before us if you don't get a move on.' He groaned as the first drops of rain began to fall. 'Here we go again, something else for Eric to take charge of.'

FOUR

Mike was taken aback as he burst through the stairway door into Alastair's small living room, where his host sat on the battered sofa beneath the open window, oblivious to the draught blowing in around him. His head was in his hands, one of his precious serpentine lighthouses in his lap, and a pile of photograph albums beside him.

Mike hovered uncertainly, torn between his burning need for a coffee and a feeling that he should say something helpful. 'Err,' he began, just as Alastair looked up, letting his hands drop and close around the piece of serpentine.

The vicar's finely drawn features were strained and white, but he attempted to smile as he saw his guest and noticed his awkwardness. 'Good morning, Mike,' he said. 'I won't ask if you slept well; I'm sure your night must have been as disturbed as mine.'

Mike had gone to bed angry and distressed, had indeed tossed and turned, until he had at last fallen into a heavy sleep, disturbed by dreams of grinning Viking warriors bearing down on him, their gleaming swords swirling around their heads. He had woken suddenly with the bedclothes wrapped tightly round his sweating body, the early morning light shining through a wide gap in the closed curtains onto his face.

'Umm,' he said noncommittally, shifting from one foot to

the other.

Alastair lifted the model lighthouse and placed it carefully on the table beside the sofa as he got up. 'He gave it to me, you know. Roger.' He gestured at the pile of albums. 'I wanted to look at the old photos.' He passed one hand across his eyes. 'Not a good idea. Breakfast,' he said with an effort, 'that's what we need. It's all ready in the dining room, but I'll just put the kettle on.'

He passed Mike to get to the kitchen, and noticed the expression of suspicious curiosity on his square face. 'I've known him for years,' Alastair explained, 'since we were students, in fact. You could say we were each here because of the other.' He broke off as he turned on the tap to fill the kettle, switching this on before shifting to lean against the work surface and look across at Mike.

'Roger knew this place as a child, from holidays with his parents.' Alastair smiled faintly. 'I find it difficult to imagine Roger when he was young, but apparently he was a keen fisherman, going out regularly with the locals. In our student days we once came down here together on vacation, and I always remembered the place. When,' he hesitated, then carried on firmly, 'when I decided my calling was in danger, it was here I chose to come to see if I could sort myself out.' His face lightened. 'And the place and the people showed me my role, so here I stayed.'

He poured water into a coffee pot, then put the kettle down and looked ruefully at Mike. 'How stupid of me, perhaps you would rather have tea?'

'No,' Mike said shortly. 'Coffee's fine. Thanks.' He stepped back from the doorway, allowing Alastair to pass him with the pot.

'Through here,' Alastair said, leading the way back across the living room and opening the other door in the far wall to reveal the dining room. It was almost filled with a table covered with a green velour cloth, chairs crammed in round it with heaps of parish magazines covering their seats. Mike looked about, feeling a faint empathy as he saw the piles of box files lying around the floor and the notebooks crammed in untidy towers on the narrow mantelpiece. He thought he was untidy, but compared to this his own cottage was neat.

'There's not much room, I'm afraid,' Alastair said apologetically, 'but I'm sure you can squeeze in. I'm always being told there'd be less paper if I computerise, but I haven't got round to it yet. Just move anything in the way.' As he spoke he thrust a roll of posters along the table until they bumped up against the electric typewriter at the far end.

Mike seized the nearest chair as Alastair put the coffee pot down on the table and edged round to sit in front of the window, almost blocking the dull daylight from the room.

'Ah,' Alastair said, reaching round to open the window, 'silly of me. Perhaps you wouldn't mind leaning back and putting the light on, Mike. It's a little gloomy in here at this time of the year.'

Mike looked over his shoulder and saw the switch, pressing it down impatiently and filling the room with a faint glow from the low wattage bulb overhead.

'Thank you, thank you,' Alastair said. He waved a hand at the cereal packet on the table. 'Now help yourself. It's nothing much, but I find it keeps me going.' He reached for the Weetabix and pushed it across to Mike. 'I did mean to go to the shop and get some more, but what with one thing and another ...'

Mike seized the packet and saw there were only two rusks left. He tipped one into the bowl in front of him and handed the box back. Flooding the bowl with milk from the bottle that Alastair passed him, he demanded, 'If Roger came down here to visit you, why the hell was he parading round in fancy dress and living in the huer's hut?'

Alastair was pouring coffee and waited until he had finished, pushing a mug over to Mike, before he replied, 'It was simple really. He liked the clothes, and he liked his privacy. He set up camp in the hut for a few weeks one year, and there was no fuss. He did it ever since, for longer and longer periods. He bothered nobody, so nobody bothered him. He didn't particularly come to see me, you know,' Alastair added. 'I think we just both found our own peace here.' He looked up at the archaeologist. 'Did you study under him?'

Mike nodded, and Alastair went on, choosing his words with care as he tipped the last rusk into his bowl, 'Then you must have seen that he became more eccentric as the years passed.'

Mike frowned. 'Yes,' he said abruptly. 'He was brilliant in his own sphere. There was nothing he didn't know about Viking life.' He smiled rather sourly. 'We used to kid him that he was a reincarnation, and I think he was actually flattered. And,' the frown deepened into a ferocious scowl, 'when I found him down here I was certain he was behind this …' Mike coughed, self-consciously repressing the words he was about to use, 'this hoax. I owe him for that, because now I'm damned sure he was killed to make sure he couldn't expose the bloody prankster. And I've no idea who it is.'

Coffee spilled from the mug Alastair had raised to his lips. 'What?' he demanded, his eyes fixed on Mike's face as he lowered the mug carefully to the table, clasping his long fingers around it. 'Why do you say that?'

Mike stared at him blankly. 'Isn't it obvious? Take one prankster with a set of Viking armour, add one Viking expert in the area who can't resist going to pry, result one dead Viking expert.'

Alastair gazed fixedly at the table now, one hand playing with his cereal spoon, shifting the uneaten rusk around in his bowl. 'Is that what the police think?'

Mike had sipped his own coffee, wincing at the sharp taste of powder rather than the ground beans he was expecting. He swallowed and growled, 'No, they bloody don't. Sorry,' he apologised half-heartedly. 'They think I did it.'

'Surely not,' Alastair exclaimed, horrified.

Mike nodded, his mouth set grimly. 'Oh yes. I didn't see it last night, but it was obvious enough when I woke up this morning. And that,' he ground his teeth, 'is why Anna stayed behind when Lucy went off to get help. To make sure I didn't interfere with the evidence.'

'No, Mike,' Alastair said firmly, 'I'm sure she stayed to help you.'

Mike groaned. 'The worst case scenario. I'm to be rescued again.'

Alastair pushed away his bowl of untouched cereal and reached for a plate of toast, which he offered across the table. Mike took a piece and bit into it without thought, chewing on the soft mouthful and swallowing it with an effort. 'No,' he said decisively, lifting his chin and glowering at Alastair. 'No, I'm not letting it happen. I've never yet managed to arrive in time to get her or Lucy out of trouble, but I'm damned if I'll let Anna take the lead role in this.'

The vicar had turned round with difficulty in his chair to peer out of the window. 'Ah, I fear your time has come, Mike. Inspector, now what is his name,' he tapped the arm of his chair thoughtfully, 'ah yes, Elliot, Inspector Elliot has just been waylaid by Thomas. No doubt he's on his way here to see us.'

Mike pushed back his chair, bumping it into the wall so that the framed print of *The Good Samaritan* slipped sideways to hang as lopsidedly as its neighbour, *The Woman at the Tomb*. 'Getting more details for my indictment,' he muttered. 'Can you see handcuffs dangling from his pocket? No,' he added, 'Elliot wouldn't spoil the set of his smart suit, he'll have brought one of his lackeys to do his dirty work.' He ran his fingers through his hair as he stood up. They clenched suddenly on his curls. 'Or he's just paying a social call on Anna,' he snarled, 'where he'll listen to her telling him how I met Roger yesterday.'

'I think,' Alastair said mildly, 'you do Anna, and perhaps Inspector Elliot, an injustice. I happen to know Anna is having

an early morning dress rehearsal for some of the women down
in the village, as so many of them have to travel a great distance
to get to work. Then she's checking the decorations in the
church afterwards. Lots of seine netting to drape, you know,'
he said vaguely, 'and all those creels to arrange. Ah, here's
the inspector come to call now.' A firm rap at the front door
with the dolphin knocker underlined his words. 'Perhaps you
wouldn't mind letting him in, you're closer than I am.'

Mike strode across the living room to pull the front door
open abruptly. The two men outside were only visible as dark
silhouettes against the light. The taller greeted him politely.
'Good morning, Professor. I was sure you'd be up and about.'

'You'd better come in,' Mike said reluctantly, standing
back to allow Inspector Elliot to enter the low-ceilinged room,
ducking his head to avoid the rafters. His well-cut grey suit
made him an incongruous figure in the cluttered old-fashioned
cottage as he stood taking in the room. The man beside him
seemed quite at home in his surroundings, his square build
and rubicund face making him seem more of a countryman,
an impression enhanced by the shrewd blue eyes that were
regarding Mike with interest.

'Ah, sit down, Rob, sit down,' Alastair said from the dining-
room doorway. 'So much safer for us tall chaps. I sometimes
have to remind myself to stand up straight outside, I get so used
to stooping in here. Oh dear,' he looked apologetic, 'I suppose I
should call you inspector now that you're here officially. When I
met you and Anna on your walking trip I little thought it would
come to this.'

'Don't worry about it,' Elliot said. 'This is Detective Sergeant
Peters, who will be looking into the case with me.'

As Alastair held out an eager hand to greet the sergeant,
Elliot hitched up his trousers as he lowered himself cautiously
into an armchair out of the direct draught from the window.
Alastair took the other one as Sergeant Peters moved to stand
near the cold hearth, where long dead ashes still lay in a

forgotten heap. Mike flung himself onto the sofa, which creaked in ominous protest.

'Ah, coffee, I'm sure you'd like some of the coffee. It's quite fresh, you know.' Alastair began to get up from his seat, to be halted by Elliot's upraised hand.

'Thank you, but no,' the inspector said politely. 'I've only just finished an excellent pot at the pub.'

'The pub,' Alastair repeated, puzzled. 'Here? Good heavens, I had no idea you were staying there already.'

'Neat work,' Mike commented sardonically.

'Not at all,' Elliot replied blandly. 'I was already booked in for the weekend, and luckily they were able to fit me in a bit earlier. Unfortunately it doesn't look as though I shall be able to spend the time as I'd planned.'

'Unfortunate,' Mike repeated, his lip curling sarcastically.

'Dear me,' Alastair said in concern. 'Yes, I remember now. I knew you were coming, of course. Dear, dear, we little thought when we planned this event that you'd have to be here on duty. Still,' he collected his thoughts with an obvious effort, 'I do hope you'll be able to join us for a while at the pageant.'

'That depends, I'm afraid, on how quickly we can sort out this nasty business.'

'Yes, yes, of course.'

Mike leaned back on the sofa, folding his hands behind his head and thrusting his legs out into the room. 'Come to take me in, Elliot? Or have you got the bastard who really did it?'

Elliot surveyed him noncommittally, a spark of humour in his grey eyes. 'You're at liberty for a while yet, Professor. I really came to show you this.' He pulled out the newspaper from under his arm, opening it to the front page as he held it out to Mike.

Mike dropped his hands as he leaned forward to take the paper, his face flushing with anger as he saw the banner headlines. *Viking King Defends Our Shores*. His lips rolled back, revealing his clenched teeth as he saw the half page picture of the figure in the cave. 'Who the hell got in there for this?' he demanded furiously, crumpling the paper.

'The byline is Tamsyn Warne,' Elliot said. 'A local journalist, I gather.' On the far side of the room Alastair put his head in his hands with a faint groan. Elliot added sharply, 'Don't mess it up, Professor, I want you to have a good look at the picture and tell me if you see any discrepancies.'

'Discrepancies?' Mike growled. 'What do you expect, that I'll see the maker's mark all of a sudden?' He smoothed out the page and glared down at the picture, his rage dissipating as he concentrated on the image staring up off the paper. His eyes narrowed and he stabbed at the page with one finger. 'See here,' he said abruptly. 'Where's the sword?'

Elliot removed the paper and looked down at the picture. 'The sword?' he queried sharply. 'What do you mean?'

'When we found that, that figure,' Mike said, pacing his words slowly and deliberately, watched closely by Sergeant Peters, 'it had one hand hovering over the sword that lay across its lap. The sword that was used to stab Bland. But,' he leaned forward to jab at the page, which Elliot quickly moved out of his reach, 'it's not under his bony fingers in this picture. And I'd swear the skeleton is leaning forward.' He frowned, one hand clenched on his knee, the other yanking thoughtfully at the neck of his jumper. 'So does that mean Bland was already lying dead at the skeleton's feet when this was taken?' He stretched further forward, grabbing at the paper. 'Here, let me see that again.'

The inspector released it swiftly, afraid it would tear. Mike smoothed the page out across his knees and stared down at it. 'No, that won't work, I can't tell. See,' he held the paper out for Elliot to look, 'the picture is from the feet up. Bland could already be lying there dead, just out of sight.' He scowled, his eyes boring into the image before he released his hold on the paper, allowing Elliot to gather it up.

Mike ran his hands through his hair, clutching it as he growled, 'And how the hell could anyone race in there, stab

Bland, stop to take a photograph and be gone before I could see him?'

'Why else would the sword have been removed?' Elliot asked. 'You didn't move it, touch it, for any reason?'

Mike sneered. 'You know better than that, Elliot. I wouldn't have touched a thing in that crevice until,' he snorted, 'until I'd got Bland down to inspect it.' He groaned suddenly. 'My God, I've got Lynette Mellors coming down today to look at the bloody bones!' He looked belligerently at Elliot. 'She's coming down from Oxford, and she's a busy woman. Any chance she can have a look at the skeleton? I want to know how old it is.'

'And you know better than that, Professor,' Elliot replied as Mike hunched up morosely. 'That crevice is a murder scene. Nothing can be touched until our investigations are complete.' As Mike groaned again, Elliot added, 'But I'm sure our pathologist will be able to give you a rough date for the bones, if that's of any use.'

Mike straightened abruptly. 'You can't touch the Viking,' he said furiously. 'I want that seen as it was found.'

'That's the other reason I'm here, Professor,' Elliot said calmly. 'I'd like an archaeologist to be present when we move the skeleton.' He held up a hand, forestalling the words that were ready to pour off Mike's tongue. 'You know we've got to examine the whole scene, and that skeleton may well be concealing something important, so it's got to be moved. And there's always a chance that the skeleton itself is the issue. You yourself doubt that it's contemporary with the armour. If it's a modern one we're potentially faced with another murder enquiry.'

Mike's brow was deeply furrowed as he listened. 'Yes,' he admitted grudgingly, 'I see. I hadn't thought of that. Then I'd better get over there before your plods damage anything.'

Elliot shook his head. 'You know better than that too, Professor. You're involved in the case. It will have to be somebody else.'

'A bloody suspect, you mean,' Mike growled. 'Alright then, get Lynette to do it. She'll probably enjoy the thrill, although she'll never let me forget it. At least I know she's competent.' He smacked his head suddenly and leaped to his feet. 'Hell, I'm supposed to be meeting her at the local airport this afternoon. What's the time now?' He peered at his watch.

'There's plenty of time,' Elliot said. 'I'd rather you stayed around, Professor. I'll send a constable to meet her. The three o'clock flight, I suppose?'

'Yes.' Mike leaned against the kitchen doorjamb, arms folded across his chest. 'Do you want me to report to the police station?' he demanded.

'Not at the moment,' Elliot replied. 'But I do want to know where you'll be today.'

Mike shrugged impatiently. 'Well, if I can't get on with examining the Viking there's nothing ...' His voice tailed off, and a look of anticipation appeared on his countenance. 'I'll be visiting Tamsyn Warne. *Ms* Warne, no doubt.'

'No, you won't,' Elliot said quietly. 'You'll leave that to me. I understand she's at the coastal watch station this morning, so I'll be seeing her there very shortly.'

'Ah, Inspector,' Alastair interrupted in a reluctant tone, 'I don't think you will, you know. She changed her place in the rota again while we were at the station last night. We've both been juggling our times a bit just lately to fit in with the pageant practices. They have to be fitted around the tides for the fishermen too, you know, so it's all rather difficult.' Alastair clasped his hands together nervously. 'I'm worried about the watch shifts getting muddled up. As it is, I had a struggle to get somebody to fill in for Tamsyn this morning. Good gracious,' he added, getting up hastily, 'I should be off. I'm on at ten for two hours.'

Elliot got up too, saying, 'One moment, vicar. I understand that you saw Roger Bland last night?'

Alastair looked taken aback. 'Yes, indeed, but how ... Oh, I expect Anna told you.'

'No,' Elliot said. 'I haven't seen Anna since last night, and she hasn't mentioned anything about this. You were seen by somebody else.'

'Then how on earth ...' Again he broke off. 'No, no, I see, you mustn't say who told you.' He nodded. 'Yes, I went up to the huer's hut, about five, I suppose, hoping to persuade Roger to walk with me to the watch station later on. He often did, you know. But last night he was set on going earlier and wouldn't wait for me. So I walked with him through the village and up towards the far entrance to the coastal path, turning off along my own path home while he went on.'

'Why wouldn't he wait?' Elliot asked quickly.

Alastair smiled faintly. 'It was his way, Inspector, as I'm sure Mike would tell you. He would do what he wanted when he chose to, not at anyone else's convenience. He wanted to go walking at that time and not later, that was quite enough to keep him to his purpose.'

'And you, vicar? What did you do when he walked on and left you?'

'I?' Alastair was startled. 'Now let me see, what did I do. I came back, yes, of course, I came back. I had a word with Anna, and then finished a letter.'

'Did you see anyone other than Anna?'

'Umm, now let me think.' After a few seconds' silence he said reluctantly, 'No, I really don't think I did. I was in the church for quite some time, too, you know, and,' he added rather sadly, 'nobody came in, nobody at all.'

'Well, it's quite possible somebody saw you, even if you were unaware of them,' Elliot said.

Mike snorted. 'Try the bloke next door. His eyes are always out on stalks.' By the fireplace Sergeant Peters suppressed a grin, raising one blunt-fingered hand to hide his mouth.

'Thomas, yes, that's quite true,' Alastair said gratefully. 'But, Inspector, does this mean that I ... that you ...'

Mike laughed suddenly. 'You and me both, Alastair. Right in the frame.'

'And both at lunch at the Rasmussen place today, I believe,' Elliot commented as he reached the front door and opened it.

Mike clutched his head. 'Damn it, I can do without that. Oh,' his hands fell, 'what the hell does it matter? Yes, I'll be there and let's hope Rasmussen doesn't really push me into murder.'

'No, no, Mike,' Alastair said anxiously, 'you mustn't even think of it. Your friends will be there, and Anna too. I'm only invited because she's going, and Eric thinks of me as her host. I don't often get to dine in such grand surroundings.'

'I've no doubt, then,' Elliot said, 'I'll be seeing you there if we have any further questions.' He raised a hand in farewell as he and Sergeant Peters set off through the little garden towards the valley path. At the gate the inspector halted and looked back. 'In fact, Professor, if you could come over earlier you could help us reconstruct your actions last night. About twelve, as I gather you're due at Rasmussen's for one.'

Mike nodded brusquely. 'I'll be there.' He watched Elliot walk away, and muttered, 'That's all I need to make my day.' He looked at Alastair and gestured towards the dining room. 'Do you need a hand with the clearing up?'

Alastair shook his head. 'Thank you, thank you, but please don't bother. I'll just put the things in the sink until later. I really must go down to the church.'

Mike thrust his hands morosely in his pockets. 'At least you're allowed to go to your place of work. What the hell am I supposed to do?'

'Perhaps,' Alastair suggested tentatively as he began to rummage in a crammed drawer in the small sideboard that stood on one side of the room, almost buried under books and papers, 'you might like to look around the village. Get the lie of the land, as it were. Do feel free to come and go here as you like. Ah,' he exclaimed triumphantly, flourishing a key which he passed to Mike, 'I knew I had a spare. I don't,' he admitted, 'always remember to lock the door, but if I do you'll still be able to get in.'

'Thanks,' Mike said, mustering a smile. 'I'll get off too.' He pounded up the stairs, slipping again near the top with a muttered expletive that echoed down into the living room.

A few minutes later he was back again, wearing the disreputable old donkey jacket that bore tears commemorating many a past excavation, to find that Alastair was no longer around. Mike called out as he opened the front door, but there was no reply so he banged it shut firmly behind him. He was turning away when he felt the heavy key bump against his thigh. Muttering under his breath, he yanked it out and shoved it into the lock, breathing heavily as he struggled to turn it. He banged the door edge angrily and felt the key move. Pulling it out and thrusting it back into his pocket he set off along the path, still wet underfoot from an overnight shower.

There was only a slight warning rustle behind the fuchsias screening the neighbouring garden before a head popped up through the dangling bells, spattering raindrops that still lingered from the night's downpour. 'Morning,' Thomas said brightly, his eyes eager, the bobble wobbling on top of his knitted hat. 'You certainly brought trouble with you, then.'

'Morning,' Mike grunted, without slowing down.

'I do hear the Viking did it himself,' Thomas called after him. 'Lets you off the hook, don't it?'

Mike's pace faltered, but when he swung round the old man had disappeared back behind his flowers. The archaeologist slowly uncurled his tightened fingers and took a deep breath. Right, he thought grimly, there's going to be plenty more of that.

He set off again, careless of the puddles he splashed through, pausing as he reached the turquoise church, wondering whether Alastair was here. He walked over to the door, cautiously pushing it open a crack to peer inside as he remembered that

Anna was due here at some time.

At first the church seemed quite empty, although in one corner a stack of fishing nets and creels lay under a shining heap of coloured floats that indicated the decorators had yet to arrive. Mike was just withdrawing his head when he saw the figure on its knees in front of the plain wooden cross on the altar. He pulled a face, as he recognised Alastair's dark head, bowed in prayer over his raised hands.

Mike pulled the door carefully shut and strode off again. His shoulders were hunched, his hands in his pockets, a scowl on his face as he passed the tearoom on his left. A woman was vigorously cleaning the tables outside, and paused to stare after him before she knocked urgently on the window, calling out to another woman, and hurrying to the low wall to lean over and point after Mike.

He was looking to neither his right nor his left, but staring straight ahead, his thoughts ranging from the Viking crevice back to his student days. Swerving to avoid another pedestrian, he narrowly missed the stack of crates outside the fish shop. Stumbling, he put out his hand to save himself from falling and pressed against the door, which swung open. He fell awkwardly down the shallow step, bumping into a man dressed in damp oilskins.

'Steady there,' the man said in the soft local burr, holding Mike off with a strong grasp. 'I know my oysters are popular, but there's plenty for everyone.'

'Sorry,' Mike said. 'I tripped.'

'That'll be Joe's crates,' a woman said behind the counter, as the door pinged shut behind the other man. 'Always catch the visitors, they do. Is there something you'd be wanting then? Mark has just brought in his oysters, so you'll have first choice. Native ones, too.'

'Thanks,' Mike said, looking appreciatively at the trays of fish behind the counter. 'I'm eating out today, but maybe I'll be in for something tomorrow.'

'You'm staying with vicar, aren't you, m'dear?' the woman said. Mike stiffened, but without waiting for an answer the woman went on, 'Not much of a hand for cooking, the vicar, but you'll get my fish just the same if you're eating at the pub.'

'Right,' Mike said, turning back to the door. 'Right.' He left with an awkward nod and continued on his way through the village, unaware that the woman from the shop had come to the door to stare cautiously after him. He paused, his eyes caught once again by the buildings at the top of the beach, where more doors were open today revealing pulleys and winches used to haul the fishing boats high up the cove in bad weather. A pair of ladders leaned against the front, each supporting a woman clutching the end of a string of brightly coloured bunting. As Mike watched them, noticing their practised competence, Anna's clear voice rang across the cove and he started, looking round quickly.

She had her back to him, her black curls lying across the shoulders of her red duffle coat, addressing a group of women by the rocks on the far side of the beach. The tide was well on the ebb, but there were fishermen busy about their boats, moving with cumbersome skill in their heavy boots and high visibility oilskins as they unloaded the last of their catches onto the trailer attached to a small tractor, waiting to pull its load up to the packing shed. The women were moving slowly past the boats, exchanging good-natured chaffing with the working men, and Mike hurried on along the street and up towards the coastal path. Casting a fleeting glance over his shoulder he noticed the scarlet flannel petticoats worn by a number of the women, their arms folded tightly across their shawls, their belligerent faces reddened under shabby black bonnets, realistic-looking gutting knives lying in a heap nearby.

Sighing loudly with relief at passing undetected, he turned onto the footpath, only to be brought up short by a barrier of striped tape. A uniformed policeman turned from the path edge where he had been watching the scene below. 'Sorry, sir,' he said as he approached Mike, 'the path's closed here for a bit.' He pointed up the slope behind Mike. 'You can reach it further round if you go on up the street and turn off at the stile.'

'No problem,' Mike said quickly. 'I wasn't going far anyway.' He stood for a moment, staring past the policeman. The only sound was the rumble of voices from the beach, and the high calls of the swirling gulls that had followed the small fishing fleet home. Now, out of the tourist season, there was little traffic in the village so the roar of a motorbike engine was loud in his ears as the machine swept past behind him.

Mike stiffened, glancing quickly round to see the bike go down the hill and up the other side, where the rider pulled it into the edge of the street and dismounted. Watched by the curious policeman, Mike moved cautiously back down the street, keeping well into the side. As he followed the movements of the rider, she pulled off her helmet and walked briskly across to the path leading to the church and Alastair's cottage. She called a greeting to the woman who was now briskly sweeping the paved forecourt of the tearoom, and paused as the woman answered.

Tamsyn Warne. Mike dredged the name up out of his memory as he edged forward, his jaw clenched. The journalist. He had no doubt who she had come to see, and his eyes narrowed as he remembered the article she had written. He was about to stride forward when he hesitated, torn between the burning urge to interrogate the woman and the abrupt determination to give her no more material.

Mike's heart sank as the woman in the tea garden pointed down the street towards him. He slid round the corner of the fish cellar onto the beach, looking round desperately. Surely I can get across the rocks over there, he thought, bounding towards them, the stones on the beach grinding under his feet. To his dismay there was no obvious way of easily getting through them. Scrambling and climbing was possible, but he would be slow and very visible. He swung round, searching for another solution. With two steps he had reached the group around Anna, now augmented by a number of men in a variety of costumes. Mike's abrupt arrival caught Anna's attention and he scowled furiously at her as she opened her mouth.

She saw the desperation in his eyes and swiftly altered what she had been about to say. 'Ah, Mike, I'm glad you've made it. We need somebody to fill in for one of the fishermen. Here, you only need a woolly hat,' she reached down to a pile of clothes and tossed him one, 'and a creel to carry.' He looked where she pointed and bent over to pick one up, shifting it to his left shoulder, screening his face completely. 'We're just going to the church to form up properly and march back down here in the correct order. I hope,' she said wryly, to a ripple of laughter. 'I'm sure you'll pick up the words of the songs.'

The group set off in a ragged line, excise men in dark tail-coats and white breeches at the front ambling beside fishermen in rough homespun trousers and coarse linen shirts, each with a brightly spotted handkerchief about their heads. Anna fell back to speak to Mike. 'What is it?' she asked urgently.

'That bloody journalist,' he muttered, jerking his head towards Tamsyn who was tracing the route he had taken up to the coastal path. Anna stared after the woman, recognising the leather trousers and jacket, and the careful braids plaited round her head. 'I expect she thinks I did it too.'

'I don't expect she cares,' Anna commented. 'All she wants is a story.'

'She's already got a damned good one,' Mike growled. 'She's got a piece about the Viking in one of the nationals – and a bloody photo too! God knows where Rasmussen's guards were when that was taken.'

Anna looked at him with an arrested expression. 'How do you know?'

'I've seen it,' he snapped. 'I'm surprised Elliot didn't show it to you over breakfast.'

She stared at him in amazement. 'I haven't seen him. Why

would he show it to me anyway?' Before Mike could reply she said quickly, 'Get going. She's coming back. She should be joining us when she's changed.'

Mike hunched his back, yanking the hat further over his head, trying to erase all signs of his red hair, as he shouldered his way through the straggle of people in the procession, leaving a wake of muttering behind him as women pulled their long skirts from under his heavy feet and a soldier struggled to rebalance the scabbard that Mike had knocked awry.

It was with relief that Mike finally muscled into the group of men dressed like himself and was swept at last into the church forecourt with them, ostensibly part of the laughing joshing mass. He moved stealthily towards the gateway while Anna formed the procession up in order, ducking his head hastily as he saw the journalist coming up the path.

Tamsyn Warne scarcely gave the strangely dressed medley a glance as she hurried past, even though a number of people called out to her. Once, Mike thought sourly, she'd probably have shown a decent interest in the scarlet petticoats, but now her mind was set on more exciting prospects. He glowered as he remembered that she was supposed to be taking part in this pageant, had actually played a large part in creating it. His teeth ground together as he realised that Tamsyn must indeed be on a hot scent. He felt a surge of rage as he guessed that it was probably himself, Mike Shannon, as Suspect Number One, not Mike Shannon, Archaeological Expert, that she had in her sights. He fancied she was almost panting with eagerness as she approached the cottage, and felt a supreme satisfaction as a bobble-hatted head popped up to intercept her.

Only a slight breeze disturbed the reeds and grasses in the Pennance garden, rippling the tranquil waters of the stairway and the lower pool, an inadequate herald for the gusts of wind that rollicked over the cliffs beyond the wall. Clouds raced across the sky as Hugh swung the garden gate closed and pulled his cap more firmly over his ears, turning up the collar of his waxed jacket as he tucked Lucy's arm through his. 'I don't think I've ever been so relieved to escape my host,' he commented dryly.

'It was a grim breakfast,' Lucy agreed, watching Ben range eagerly ahead of them over the field, sending a flock of redwings into the air, calling in alarm. 'But you've got to feel sorry for him.' Hugh tore his attention away from the birds and looked at her, one eyebrow raised quizzically. 'You have,' his wife insisted. 'This business about Roger Bland seems to have hit him really hard.'

'Adverse publicity,' Hugh commented cynically. 'Especially as Eric knew the bloke. The papers will pick that up fast enough. You can imagine the headlines.'

Lucy tugged reprovingly on his arm as she continued, 'They did go back a long way together even if they haven't been close lately. And for Eric to have family troubles too seems tough.'

Hugh's lips twitched as he looked at her pointed face, the lightly tanned skin already tinged with pink from the wind. 'That's an extremely understated way to describe getting a text from his wife announcing that she's not coming back, and then finding he's overlooked his daughter's eighteenth birthday.'

'Rosen didn't seem fussed, though,' Lucy observed thoughtfully. 'I'd have been gutted if my father had forgotten any of my birthdays, let alone a significant one.'

'I imagine she wasn't expecting anything else,' Hugh said, opening the gate onto the coastal path. 'It's probably happened before. Although I'm can't think why Eric doesn't have a secretary to remind him of these things.'

'He told me that with the internet it's easier to manage his own communications, and I think he likes to be in charge. And,' Lucy added, falling into step behind Hugh, 'he probably expects his wife to pick up on family and social dates.'

'Hmm,' Hugh murmured as they picked their way round the rocky outcrop, the granite underfoot slippery from sea spray.

His eyes lifted, automatically scanning the sea birds wheeling and skimming over the water in the inlet. 'Look.' He stopped so abruptly that Lucy almost trod on his heels. 'Out there.' One of his hands pointed to the open sea, where the blue water heaved hypnotically. 'Gannets diving, out over that calm patch of water.'

Lucy looked too, her eyes narrowing, quickly pinpointing the large birds that hovered high above the water before plummeting at great speed into the depths and rising again. 'Five, six,' she counted. 'There must be quite a shoal of fish there.' They stood for a while watching the display, Ben sniffing happily round the bushes, before she said reluctantly, 'We should get on, Hugh. You spent a long time checking your emails, so we're cutting it fine now. We don't want to be late for lunch.'

'Hmm,' he murmured again, tearing his gaze away from the birds and off into the gully to the police cordon where a uniformed policeman stood watching them. 'Well, I suppose Elliot's summons certainly did us a favour by getting us out of the house, so we shouldn't hold up his reconstruction.'

Ben raced ahead to the constable, a young man barely out of his teens, his pale face serious as he held up a hand to stop them. Before he could speak, Hugh greeted him cordially, 'Good morning, we're here for Inspector Elliot's reconstruction. Lucy Rossington,' he gestured at his wife, 'and Hugh Carey.'

'Oh yes, Mr Carey,' the policeman said, lifting the fluttering tape with one hand for them to pass through. 'The inspector said you'd be coming. He's with the Viking.'

'Thanks,' Hugh said, lips twitching as he paused to survey the gully, noting how more tracks had appeared through the bracken. 'I suppose this has all been searched.'

The policeman nodded, one hand stroking the collie. 'As soon as it was light,' he said. 'It's alright to go across the slope to the crevice.'

'Fine,' Hugh said. 'Have you had many visitors?'

'Not really. A few walkers who've ignored the warning sign

further back along the path, but mainly people try to come through from Portharrock. I think there's quite a crowd up at that end, hoping to see something.'

'There's bound to be,' Hugh said. 'People are always curious. I'm glad the weather's holding up for you. It would be bleak up here in the rain. Well, we'd better get going.' He lifted a hand in farewell as he led the way down into the gully, Lucy following close behind with Ben at her heels.

They leaped easily over the stream, now considerably fuller and faster after the overnight rain, and approached the entrance to the crevice. Another police constable waited there for them, a young woman with short fair hair standing confidently beside the column of rock.

'Lucy Rossington and Hugh Carey,' Hugh announced. 'Your colleague sent us on down for the inspector's reconstruction.'

'Yes, sir,' the constable said, 'you're to go on in.'

Another deeper voice spoke from within the crevice, the words strangely distorted by the rock walls, as a square figure eased its way out into the open by the column. 'Mr Carey, well, this is just like old times. How are you?'

Sergeant Peters held out a hand, shaking both of theirs with pleasure, as they greeted him. 'Come on through. Inspector Elliot's with the Viking, who's just having his photo taken again – officially this time.'

'Really,' Hugh murmured, as he and Lucy followed the sergeant, passing by the outer pillar and carefully avoiding the jutting rock finger, 'I think we see more of the county police than we do of our friends.'

The words were magnified by the rocky walls of the crevice and came out louder than he had expected, reaching the two men before them, standing in front of the Viking. Inspector Elliot's head turned towards them. 'I wonder why that is,' he mused. 'One of you always seems to have a finger in a police pie.'

His cool grey eyes warmed a little as he regarded them.

'Well, let's see if you can help me here. Would you look at the Viking carefully and tell me how you saw him the first time and what is different now. Especially you, Miss Rossington, as you managed to be on the scene when the Viking was discovered and again soon after Mr Bland was murdered.'

The other man had fallen back with his camera paraphernalia and left the crevice, which still felt uncomfortably crowded with Sergeant Peters' solid bulk behind them. Lucy's eyes moved from the patch of dried blood on the floor to stare at the figure, still seated on the makeshift throne in its rudimentary boat, but now tilted at a drunken angle. 'Well, obviously the sword's gone now,' she said slowly, her brow furrowing. 'And his arm has moved, which may be why he's fallen forward a bit. I don't see anything else different.'

'Where was the sword when you first saw the figure?'

'It lay across his lap, with his hand resting above it.' She pointed. 'See, those rocks have been knocked away, and the arm is hanging down. When I first saw him they were piled up more, and part of his arm lay along them, as if it was on a chair's arm-rest.' She drew in a breath and let it out again, a puzzled expression on her face.

'What is it?' the inspector asked.

'Why has he sagged so much?' Lucy demanded. She shivered. 'It's as if he got up and then sat down again differently.'

Hugh studied the figure curiously and suddenly leaned closer. 'Hmm,' he murmured, 'I think the sword probably held the Viking in place. 'It's a heavy piece of work and once it was taken out of the equation it was likely that the figure would collapse, perhaps quite gradually.'

'Yes, that's what we thought,' Elliot agreed. 'And see here,' he pointed at the patches of rusty chain mail across the skeleton's lap. 'There are some fresh marks on this, so it looks as though the sword was pulled away with haste and little care.'

Hugh inspected the marks closely, then turned to the inspector. 'And what was Bland doing while this happened? He must surely have been incapacitated before the blow was struck. There wasn't time for a struggle or for him to be laid out as neatly as Lucy described.'

'Have you asked Mike?' Lucy said. 'He may have noticed more than I did.'

'Perhaps,' Elliot conceded. 'We'll invite him to have a look later. In the meantime, please don't mention anything you've just told me.'

'Of course we won't,' Lucy said as Hugh nodded in agreement.

He smiled crookedly at Elliot, but his eyes were watchful. 'I bet you're having a devil of a job keeping Mike away.'

'He's being reasonable,' Elliot replied noncommittally. 'In fact, he should be here shortly. I want to recreate his actions and time them. And,' he looked at Lucy, 'I'd like you to stand on the far corner of the gully until you see me wave my hand-kerchief, then come down and do just what you did then. And if you have to, deter any visitors.'

'I suppose,' Hugh said quietly, 'he was still alive when he was stabbed.'

'Yes,' Elliot said decisively. 'There was too much blood from the wound for him to have been dead.'

'How about drugged?' Hugh raised a querying eyebrow.

The inspector met his eyes for a moment, his own showing an appreciative glint. 'We shan't know until we get the pathology report,' he said. 'And that's likely to be a couple of days at least, given the lab's current workload.' He ushered them out past the policewoman, who spoke to him in a low voice.

The inspector glanced at the top of the gully, and said smoothly, 'And here is the professor, well ahead of his time. Kittoe is taking him along the footpath up to the far stile. Just as well we're ready to go ahead. Tom, you're sure everyone knows the ropes?'

The sergeant nodded. 'Yes, sir. Everyone's ready.'

Elliot turned to the waiting policewoman. 'Then you'd

better get into position, Carlus, and wait for Kittoe to appear in the crevice. Go easy on the murder, Constable,' he advised blandly, as she entered the crevice, 'and be as nippy as you can.'

With a wave of her hand Lucy went swiftly off down the gully towards the outcrop of rock on the eastern edge, Ben leaping happily through the heather beside her. The others followed the track up the western slope towards the serpentine quarry and as they neared the field the sound of Mike's argumentative voice reached them. 'What do you mean, wait here? Elliot wanted me to come over, so where is he?'

'Right here, Professor,' the inspector said, appearing over the brim of the gully with Hugh, much to the relief of Constable Kittoe whose face was blotched red and anxious as he tried to keep Mike by the stile. The barbed wire strands had been peeled back from one section of the fence, allowing easier movement between the gully and the field. The quarry was deserted, its rocky ledges and pits shining damply, with here and there a gull standing around, watching the human activity with curiosity.

'I'm glad you were able to come so promptly,' Elliot said as he reached Mike and Kittoe. 'We're all ready for action, so we can go straight ahead.'

Mike glowered at him. 'Where are we starting? Am I supposed to chase your constable all the way from the coastal watch station?' He glared at the unfortunate Kittoe, who looked even more anxious.

'I don't see the need for that amount of action just yet,' Elliot said, looking across the gully to check that Lucy was in position. 'If you go back to the stile and start the chase from there, it should be sufficient for now. Just a moment,' he added quickly as Mike turned away, 'we need to place Bland before you start. As you came over the stile, where was he?'

Mike's eyes narrowed as he measured the distance mentally. 'There, on the edge of the gully, I think,' he said. 'Just about where you came up. I saw him from the corner of the path,' he waved energetically back towards the sea, 'when he turned off over the stile. That was when I realised where he was going.' His face darkened with remembered anger.

'How quickly were you moving? Walking or running?' Elliot asked.

'A fast walk most of the time,' Mike said after a second's consideration. 'I wasn't hanging around looking at the views. In some places I suppose I went a bit more slowly, depending on how bright the moonlight was. It was good going except a couple of times when the clouds came over. There was a storm brewing, but the rain didn't fall until later.'

'Did Bland know you were behind him? Did you call out?'

'No, I didn't,' Mike said shortly. 'I didn't want the bastard slipping away from me again.'

Hugh shut his eyes in disbelief, then opened them again, watching his friend in fascinated horror as Mike continued roughly, 'And how do I know if he heard me? Certainly I wasn't trying to be quiet, but the sound of the sea probably covered any noise I made. Maybe,' he ended sardonically, 'we should start from the beginning of the path and find out. I'm sure your constable would enjoy a scenic walk.'

'So Bland was walking, was he?' Elliot asked.

Mike ran his hands irritably through his tousled hair. 'I guess so. There was no reason for him to be going any faster. But,' he said slowly, 'I certainly wasn't gaining on him, so he must have been going at a fair whack. I wasn't fussed about catching him up as long as I could see where he was going. I only ran a bit across this field once I knew what he was up to.'

'Right,' the inspector said decisively. 'Let's get on with this. Kittoe, go over to the edge of the gully. Professor, if you'd take up your position, I'll raise my hand and when I drop it, take it as your signal to start.'

Mike snorted as he turned away, but lingered as Hugh asked suddenly, 'May I ask Mike one question, Elliot?'

Elliot nodded, and Mike looked at his friend, demanding abruptly, 'Well?'

'You were in a great hurry,' Hugh said thoughtfully. 'Did you fall or trip at all on the rough ground?'

Mike glowered at him. 'I'm not an imbecile, you know. Only on the bloody stile. Though it was as well the sky was clear then, otherwise I might have ended up in that damned quarry.'

Hugh nodded, satisfied, and Mike strode off to the stile. As they watched him, Hugh said quietly to Elliot, 'So Bland probably did hear him at that stage, if not before. Knowing Mike, he wouldn't have slipped quietly.'

'And Bland would have put on a spurt of speed if he did hear him,' Elliot conceded, raising his hand as Mike climbed the stile and swung round to face them. 'Did you get that, Kittoe? Run as fast as you can as soon as the professor hits the ground.'

'Yes, sir.' The constable tugged his padded waistcoat down nervously as he hovered by the track down into the gully.

Elliot dropped his hand. 'Now, Kittoe. Go.'

The constable disappeared over the edge and Mike pounded towards them, his face already scarlet. Hugh felt a moment of amusement as he realised Kittoe would run as fast as possible to avoid feeling Mike's hot breath on his neck, fearing how realistic Mike's re-enactment might become. He wondered if Elliot realised that too.

Mike passed them without looking up, his eyes fixed on the track through the gully. Below him, Kittoe had just reached the crevice and was disappearing from sight. Elliot glanced at his watch as he pulled his handkerchief out of his pocket, then returned his attention to Mike who was rushing down the track, slipping noisily on a little loose shale. As they watched from above they saw a figure slide out of the crevice by the granite pillar and crouch out of sight beyond a clump of hawthorn and sloe bushes. Mike brushed roughly past a gorse bush, showering the ground behind him with fallen yellow flowers, and raced over the last stretch to the entrance. He hesitated, and Hugh wondered whether he had seen Carlus, then he pushed his way into the crevice without any caution. A muffled curse reached the men standing above the gully.

Hugh began to rub his ear thoughtfully as he realised Mike had forgotten the projecting finger of rock, and grinned slightly as the sound of Mike's distorted voice reached them again. He wondered briefly if Kittoe was expected to play dead through the diatribe that was being loosed over his head. Beside him Elliot waved his handkerchief and Lucy began to walk down the path from the far side of the gully, Ben leading the way as she leaped lightly over the stream and picked her way across the slope below them. The dog paused at the pillar until she reached him, when they both vanished into the cave in their turn.

'Right,' Elliot said decisively, striding down the gully with Hugh at his heels as Carlus came out of cover.

'That finger of rock just past the entrance to the crevice,' Hugh said, 'it catches the unwary.'

Elliot glanced over his shoulder, amusement in his cool grey eyes. 'Yes. We've checked it over and got some interesting strands of material. Definitely Bland's cloak, but also others we've yet to match.'

Carlus had come up to meet them, and the inspector demanded, 'He saw you?'

'Yes, sir. Only just though. But there was no way I could avoid Miss Rossington. Nowhere to hide or anything as she approached from that side.'

'So, when it was dark,' Hugh mused, 'it might just have been possible for somebody to slip out of the crevice unnoticed.'

Elliot moved on as he replied, 'Possible, yes, but it's all very tight. And where did they go without Anna and Lucy seeing them?'

Hugh was close behind him. 'Up the gully. It's the only possibility. And I believe it's the way the footpath used to go until Rasmussen diverted it.'

'Yes,' Carlus said. 'It went across the fields below Pennance and out into the lane beyond the house. There was a lot of bother here when Mr Rasmussen had the route changed. It was felt he deliberately tried to make life difficult for the serpentine diggers by putting the path in the field they wanted to work.'

Hugh noted this without comment, saying as they reached the crevice, 'Rasmussen has CCTV. I don't know what area it covers, but it would be worth having a look to see if it picked up anything.'

Ben appeared in the crevice entrance with Lucy close behind him. She was half-turned back to Mike, whom she seemed to be dragging out. 'Come on,' she said crossly. 'Let's get to the others. Leave him alone, Mike.'

'It's alright, Lucy, we're here,' Elliot said. 'But it'll be easier to talk outside. And a relief to Kittoe, no doubt.'

Mike shot out, brushing past her as he said furiously, 'What the hell did you mean by it, Elliot? It gave me a hell of a turn to see that bloody constable on his back clutching a sword. Were you expecting me to crumble and confess?'

'We needed to re-enact as closely as we can all the actions of last night, so we borrowed a sword from a local theatre,' Elliot explained patiently. 'You can surely see yourself how tight the timing is; after all you spotted Carlus slipping out.'

Mike's expression changed, the fury slipping away. 'No,' he said flatly. 'I didn't see her come out, but I saw her in the bushes, and she must have bumped into Lucy too. That finishes me, doesn't it?'

'Is this a confession after all, Professor?'

'No, it bloody isn't,' Mike shouted, clenching his fists.

'I didn't think so,' Elliot commented. 'And don't despair yet. The timing is very close, but it was dark. I suppose you can't remember any movement by the bushes?'

Mike brushed a hand across his forehead. 'No,' he said wearily. 'I can't even remember if the sky was clear or not just then.'

'Then we'll just keep on checking details,' Elliot said, 'while you all get up to Rasmussen's for lunch. I'll no doubt see you there later.'

Mike groaned as Lucy took his arm, pulling him down the slope. 'What a bloody bloody day! I knew this damned Viking meant trouble.'

FIVE

Sun was breaking through the clouds so that the garden below brightened as Lucy and Hugh led the way along the terrace to the front of Pennance. Ben lingered beside Mike, who was dragging along reluctantly in their wake, studying the mosaic patio before stalking up the steps to the terrace and pausing again to read the faded inscription on the corner obelisk.

As Mike caught up with them he spotted Alastair in the drive, getting out of the old Volvo Anna used during her stays in the country. 'It's about time she stopped borrowing her father's car,' Mike muttered. He stood watching Alastair hold open the driver's door as Anna swung her long legs out and stood up gracefully, just as the excited collie reached her. 'She's always down here these days, it's about time she got one of her own.' Mike scowled at her as she moved towards the house, taking in the glass walls and sedum-covered roofs of the central pavilion and its satellite units with a fascinated gaze.

'It's quite something, isn't it?' she said, Ben ambling beside her as she strolled over to join them, bringing a waft of her usual subtle scent with her. Alastair walked with her, his finely drawn features looking a little strained as he exchanged greetings with Lucy and Hugh. Anna's blue eyes, though, sparkled as she asked innocently, 'Still avoiding Tamsyn Warne, Mike?'

His scowl deepened and Anna gurgled with laughter. 'Mike

makes a very good fisherman when he has to, although I don't know that I'd trust him to catch my supper,' she explained to the others. 'All it needs is the right stimulus. The local journalist provided it.'

'Right now I'd do almost anything to avoid that woman,' Mike muttered. 'Even take part in your pageant.'

'Oh dear,' Alastair murmured. 'I wondered why Tamsyn rearranged her watch times. She's normally very meticulous about her shifts, and,' he hesitated before adding quietly, 'and other people often don't like working with her. She can be a little too forthright about her Cornishness, especially to incomers.' He sighed wearily. 'I suppose she's following up this story of hers.'

'I shouldn't mention her here,' Hugh warned. 'I don't know whether Rasmussen has seen the papers yet. But I'd guess that he reads them as soon as they arrive, so Tamsyn won't be particularly popular with him either.'

'What's in the paper?' Anna demanded. 'I haven't seen it. Mike mentioned something about it, but you know him, he didn't say what he was on about.'

'We haven't seen it either,' Lucy assured her, ignoring Mike's glowering expression, 'but Rob Elliot showed it to Mike. Tamsyn sent in a piece about the Viking, with an amazing photo of the skeleton in his armour, and of course it's on the front page.' Her eyes met Anna's fleetingly and saw the flash of surprise in them.

They had moved through the slender columns of the entrance courtyard, their voices drowning the murmur of flowing water in the narrow pools on either side of the path. As they reached the front door it slid open, to a gasp of astonishment from Anna, which caused a slight smile to touch Eric Rasmussen's thin lips as he came forward to greet them.

'You must be Anna,' he said, appraising her shapely figure in its ruby cord smock with open appreciation as they shook hands. 'I'm so glad you could come. I've been hearing great things about this pageant of yours.'

'Not mine,' she replied immediately. 'I'm only refining the material, and helping with the production. All the real work was done by Alastair and Mark Teague and Tamsyn Warne.'

Eric Rasmussen drew in his breath with a sharp hiss and looked beyond Anna, brandishing the newspaper he held in one hand. 'Have you seen this?' he demanded. 'Tamsyn Warne has been busy. I haven't been able to get hold of her yet, but she'll have some answers to give when I do.'

Hugh took the paper and handed it to Lucy. 'Only Mike's seen it, so we'll all be glad to look at it. We bumped into your other guests on the doorstep.'

Eric visibly pulled himself together and took Anna's arm to lead the way to the chairs in the sitting area. As she sat down gracefully, creating a bright splash of colour on one of the cream linen chairs, he bent over her saying confidentially, 'You must forgive me, Anna, it's been a difficult day.'

Mike snorted and Eric turned to him. 'Ah yes, Mike, I suppose this is as awkward for you as it is for me. But don't worry, I'll get to the bottom of it pretty quickly.'

'Where were the guards you posted around the site? They were obviously missing last night when Bland was murdered. Did you tell them to stay overnight?' Hugh asked, quickly scanning the paper that Lucy had passed back to him.

'I don't know where they were,' Eric replied shortly. 'I'd definitely arranged for somebody to be there all the time, so I can't explain why the site was left unguarded. Apparently the two men involved went off to work at the oyster fishery early this morning. I've been in touch with Teague, but he wasn't very helpful, so I'll have to wait until they've finished there to hear what they've got to say. Look,' he said more genially, 'why don't you sit down and have a drink before lunch? I have a very nice local white wine, no air miles behind it.'

Mike's eyes rolled upwards in annoyance at Eric's standard remark, but the others chose their seats as Eric moved to the sideboard and picked up a bottle from the ice bucket. He poured the wine into fragile glasses and Hugh went over to hand them around, watched curiously by Ben, who only lowered his head to his paws when Hugh at last sat down with his own drink.

Eric took up his stance at the front of the sitting area. 'Well, Anna,' he said, raising his own glass, 'we should drink to the success of your pageant. I believe you're gaining a reputation for having a magic touch. Alastair was lucky to get your help.'

Above the murmur of the repeated toast, Anna sat up straighter on the wide chair, tucking her black-booted legs more neatly against the side as she said clearly, 'I'm enjoying the whole thing, and although the real hard work has been done by a few other people it's really Alastair's brainchild. Without him we wouldn't be doing this. So let's raise our glasses and have another sip of this delicious wine in honour of all his efforts. The man behind it all, Alastair.'

The vicar's face flushed uncomfortably as they lifted their glasses to him and drank. Before he could speak Eric turned to Hugh, pointing to the paper that Lucy had handed on to Anna as he said, 'Damnable, isn't it?'

'She makes a good story of it,' Anna said thoughtfully as she skimmed through the words. Her eyes rested again on the photograph, which showed the Viking's threatening stare very effectively, and her brows drew together as she studied it.

'Is Rosen joining us for lunch?' Lucy asked quickly, suddenly anxious that Anna had noticed the missing sword in the photograph, and mindful of Inspector Elliot's request not to discuss it or anything else to do with the skeleton.

Eric glanced at her ruefully. 'No, I'm afraid she isn't. I suggested we could make a celebratory meal of it, but she said she has better ways of marking her eighteenth birthday.'

Anna let the paper fall onto the floor beside her. 'Is it today?' she exclaimed. 'Oh dear, I should have brought something for her.'

Mike leaned over and picked up the paper without a word, as Eric said, 'That's kind of you, Anna, but there's no way you could have known. Especially,' he spread his hands, 'as I forgot the day too. I must think of something she'd like and try to redeem myself.'

'What's she planned to do?' Hugh asked, while in the background Alastair muttered, 'Dear, dear,' in a distressed tone.

'I'd be the last to know,' Eric said. 'No doubt she's off with those louts from the village, but I suppose I can't complain when I've let her down so abysmally.' He frowned. 'I've always been bad at remembering anniversaries, and until my wife's card arrived for Rosen I just had no idea it was so soon.' His frown deepened. 'I would have thought …' he began, breaking off his comment with an effort. 'No matter. I'm sure we'll recover.'

Mike had been ignoring the conversation as he went through the article in the newspaper again, the scowl on his face deepening as he read. Finally he screwed the paper up and threw it furiously across the room.

'I know, Mike,' Eric said soothingly, retrieving the paper and smoothing it out as he laid it on the table, 'but we'll have to play this carefully. There's no point losing our tempers with Tamsyn, it will only give her more material.'

Mike snorted, but his attention was distracted by the opening of the kitchen door. The collie raised his head, nostrils twitching, to stare towards it as a dark-haired woman peered through, waiting for Eric to turn towards her. When he did so he nodded slightly, and she disappeared from view.

'Jenny, who comes in from the village when I have a party,' he said, 'indicating that lunch is ready.' He gestured towards the table in the dining area, and waited to escort Anna as she stood up, holding her barely touched glass. As his eyes fell on it, Eric said, 'I hope it's to your taste, Anna.'

She smiled brilliantly at him as they passed the tall vase, her eyes resting appreciatively on its swirling greens and blues. 'It's delicious, but as I'm driving I won't have more than this, so I'm making it last.' She eyed the colourful mats on the table with approval, noting the wide bowls of green salad and the generous provision of wine bottles and water jugs.

'No, no, don't worry about it,' he said, waiting as she sat down on one of the low-backed wooden chairs on the far side of the table. 'I can easily arrange for somebody to drive you back.'

Eric gestured Lucy into the seat on his other side, before he sat down between them at the head of the table. Ben slipped round Lucy and under the table to sit over her feet. Mike quickly took the place beyond Lucy, leaving Hugh to stroll to the foot of the table as Alastair hurried round to sit beside Anna.

She was saying, 'Thank you, Eric, but I've got some last minute touches to make to the pageant this afternoon, and it's better that I keep my wits about me.'

Her eyes widened as Jenny brought in a large earthenware tureen, a distinctive fishy smell gradually overwhelming the scent from the vase of jasmine in the centre of the table. Jenny placed it down carefully on the unusual mat set in front of Eric, thick cork on tiny casters. 'Although that's going to be difficult if I over-indulge in oysters.'

Eric's tight lips relaxed. 'I'm glad you're fond of them. I'm very partial to them too, especially in this stew.' He smiled slightly. 'Mark Teague always sends me Pacific oysters rather than the native ones, a small way to show his dislike, but I don't let it bother me. I like to support local businesses, and Mark Teague is certainly enterprising, so I don't let emotion get in my way. His business seems to be doing very well, I'm glad to say, and I'm happy to add my mite to his success.'

Eric pushed the tureen towards her, and it rolled gently on its castored mat. She smiled at the sight of it, and his face showed a hint of humour as he enjoyed her surprise. 'A little invention of mine. Everything's designed to make self-service easier. That's why I like casseroles, so much easier for entertaining, and for the local women to prepare,' he said as she lifted the lid, taking up the ladle attached to the side as steam rose from the contents and wreathed around her black curls. 'Do take as much as you like,' Eric urged. 'I'm relying on you all to make sure I don't slide from gourmet to gourmand.'

Jenny brought in a second tureen, placing it on another castored mat at the far end of the table as Anna heaped oysters onto her plate. 'Fish casserole,' Eric said, 'for those of you who prefer to miss the oysters.' Lucy looked relieved, and he smiled at her understandingly. 'I know not everybody shares my taste.' He nodded to Hugh, seated at the foot of the table between Mike and Alastair. 'Perhaps you'd send it round, Hugh.'

'The mats are very clever,' Lucy commented, watching her husband serve himself.

'Yes, I'm pleased with them,' Eric said. 'Cork from oaks in Spain. It's so important to keep them productive, especially now wine producers are using plastic and screw tops. I'm thinking of patenting the idea.'

Anna had passed the tureen of oysters on to Alastair, who helped himself to a few, then a few more. As he pushed the tureen to Hugh he murmured, 'Gluttony is, I know, a sin, but I'm always sorely tempted by these.'

'It's relative,' Hugh commented, taking a few and passing the tureen on. 'A few centuries ago London apprentices would have paid you to take their share. They were so despairing of their endless diet of oysters it became an article of indenture that they shouldn't have to eat them every day.'

Alastair smiled as the tureen passed on untouched by Mike or Lucy, who were both helping themselves from the fish casserole. 'Yes, you are right,' he said. 'False humility is also a sin.' He bent his head in an impromptu silent prayer over his food.

Eric had taken a large portion of oyster stew and picked up his cutlery, but paused, waiting silently until Alastair lifted his head and looked along the table at his host. Eric laid down the knife and fork he held and straightened his shoulders. 'I'm sorry,' he said slowly and deliberately, 'I had hoped this would be a congenial meal for us all, but I feel I can't go on without asking you all to spend a moment remembering Roger Bland.'

He glanced at Mike, 'A colleague of yours and a friend from long ago for both Alastair and me. May his spirit rest in peace, wherever it now is.' He picked up his glass and said, 'Roger'.

The guests held their glasses high and repeated, 'Roger'. Mike tossed his wine down his throat, barely tasting it, and brought the glass back to the table so heavily Lucy glanced at it, expecting the stem to have snapped.

'And now,' Eric said, picking up his cutlery again, 'let's see if we can regain a semblance of pleasant company enjoying lunch. Roger would have been the last to wish us to spoil fine food.'

'Hmmph,' Mike said disagreeably as he refilled his glass. 'His character had obviously changed over the years. By the time I knew him he would have gained immense pleasure from the thought of us choking over fish bones at his wake.'

'He laboured under a sense of injustice,' Alastair said quietly. 'He felt life hadn't treated him fairly.' His hand hesitated with an oyster on his fork, then he slipped it into his mouth and swallowed. 'Many of us feel that at times, but Roger's life was blighted by his failure to rise in his profession.'

'He rose quite well enough,' Mike said thickly. 'There are only so many places at the top.'

'Indeed,' Eric agreed, 'and Anna is an excellent example of how one can prosper in either direction.' As Mike choked on the mouthful of wine he had just gulped, Eric said, 'After the reviews of your performance in *The Queen's Necklace*, it was predicted you'd go on to great things. Yet you've branched out into productions of regional performances. Wasn't success to your taste?'

'Oh yes,' she said serenely, scooping up her last oyster. 'I like my projects to be successful. There are just so many things I want to do, that the most obvious career path sometimes seems rather boring.'

'I can appreciate that,' he said. 'One day you'll find something that matters more than you expect. And nothing else will count.'

'Is that what happened to you?' Anna asked, wondering if he was going to pass the oyster stew back to her. Deciding informality was the rule she reached out to the tureen, pulling it towards her and just catching it as the castored mat shot the lightened pot over faster than she expected.

'Yes,' he said, leaving most of his oysters untouched and helping himself to salad as Anna ladled more stew onto her plate. 'Now I can't think of anything more important than preventing mankind from destroying the planet, however it was created.' He glanced wryly at Alastair, to whom Anna had passed the tureen. 'It touches everything we do and are. It affects my every waking moment. And,' he added ruefully, 'Rosen thinks it supersedes any concern for my family.'

'She's an interesting girl,' Anna commented.

'You've met her?' he queried quickly.

'Yes, in the pub at Polkenan last night,' Anna replied, wondering if she had said too much.

'With young Teague,' he said tightly. 'Wasn't she?'

'I think so,' Anna said. 'I don't really know many people down here. They seemed happy enough together anyway. Don't you approve?'

'She's only taken up with him to annoy me,' Eric said sharply. 'Maria, Rosen's stepmother, says Rosen wants more of my attention and thinks taking up with young Teague will help her get it.' He shrugged. 'My fault again, but it's difficult to know what to do with a daughter. Her own mother's dead, and Rosen never really got on well with my second wife. She's managed to rub along alright with Maria, but more because they mutually ignore each other than anything else.'

Anna had a brief picture of the spare, etiolated man beside her transformed into Henry VIII with his growing list of wives, and managed to suppress the spurt of laughter that welled up in her chest.

'Teague,' Mike snapped, aroused from his state of silent but oppressive disapproval. 'What have you got against him?'

Eric turned away from Anna, looking slightly taken aback. 'Nothing as such,' he said. 'I just don't think he's going to help Rosen make useful choices about her life. Of course,' he added comprehendingly, 'it was Kevin Teague who found the Viking, wasn't it? I see what you're thinking, Mike.' He frowned thoughtfully, twirling his glass in his fingers. 'Hmm, I wouldn't have thought he had the brains to set up that sort of scam. But perhaps,' he continued slowly, 'he would be the ideal person to find it. And, of course,' his fingers froze on his glass, 'he could have primed Tamsyn Ware before he made the discovery. I believe his uncle is very friendly with her.' Eric carefully put the glass down and pressed his fingers to his forehead. 'Yes, that is possible, isn't it?' He looked at Mike questioningly.

The archaeologist was nodding vigorously. 'And the bloody photograph could have been taken in advance too,' he said, running his fingers through his hair. 'No, that's not possible.'

'Ouff, sorry, Mike,' Lucy exclaimed as her glass fell, tipping wine across the wooden surface of the table. 'You caught my elbow.' At her feet, Ben sat up, but she leaned down to speak to him and he lowered himself to the floor again with an audible sigh of resignation.

'No matter,' Eric said quietly, pressing a button hidden under the table. The panel to the kitchen opened, and Jenny's head poked cautiously out. 'A cloth, please, Jenny. Just a minor accident with the wine.'

Jenny came straight out of the kitchen, her dark eyes fixed on the table. She edged behind Mike's chair, pulling a cloth from the pocket in front of her striped butcher's apron, and slipped between him and Lucy to mop up the spill, starting slightly as she saw Ben watching her.

'Sorry,' Mike said, sounding anything but regretful as he glanced at Lucy. 'But if you must wave your glass around ...'

'No,' Eric interrupted as Jenny returned to the kitchen, shutting the door behind her, 'Lucy was being kind, creating a diversion and sacrificing her wine. It's Rosen, isn't it? You think she's responsible for the photograph.'

Mike was staring between the two of them, perplexed and increasingly annoyed. 'Your daughter?' he demanded disbelievingly. 'Why would she take it?'

'She has a fantastic idea about a career in photography, the latest whim,' Eric said tersely, 'and not the faintest idea of how difficult it would be to succeed in it.' He sighed. 'And she may have wanted to get at me. But I can't really believe she'd go that far.'

A silence fell, broken almost immediately as a silvery note of music shimmered through the pavilion. Eric glanced at his watch with a shade of annoyance. 'I expect that's the police,' he said, glancing at the CCTV camera behind him. 'Inspector Elliot said he would come up after lunch, so he's been remarkably prompt.' He looked round at the cleared plates and a faint smile touched his mouth. 'I'm glad Jenny will see her efforts have been appreciated. Sadly my own appetite is too indifferent to make cooks feel rewarded.' He got to his feet, adding, 'Fortunately my dessert offerings are always simple, cheese and fruit, so nothing will be spoiled. Perhaps we can persuade the inspector to join us.'

'He won't eat with his suspects,' Mike said sharply, before glancing at Anna. 'Unless the temptation overcomes him.' He scowled as she smiled sweetly at him, while she moved slightly to allow Jenny to take away the oyster tureen.

Ben emerged from under the table to watch Eric cross the sitting area to open the front door. They heard him greeting the inspector but as the door closed the conversation became lower, inaudible to those listening around the dining table. It was only when two pairs of footsteps crossed the sitting area towards them that their frozen postures relaxed. Ben pattered over to greet the inspector and they all swivelled round to watch the men approach, while Jenny continued to clear the table without any sign of interest.

Elliot stopped at the end of the table as Ben went back to

his place beside Lucy. 'Well,' he said blandly, 'I'm glad I haven't actually caught you while you're still eating. Mr Rasmussen,' he nodded politely to the man beside him, 'has assured me you'll survive until the next course while I run through a few points with you.'

'Unless you'd care to join us,' Eric said, as the sliding panel closed finally behind Jenny, who had left the table clear but for the bottles of wine and jugs of water.

'That's kind, but no thank you,' Elliot said.

Mike shot a triumphant look at Anna, saying, 'Duty first, you see.'

Elliot surveyed him impassively as Eric pulled up another chair, inserting it between Anna and Alastair. 'Do at least take a seat,' he urged.

'Thank you,' Elliot said, sitting down in Eric's own seat at the head of the table.

Lucy's lips twitched as she saw how nonplussed Eric was, although he recovered immediately and sat down in the chair whose back he had been gripping tightly. He reasserted his authority automatically, saying, 'The inspector has some more questions that he wants answered, but doesn't want to see us individually ...'

'Yet,' Mike interrupted.

'So,' Eric continued, unperturbed, 'I'll pass you over to him.'

'As Mr Rasmussen has told you,' Elliot gathered the reins of the discussion into his own competent hands, 'there are some loose ends to tie up.'

Mike snorted. 'Such as who did it.'

'If you know that, Professor, I would expect you to have told me already,' Elliot answered. 'As you haven't, instead you can tell me what caused the violent argument you had with Roger Bland at the huer's hut.'

Mike shot a look of such loathing at Anna that she almost recoiled. An expression of anger spread across her face as she glared back at him.

Noting the interchange Elliot said, 'My informants had information to this effect, but I haven't yet been able to speak to the original source, so your frankness will be welcome, Professor.'

Lucy bit back a laugh at the expression on Mike's face as he worked this out. 'You mean the whole bloody village is talking about it.' He glared furiously at the inspector, then blurted, 'It wasn't much of an argument. I hadn't the faintest idea the old fool,' Alastair's breath hissed as he drew it in sharply, 'was here when I was wasting my time trying to trace him through Oxford. And I certainly didn't know he made a habit of swanning around in fancy dress.' He scowled as he remembered the occasion. 'I'd just gone for a walk when I spotted the hut and remembered Lucy had mentioned it earlier. I went to have a look at it and he popped out, all wrapped up like the villain from a bad opera.' His hands clenched on the table, then relaxed as he gave a grunt of amusement. 'I don't know which of us was more startled, but I didn't have time to find out what he was up to.' He glanced at Anna crossly. 'He was always slippery as an eel when you asked him questions at the best of times. And at the hut it was obvious he didn't want to tell me anything, and took the first chance to slip off.'

'That was when I appeared, wasn't it?' Anna asked. 'When I heard you shouting at him.' Mike nodded curtly. 'If he'd known you for so many years I expect he was used to your bluster,' she said coolly. 'He certainly wasn't cowering in fright when I arrived.'

Elliot's eyes met hers for a second, before moving back to the archaeologist. 'Did you see him again?'

'I went up there from the pub last night,' Mike replied reluctantly, 'before I went along the coastal path to meet up with Hugh.'

'What happened?'

'He wasn't there,' Mike said shortly. 'The place was in darkness. I didn't hang around. Anyway,' he added, 'he must have been well off on the coastal path by then.'

'What time was it?'

'I don't know. I don't go around looking at my watch all the time,' Mike retorted brusquely.

'Roughly then.'

Mike shrugged. 'Between seven and eight, I suppose.'

'We can do better than that,' Lucy said, glancing at Anna for her agreement, one hand on Ben's soft head as he pressed against her legs. 'We got to the pub about six forty five, ate our meal and left again just after seven fifteen. I did happen to look at my watch because I knew Alastair's shift at the coastal watch ended at eight o'clock, so he and Hugh would be almost ready to leave when we got there. And Mike can't have been gone more than fifteen minutes before that.'

'About seven o'clock then. Do you agree with Lucy's calculations?' Elliot asked Anna.

'Yes.' He waited, but she added nothing further.

'You can't have had time for pudding,' he commented quietly. 'What made you leave the pub so quickly?'

Anna bit her lip. This was the trouble with friendships. People got to know things about you. Like the fact that she would never forgo a pudding. It really wasn't fair of Rob to use information he'd obtained privately.

'It was a nice evening,' Lucy said, 'and we thought it would be fun to meet Alastair and Hugh to walk back together.'

'Did Professor Shannon enter your thoughts?' Elliot asked softly. 'After all, you all went to the pub together and then he left fairly rapidly. Did you know he was going to look for Roger Bland?'

'We didn't know and he hadn't said so,' Lucy said carefully. She added valiantly, 'It was his idea to go and meet the others, and after he'd gone we thought we would follow too and catch up with them all.'

Elliot waited, leaning back in his chair, idly twiddling a spoon as he looked at the faces around the table. Anna lifted her chin slightly as she met his eyes. Eric's expression was impenetrable as he studied the inspector. Alastair looked strained as he gazed at the table, the fingers of one hand absently pleating a trouser leg. Hugh returned Elliot's look, one eyebrow raised quizzically, while Lucy was studiously peering into her wine. Mike was pulling thoughtfully at his jutting lower lip, staring uncertainly at Anna who was avoiding his eyes.

'That gives me a very clear picture,' Elliot said blandly, watching Mike shift uneasily in his seat.

Anna tried to shut out of her mind the vivid images she had of last night. Mike storming out of the pub and up to the huer's hut. Mike raging back into the village and westwards on the coastal path in the footsteps of the man who died only a short time later. She and Lucy setting out on Mike's heels, unaware of what they were so shortly to find.

'But of course Roger wasn't at the hut when Mike went up, Inspector,' Alastair said, his fingers suddenly stilled. 'You know I told you that when I went up to see him at about five o'clock he was just setting off then. It was too early for me to go over with him for my spell at the watch station, but I definitely saw him go off along the coastal path. So he would have been well out of Mike's way later on.'

'You saw him set off,' Elliot pointed out. 'You don't know how far he went, or whether he came back to the hut or the village.'

'No,' Alastair agreed, puzzled, 'but why would he come back once he'd started?'

'Who knows?' Elliot replied. 'Maybe he'd forgotten something, maybe he had an appointment and wanted to get you out of the way before he returned for it.'

Mike leaned back, crossing his arms over his chest as he listened, his expression sardonic. 'With me?' he asked. 'Is that what you think?'

'I have to think of all the possibilities at this stage,' Elliot answered, unperturbed. 'If Bland had come back for whatever reason, it would seem likely that he'd bump into you.'

'He didn't,' Mike said curtly.

'Then we still have to account for his time,' Elliot said. 'I understand that it takes thirty to forty minutes to walk along the cliff path from Polkenan to the far side of Portharrock, and if he'd taken the inland path it would have been ten minutes or so longer. Although we know he was coming back along the cliff path at about seven fifty we've no proof yet which way he went out. And either route means that nearly two hours need to be accounted for.'

Silence fell across the dining area as the others absorbed this. Hugh spoke first, asking, 'Could he have gone anywhere else in Polkenan? Your theory about his return is plausible, but he could have been visiting anyone.'

'We're checking, of course,' Elliot said. 'Somebody will have seen him. The house to house calls will pick that up.'

'If you're lucky,' Mike snapped.

Anna's eyes lifted to his flushed face. If you're lucky, she thought. I wonder if you see how well you're fitting into the frame.

'The other main point I hope you can clear up, Mr Rasmussen,' the inspector said. As he continued all eyes turned to Eric. 'We talked with the men you'd appointed as night guards at the Viking site, and they say that you told them not to bother after all, that there was little likelihood of intruders finding the cave in the dark.'

Eric stared at him in blank shock. 'But that's nonsense!' he exclaimed. 'I didn't say anything of the sort.'

The inspector studied him for a moment. 'Apparently the message came via your daughter, when she saw them at the oyster fishery where they were working during the day.'

The effect was obvious. Eric's face was a pasty white, but he rallied quickly, pressing his fingers to his forehead in thought. 'Rosen must have misunderstood me,' he said awkwardly. 'No doubt I wondered aloud if a night guard was necessary, and she thought I didn't want one.' He let his hand fall to his knee as he achieved a painful smile. 'We aren't communicating too well at the moment, I'm afraid. I should be more careful in my dealings with her.'

'I see,' Elliot said. 'Can I have a word with Miss Rasmussen? That should clear the matter up.'

'She isn't here,' Eric replied. 'And I don't know where she is right now. We had an upset this morning and she's gone off in a bit of a temper.' He gathered his forces and sat up straighter. 'Surely it can't be important?'

'It's always important to get all the facts right,' Elliot said, 'however little they may seem.'

'Of course,' Eric agreed. 'All I can do then is let you know when she comes home so that you can talk to her. Or would you prefer me to bring her to the police station?'

'Call me when she gets back,' Elliot said. 'I'll be in the area, so it's easier for me to come here. One more thing, Mr Rasmussen.' He gestured towards the screen in the corner of the room. 'What area does your CCTV cover?'

Eric spread his hands apologetically as he replied, 'Only the main drive, I'm afraid. I like to be forewarned of visitors, but I don't really expect them to come in from the cliffs so I haven't had the cameras directed that way.' His thin lips tightened for a second before he added, 'And I'm afraid the tapes are wiped clean automatically every morning for reuse. I didn't think to keep them. But,' he concluded, 'I was here all evening working in my study until Lucy and Hugh came back with the news, and I'm sure I'd have noticed anybody on the terrace.'

'It was only a long shot,' Elliot admitted, pushing back his chair and standing up. 'I must ask all of you to let me know if anything more occurs to you about the matter.'

He inclined his head in farewell and began to make his way across the sitting area. Eric got quickly to his feet, but Anna was before him, stepping swiftly round the table and after the inspector, her shoes tapping lightly across the floor. Eric halted in surprise, but Hugh said quietly, 'They're friends. I expect she's keen to find out if he's got any chance of getting to the pageant.'

Mike snorted.

The living room of Alastair's cottage was dark and Mike felt impatiently along the wall for a light switch, knocking a couple of the crowded picture frames even more askew. At last his fingers found the switch and pressed down, so that a dingy brightness spread around the room, striking tiny shining gleams from the serpentine lighthouses that watched endlessly from their stations around the walls.

Behind him Alastair tripped on the low step, banging his head hard on the front door lintel. 'Dear, dear,' he said ruefully. 'I should be used to the hazards here by now. I do hope it wasn't Eric's wine.'

Mike glanced at him, noting how pale he was. 'I'll make some coffee, shall I?' he offered gruffly. 'Elliot's interrogation technique is enough to wear anyone out.'

'No, no, he was most courteous,' Alastair protested, sinking down onto the sofa. 'Coffee, ah, do make some, but not for me, Mike. I have a little weakness, you see.' He looked conspiratorially at Mike, who tried not to appear startled. 'I like a glass of cherry brandy after my evening meal, a very small glass, my reward for surviving the day.' He smiled suddenly up at Mike, 'The pub's pint of prawns are always a favourite of mine, so I'm most grateful to you for the treat. Just what I needed. After Eric's lunch I can't believe I managed to eat any more.' He began to get up, pushing his hands down onto the sofa to lever himself forward.

'Stay there,' Mike ordered. 'I'll get your indulgence if you tell me where it is.'

Alastair subsided gratefully. 'Thank you. I must admit I've been feeling a little unwell for a while. Maybe I should have accepted Anna's offer of a lift home after all. But walking usually clears my head.' He shivered suddenly and turned round awkwardly to shut the window behind him. 'The wind's come up very strongly, so it looks as though Mark's prediction is going to be correct. Ah, of course, you were there too, when he told us there's a storm brewing. I suppose he's come over for a drink at the pub. *The Three Tuns* is popular all along the coast.' Alastair became aware that Mike was shifting impatiently from foot to foot, and waved a hand apologetically. 'So sorry. My drink, yes, my cherry brandy. In the kitchen, by the back door. The glass is beside the bottle.'

Mike took three long strides into the kitchen where he filled the kettle and switched it on, before turning to survey the breakfast debris piled into the sink, the untidy heaps of opened envelopes and food packets on the formica worktops. He hesitated uncertainly, surveying the clutter, then wrenched open cupboard doors until he saw the squat bottle sitting on a shelf beside several tins of cat food. As he took it out he spotted the tiny glass behind it and snatched that up too.

From the living room Alastair called, 'Do have some yourself if you like it.'

Mike shuddered at the thought as he tipped the open bottle over the glass. 'Thanks. Coffee's what I need right now.' Only a trickle of viscous liquid slid slowly out of the bottle, so he upended it, watching impatiently as the small glass filled up. 'There's only just enough cherry brandy,' he shouted over his shoulder. 'Have you got another bottle?' He heard Alastair murmuring in the living room, and stepped back to the doorway to catch his words.

'Dear me,' Alastair was saying, almost to himself, as he clutched the pile of albums he had moved onto his lap, 'I quite thought there was plenty there.' Suddenly aware of Mike looming in the doorway, he glanced up, gathering his thoughts. 'No, no, I don't keep more than one bottle at a time, but I'm quite happy with just a little taste. I must remember to buy another at the shop. They keep a supply specially for me.'

He looked down again at the albums, sighing as Mike brought the glass over to him, nudging aside a couple of lighthouses as he placed it on a crowded table near the sofa. 'My memory seems to be getting worse. I quite thought I'd found the book I wanted this morning. Never mind,' he added, lifting one and almost dropping it as he put it down on the floor, 'it must be here somewhere.' He bent over to push the discarded album more neatly against the sofa and sat up again, a surprised look on his face as he began to hiccough. 'Dear … hic … me,' he began, starting violently as Mike clapped his hands loudly beside his ear.

The remaining albums slid forward and Mike caught them, heaving them back onto Alastair's lap. 'It's the best remedy,' he said. 'See, you've stopped.'

Alastair waited a moment, considering. 'You're right,' he said in surprise. 'I haven't had hiccoughs since I was a child.' He reached out for his glass, sipping gratefully at the brandy. 'This wasn't a remedy then, of course, but I find it cures most ills now.' He took another sip, putting the glass down again carefully. 'I thought Anna was looking rather tired at the pub. She said she had a niggling headache, but I hope she isn't working too hard.'

Mike had returned to the kitchen. He rinsed a couple of glasses as he mumbled, 'Socialising more like.' The kettle boiled and he gave up his desultory attempt at washing up to spoon instant coffee into a mug with a grimace of disgust, before adding hot water.

As he came back into the living room he saw Alastair push the albums off his lap and stand up shakily. 'I must leave this to another time,' he said, running his hand over his face. 'Looking up old memories is perhaps not always a good thing anyway. If you'll forgive me, Mike, I must go up to bed. I think poor Roger's death has been more of a shock to me than I realised.'

He tripped over the album on the floor, catching at the table and knocking it over, serpentine lighthouses bouncing in all directions across the worn carpet, empty glass rolling away. 'Dear, dear,' he said in distress, leaning against the arm of the sofa. 'How clumsy of me.'

'Don't worry,' Mike said gruffly, finding space to put his mug down on the mantelpiece, 'I'll see to it. You get off to bed.'

'I ... well, yes, thank you,' Alastair said, walking unsteadily towards the stairway door. 'I do hope I'm not coming down with anything,' he murmured as he slipped under the curtain. 'It would make life so difficult for Anna.'

Mike snorted as he righted the table and bent to pick up the serpentine pieces, pausing for a second when he heard Alastair slip on the stairs, half expecting him to come tumbling down. He put the lighthouses back on the table, listening until he heard Alastair's bedroom door open. He stepped towards the mantelpiece, reaching for his mug, but cursed as glass crunched underfoot. Muttering under his breath he picked up the pieces, grabbing a piece of newspaper to wrap round them as he stalked into the kitchen to find a bin.

When he returned he flung himself into an armchair, then got up crossly to fetch his coffee. He sat down again more care-fully, nursing the mug. Outside the wind had grown stronger, buffeting the cottage, making the windows rattle in their frames. Now it was carrying rain too, hurling it against the panes in great spattering flurries. No other sound disturbed Mike as he sat in the dimly lit room, surrounded with the clutter of another man's life as he tried to sort out the latest problem in his own.

Mike drained his coffee, putting the mug down on the floor by his feet. He tried to marshal his thoughts but gradually his head sank on his chest and soon the sound of his heavy snoring filled the room, battling with the elemental noises outside.

He was not sure what woke him. Sitting bemused for a moment, working out where he was, he glanced at his watch and frowned. Eleven o'clock. Again something, a movement, a faint noise, impinged on his consciousness, and he shook his head, trying to shake off his drowsiness. Sitting up stiffly he listened more carefully. The wind had fallen, the rain stopped, but the noise that had awoken him came again. Now he knew what it was.

He got up quickly and strode to the stairs, wrenching the curtain aside so roughly that he pulled half of it off its rings. He mounted the steep stairs two at a time and hesitated. The sound came again, now definitely the sound of violent retching, and Mike pushed Alastair's bedroom door open, pausing at the dreadful scene in front of him.

The curtains at the tiny window were open and rainwater had trickled from the sill down the wall to collect in pools on the floor below. Fitful gleams of moonlight shone through the darkness outside, revealing and then screening the man hunched on the floor. The bed clothes trailed to the ground beside him, still grasped in one hand. As Mike found and pressed the light switch Alastair came clearly into view, a wracked figure in threadbare pyjamas, convulsed with pain.

Mike strode forward and bent over the vicar, who raised a tortured face and tried to speak. The attempt was broken by another convulsion that ended in renewed retching. Horrified, Mike said loudly, 'I'll ring for an ambulance. Wait here.'

As he rushed from the room he swore softly at the futility of his instruction as he raced dangerously down the stairs. In the crowded living room he looked around desperately, wondering where in all the clutter the telephone was. At last he saw it, half hidden by a stack of papers on a bookcase near the window. Shoving the papers off Mike grabbed the receiver and punched out the emergency code.

He took a deep breath as his call was answered, and explained the situation with commendable brevity. As he replaced the receiver he felt a slight sense of relief, knowing that help was on the way and mentally repeating the instructions he had been given. He hurried into the kitchen, cursing as he stumbled over a pair of Alastair's shoes. He looked around the tiny room helplessly. Where the hell does he keep it, he thought desperately.

Mike began to shove around the litter on the worktops. Empty sauce bottles, opened tins, bags of rice lay everywhere, and he pushed them into even further disorder. By the time he had reached the far end of the kitchen his temper was fraying and his actions were becoming wilder. It was the cherry brandy bottle that fell to the floor, smashing into large pieces. Brought up short, Mike bent to pick them up and drop them in the bin, before he forced himself to stand still and look around. And there it was, beside the sink of all places.

He grabbed the tub of salt and turned on the hot tap, running the water as he poured a heap of salt into a small bowl. Testing the water, and relieved to find it warm, he poured some onto the salt, seizing a spatula to stir it. A red smear on the outside of the bowl caught his attention and he peered crossly at it. If he had to start again because Alastair could not keep his crockery clean …

With relief Mike realised it was his own blood. Lifting the hand that grasped the bowl he saw a deep cut across his thumb, and guessed he had got it from one of the pieces of broken bottle. He sucked it vigorously as he stared into the murky water, wondering if the salt had dissolved enough. What the hell, he thought wildly, and dropped the spatula. He grabbed the first spoon he saw, a battered silver one with a tiny gilded saint's figure on the handle, seized the bowl and hurried back upstairs, spilling water here and there as he went.

In the bedroom Alastair was where Mike had left him, but he had fallen to one side and Mike's heart missed a beat as he saw how still the vicar lay. Come on, come on, he thought, willing the paramedics to arrive.

As he bent over the prone form he felt immense relief as the free hand twitched feebly. 'The ambulance is on its way,' Mike said, astounded to hear how normal he sounded, 'but we've got to get this down you, Alastair. It'll help.' He put the bowl on the floor and tried to lift the vicar from the contorted position in which he lay. Alastair was less rigid than before and Mike was able to prise the bedclothes from his clutching fingers and roll him slightly over, supporting him against his shoulder as he lifted the spoon. The salt water trickled mainly down Alastair's chin and he coughed weakly. As he tried to protest Mike spooned more liquid into his mouth and Alastair swallowed it with difficulty, twisting his head feebly away from Mike. Again Mike forced the water into Alastair's mouth, but this time most of it ran back out.

The sound of a screaming siren broke the silence, followed almost immediately by feet running heavily down the path. Mike felt relief wash over him, then he tensed, wondering whether the front door was locked. He waited, still trying to drip the liquid into Alastair's mouth, until a sudden convulsion racked the vicar again, wrenching him from Mike's restraining arms.

Mike put down the bowl and leaped to his feet as the front door burst open. 'Here!' he yelled, rushing out to the tiny landing. 'Up here.' Footsteps pounded up the stairs and he waved the two paramedics through into Alastair's bedroom.

He followed them in, explaining tersely what had happened and what he had done as he edged round the little knot of people in the centre of the room. He banged the window shut and stood in front of it, still feeling the chill night air blowing through the cracks in the frame onto his back as he watched them bend over Alastair.

'What's he eaten today?' one of the paramedics demanded.

Mike groaned inwardly. 'Prawns,' he said. 'A pint of them.'

'When?'

'This evening, at the pub. About sevenish, I suppose,' Mike said.

'Anything else? Earlier?' the paramedic demanded as he brought out a needle and small bottle.

Mike turned abruptly to look out of the window. 'Oysters at lunch time,' he said.

Behind him the other paramedic grunted. Mike's attention was caught by the single light that shone out in the darkness. Next door, at the back. Bloody Thomas, he thought savagely. Doesn't miss a thing.

Suddenly the light seemed to swim in front of his eyes as the thought struck him. Not Thomas. Thomas slept at the front. Thomas slept heavily. Anna slept at the back. Anna. Anna eating oysters, matching Alastair's consumption at lunch time.

He whipped round. 'Is it shellfish poisoning?' he demanded curtly.

'Looks like it,' one of the paramedics replied shortly. 'Probably the oysters. Did you eat them too?'

'No,' Mike said. 'But the woman next door did, and her light's on too.'

'Get round there then,' the man said, glancing up. 'It could be her lucky night. She might not be in a fit state to call us herself.'

Mike had gone before he finished speaking, thundering down the stairs, across the crowded living room, out of the open front door to splash through the puddles outside. Within seconds he was hammering on the front door of the neighbouring cottage. There was no response, so he glared round, wondering what to do. His desperate gaze fell on the painted stones edging the narrow flower beds and he seized one, using it with great force on the door. At last a window upstairs opened, and a head poked out as a woman's thin voice asked nervously, 'Who is it?'

'Mike Shannon,' he roared. 'Staying with the vicar. He's very ill. We think Anna, your visitor, may be too. Let me in to see.'

'I'll go to look,' the woman said anxiously.

'No, let me in,' he shouted. 'There's no time to waste. She could be dying.'

It was the magic word. The woman's head disappeared and shortly afterwards the front door opened slowly. Mike pushed it back, almost squashing the elderly woman against the wall as he burst in, racing up the stairs, halting at the top to yell, 'Is she in the back room?'

'Yes,' the woman puffed, following him as quickly as she could. 'Her light's on. You can see.'

Mike thrust open the door at the back of the landing, and stopped as if he had been electrocuted. It was almost the matching image of the scene he had just left. But Anna had got further than Alastair. She had obviously fallen out of bed too, but had managed to crawl towards the door, the landing door, not the bathroom one in the other direction, so Mike guessed she had wanted help.

He fell to his knees beside her sprawled figure and gently lifted her limp body, laying her head against his shoulder. Her black curls fell softly around her face, white and twisted, and her limbs were slack in her gaily patterned flannel pyjamas.

'Poor dear,' Janet whispered. 'What can I get for her?'

Behind her Thomas's voice could be heard, querulously demanding, 'What's going on? Janet, where d'you be?' His tone rose at the sound of footsteps on the stairs, 'Here, who are you, coming into my house?'

One of the paramedics appeared in Anna's room. 'Right,' he said, moving quickly to examine her, taking her pulse, lifting an eyelid, checking her heart. He nodded to Mike as he pulled out a second needle and bottle, 'Lucky you thought of her, mate. We'll take her with us. Any others at this lunch?'

'God,' Mike groaned as the second paramedic appeared with another stretcher. 'Yes. It was at Eric Rasmussen's place, Pennance, outside Portharrock. I didn't eat any of the bloody things, but he did and I think one of the other guests did, Hugh Carey.'

Anna was being lifted carefully onto the stretcher as Mike stood up. 'I'll ring them,' he said.

'Do that,' the first paramedic said. 'We'll warn the ambulance station that another call will come in. Anyone who's eaten them will be affected badly if they're the source of the poisoning.'

Mike followed them down the stairs and out onto the path, watching Anna's still face above the neatly tucked blanket as they loaded her into the ambulance, which the driver had managed to reverse most of the way down the path. 'She'll get over it, won't she?' he demanded urgently.

One of the paramedics had leaped into the front passenger seat and the second paused as he closed the back doors. He met Mike's eyes briefly. 'I won't kid you, mate. She's bad. Get in touch with her family, if you know them. But there's always hope. And you found her in good time. If she'd been left all night the chances are she'd have been dead by morning.'

Mike stepped back, shaken, as the ambulance drove off. He pulled himself together and ran back to Alastair's cottage, ignoring Thomas who was leaning precariously over his garden gate, the light from his own cottage falling on his gaudily striped nightshirt.

SIX

Inspector Elliot paused on the steps of the hospital, looking around the car park, quiet and still in the early morning. The wet tarmac shone in the bright overhead lighting, which etched stark shadows beyond the few cars that were there at this hour. Elliot could not immediately see the one he was looking for. His eyes lingered on Hugh's silver-grey Audi, where Ben was clearly visible on the driver's seat, looking out of the window. Elliot's gaze moved on, falling next on a red Passat parked askew across the yellow striped zone near the pedestrian crossing, and he ran quickly down the remaining steps and strode towards it, his footsteps ringing out loudly.

Mike levered himself out of the driver's seat and turned to face him, still clutching his mobile phone. 'Well?' he demanded hoarsely.

'Hugh's only got a mild dose, so he should be fine. Rasmussen too. But Anna and the vicar are in a bad way,' Elliot said bleakly.

'Have the doctors said what it is?' Mike asked urgently.

'Shellfish poisoning,' Elliot replied briefly.

Mike's expression lightened. 'So they'll recover,' he said, trying to sound convincing. 'Not many people die of that, do they?'

The bones of Elliot's face grew more prominent against the

tightened skin. 'Apparently there's more than one kind, and they're suffering from one of the worst types. Any luck raising her father? The hospital are keen he should be here.'

Mike stared, swallowing hard as his lips grew very white. 'No.' He shook the phone in frustration. 'I've tried his home number and his mobile, and left messages on both.'

'Well, you can't do any more,' Elliot said. 'I'll put out an alert. We're already searching for Drewe's next of kin as nobody seems to know them, not even the old bloke next to the vicar's cottage. Drewe's in the worst state of them all, the doctor was muttering about extreme sensitivity.' He jerked his head at the hospital. 'Get in there now. She may come round.'

Mike nodded and moved towards the steps, swinging back as he realised the inspector was walking away to the car parked in one of the consultant's spaces. 'Elliot, where are you going?'

Elliot halted and looked round. 'This is my case,' he said levelly. 'I've set in hand all I could, but I need to be there to run it.'

Mike stared at him. He held out the phone that was still clamped tightly in his hand. 'Put in your number,' he said. 'If, when she comes round or … if there's any change, I'll call you.'

'Thanks.' Elliot took the phone, tapped in his number and handed it back. 'Give her my love if you can.' His mouth narrowed and he turned away as the archaeologist nodded sharply.

The stark white walls and gleaming floors dazzled Mike's eyes as he bounded through the hospital corridors, oblivious to the courtyard gardens where the plants were lit gently by low round globes, to the watercolours on the walls of the cliffs and the sea, the valleys and the hills that many of the patients knew and loved. Turning right into the emergency unit he saw Lucy on one of the chairs in the waiting area, staring straight ahead, her hands tightly clasped in her lap.

As he approached her she turned her head towards him, and he was horrified to see how scared and desperate she looked.

'Hugh?' he demanded urgently.

'He's going to be okay, and so is Eric. I think they didn't eat so many of the oysters,' she said, her hand grasping his arm as he sat down next to her, the plastic chair knocking against her own. 'But Alastair is very bad, and Anna …' She broke off as a doctor appeared from the emergency unit, his white coat flapping against his legs as he walked over to them. She looked fixedly at his weary face, unable to ask, her hand tightening painfully on Mike's arm.

The doctor glanced from Lucy to Mike. 'Any news of her father?' he asked.

'No,' Mike said glumly. 'I've left messages where I can. The police are looking for him now.'

'Mike!' Lucy exclaimed. 'He may be at Fran's.'

He stared at her blankly. 'Who's she?'

'Mike, you know,' Lucy said urgently. 'Our neighbour at home, at Withern. Colonel Evesleigh's been seeing a lot of her, and I know Anna's been wondering if they're an item.'

Mike glared. 'Well, why didn't you say so before? Have you got her number?'

Lucy already had her phone out, releasing her grip on his arm to scroll down through the numbers. 'Here it is.'

'Give it to me,' the doctor said, holding out his hand. 'I'll get one of the nurses to ring it.'

Mike's jaw tightened, as the doctor strode through the door at the end of the corridor. When he returned Mike demanded, 'Is it that urgent?'

The doctor sighed as he returned Lucy's mobile to her. 'This is amnesic shellfish poisoning. They were all lucky to get here so quickly, but there's no known antidote to the poison, domoic acid. I can only say it would be a good thing if Miss Evesleigh's father gets here as soon as possible.'

A stifled sob escaped Lucy's lips, but she immediately sat up straighter. 'Would it help if we were with her, Dr Brady?' she asked. 'I've known her since we were little, and she's very dear to us both.'

The doctor hesitated. 'I don't know,' he said slowly. 'She isn't conscious, and it would be very irregular.'

'Damn that,' Mike burst out. 'Would it help her?'

The doctor lifted his hands in a weary gesture. 'Who knows?' He considered them. 'Alright,' he said abruptly. 'She's sliding into a coma. If you can prevent that she may have a chance. Only a small one,' he warned as they got eagerly to their feet. 'There's still a strong chance of other complications.' He turned, pushing open the swing door into the emergency room and they followed closely behind him, both stopping short at the sight that met their eyes.

The small room was almost filled with equipment that surrounded the narrow bed in its centre. This was where Anna lay, attached, it seemed to their horrified eyes, by tubes to every piece of the equipment that circled the bed.

Doctor Brady pulled forward a chair, pushing it in close to Anna's head. 'Her stomach's been pumped. Now we're draining fluid from her lungs,' he explained in a low voice, 'and monitoring her heart and blood pressure. It's only a question of waiting. Talk to her about anything, just try to keep her with us.'

Lucy sat down and hesitated before gently reaching out for one of Anna's hands, neatly folded across the sheet. She was careful not to dislodge the tubes but clasped the limp fingers warmly. She racked her brains for something to say, then moistened her dry lips with the tip of her tongue.

'We're both here, Anna,' she said quietly. 'Mike and I. It isn't long now until the Polkenan pageant, and we're looking forward to seeing it. You've done wonders with the programme, people are talking about it all along the coast.' She paused, peering hopefully at Anna's still white face, motionless against her black hair, which lay flat against the pillow, without any of its usual vibrancy. 'The finale on the beach is going to be stunning, with the boats all lined up for the blessing.'

The doctor moved forward, leaning over Anna, raising one eyelid. He let it fall and moved back, shaking his head.

'Lucy, you're not getting through,' Mike said impatiently. 'Let me have a go.' Without waiting for a reply he leaned over Lucy's shoulder, saying loudly, 'This bloody pageant is going to be a right farce, I could have told you that.'

Lucy flinched from the voice that resounded in her ear, and expostulated softly, 'Mike ...'

He ignored her. 'And you won't even be there to carry the can now you've made such a pig of yourself over oysters.'

Lucy began to slide out of the seat, keen to avoid being deafened, but stopped suddenly, staring at Anna's hands. 'She moved,' she whispered. 'I'm sure her fingers twitched.'

The doctor motioned to Mike, 'Carry on,' he said urgently.

Mike swallowed hard, his eyes fixed on Anna's face. 'Messing around in a fishing village,' he said scathingly. 'You're never going to do a real job of work again, are you? You just can't settle to one thing, whether it's work or play, hopping from one place to another, never settling with one bloke, always letting them get away.'

This time there was no doubt. The hands that lay on the bedspread jerked noticeably and Anna's eyelids quivered.

'Yes,' Doctor Brady said jubilantly. 'You're getting through. Keep going.'

Lucy was out of the seat now, pushing Mike into her place. He gingerly picked up Anna's hand. 'And look at this,' he squeezed it cautiously. 'You look as though you've never done any hard work in your life.'

Lucy leaned against his back, watching as Anna's eyelids rolled right up, revealing dark blue eyes that struggled to focus on Mike's face as her mouth trembled.

'You don't know anything.' The words were so faint they had to bend over Anna to catch them. 'Let go, Mike, you're hurting me.'

With an apologetic mutter, he released her fingers and sat

back in the chair. The doctor took over, saying sharply, 'That's enough, you've done all you can. Wait outside now.'

Mike swivelled round and slid out of the chair, picking his way awkwardly through the medical paraphernalia to the door. Lucy followed more slowly, looking back several times to where the doctor was talking to Anna.

In the waiting area Lucy's heart missed a beat as she saw Mike slumped against the wall, his forehead resting on his arms. He pushed himself stiffly upright as he heard her gasp, and ran a hand across his face, rasping on the reddish gold stubble on his cheeks.

'Is it enough?' he demanded. 'She won't relapse, will she?'

Doctor Brady came out of the emergency room in time to hear this, shutting the door behind him, and answering wearily, 'We can't tell that. But I hadn't much hope that you'd get any reaction. The risk of her slipping into a coma is passing.' He paused, shooting an amused look at Mike. 'It's the first time I've come across your approach, Mr Shannon. There's no doubt though that it was effective.'

Mike's guarded expression relaxed, but Brady went on, 'In the absence of Miss Evesleigh's father, I think it only fair to warn you that she still has a long way to go. And,' he said heavily, 'there may be permanent after-effects.'

'Like what?' Lucy asked anxiously.

He shrugged evasively. 'It's difficult to be sure. There may be some memory loss, some nerve damage.'

'She remembered me well enough,' Mike pointed out. 'Surely that's a good sign.'

The doctor shrugged again. 'Let's hope so. Now, if you'll excuse me, I must see the other patients. I suppose,' he said over his shoulder to Mike, 'your approach won't work with Mr Drewe?'

'Afraid not,' Mike replied. 'I barely know him.'

'Ah, well.' Dr Brady disappeared into the neighbouring room.

Mike looked at Lucy, noticing for the first time how tired her pointed face was. 'What do you want to do?' he asked gruffly. 'Check on Hugh?'

'Yes,' she replied. 'They said he'd sleep for some time, and Eric too, but I'd just like to see him. Eric,' she repeated, looking startled. 'Nobody's thought to notify Rosen.'

'Had she turned up then?' Mike asked, walking beside her along the corridors. 'I thought she'd gone out on the razzle with the boyfriend.'

Lucy's brows drew together. 'I didn't think to look before I left Pennance,' she admitted. 'It was quite late, but Hugh and I hadn't gone to bed. We hadn't even got undressed because we'd been talking for ages after Eric had gone to work in his unit. Hugh hadn't been feeling too well earlier when we went for a walk to enjoy the moonlight, before the rain really blew in. He was getting much worse by the time you rang, so I called an ambulance and then went to check on Eric. I wouldn't have thought of shellfish poisoning immediately,' she admitted, 'so it's as well you did call. I probably wouldn't have called an ambulance otherwise, I'd have tried a doctor instead. And then it might have been too late.' She pushed a strand of chestnut hair out of her eyes, tucking it behind one ear as she stopped at the entrance to a small ward, peering through the glass panels to the nearest bed.

Hugh lay, like Anna, on his back, neatly tucked under the sheets, but his pale face looked more relaxed as he slept, his chest rising and falling gently as they watched. The nurse at the nearby desk rose and came over to them. 'He's sleeping soundly,' she said quietly, 'and so is Mr Rasmussen. They're over the worst, although they'll be feeling pretty rough when they wake up.'

As long as they do wake up, Lucy thought with relief, smiling at the nurse and moving on with Mike. They walked slowly down the stairs towards the entrance as Lucy said suddenly, 'I couldn't believe it when I went into Eric's private

unit and found him in his study beside his desk, still fully
dressed. He must have been working for hours. Anyway, he was
showing the same symptoms as Hugh, throwing up and having
bad stomach cramps. The ambulance arrived then, in very good
time as apparently your paramedics had warned there might be
another call-out in the area. I never thought of seeing if Rosen
was there. Surely, though, if she was,' Lucy added thoughtfully,
'she'd have heard the racket and come out?'

'Of course she would,' Mike said bracingly. 'And if she's
not at Pennance there's not much we can do to find her,' he
glanced at his watch, 'at five o'clock in the morning. Let's get
some breakfast.'

Lucy gave a shaky laugh. 'You're as bad as Will,' she said,
'always thinking of your next meal.'

'At least I haven't …' Mike broke off. 'When's he coming?
That brother of yours will be just what we need in this chaos.'

'What's today?' Lucy asked. 'Wednesday, isn't it? I've quite
lost track.'

Mike nodded, and she said, 'Well, you've got a couple of
days to get it sorted out. He's coming over for the weekend with
Gran. Though I think we ought to put them off.'

'You'll never keep Will out of this once he knows what's
happened,' Mike said bluntly. 'Anyway, let's fortify ourselves
now. Do you want to try the hospital café?'

'No,' Lucy replied at once. 'I'd like to get right out of here.
And I ought to take poor Ben out to stretch his legs. He's been
shut in Hugh's car for hours. Poor dog, he knew something was
wrong, and just leaped in the car with me when I left to follow
the ambulance.'

'We could go back to Alastair's cottage,' Mike suggested
doubtfully, as they went out of the door and started to descend
the steps, 'although the bloody bloke next door has probably
got it staked out. And Alastair doesn't go in for much in the
food line. I should think his cupboards are pretty bare.'

'I don't think we should use his home while he's in here and so ill,' Lucy said. She bit her lip thoughtfully. 'We could go back to Pennance, of course, but to be honest I'll be glad to get away from the place. It's so smart and spartan that I never feel quite comfortable there. And Eric seems to have been having such a run of bad luck that I really feel we should leave anyway.' Her face lit up as they approached the Audi, where Ben was waiting eagerly for them, his breath misting the window and his nose leaving damp marks on the glass. 'I know, Mike. There's a café beyond Portharrock, on the cliffs above the little harbour. We can go down and give Ben a bit of a run while we wait for it to open up. I've had lunch and tea there with Hugh, and I'm sure it does breakfast too. The food's fantastic.'

'Sounds okay. We'll take my car, you can leave yours here until we get back,' Mike said. 'Get that dog into mine while I update Elliot on Anna's state.' He surveyed the Audi as Lucy opened the driver's door and the excited collie sprang out. 'Hugh's likely to have a heart attack when he sees the mess he's made. Just as well,' he added sarcastically, 'that I don't fuss about mine. Put him on the back seat, the boot's full of tools.'

Lucy stroked Ben soothingly as she watched Mike stride away, pulling his phone out of the pocket of his donkey jacket. When he began to speak she walked briskly over to the grass verge beyond the cars, letting Ben sniff the smells and cock his leg with immense relief.

Sunlight was creeping up the sky to turn the sea into a rumpled opalescent coverlet as Lucy stared out over the water to the far horizon, only a fraction of her attention on the collie as he wandered over the rough turf of the cliff top. She lifted her face to the mild wind blowing inshore, glad to feel it on her skin. Gulls were patterning the pale blue sky, weaving webs between the drifting puffball clouds, stained a clear rosy pink. The only evidence of the wildness of the night was the fresh layer of seaweed and wooden debris that coated the rocks below.

Beside her Mike shifted impatiently. 'Come on, Lucy,' he

said. 'The café's just opening up.'

Lucy glanced at her watch, feeling a sense of disbelief at how early it was. 'Okay,' she said, turning to glance across the circle of beaten earth that served as a car park. Mike's Passat stood there and had been joined by an elderly jeep, parked in front of the weathered shack on the far side. Its shutters were open and the rattle of metal indicated that tables were being put out on the terrace behind it.

She called Ben as she pushed her hands into the pockets of her fleece and strolled back across the headland, Mike restraining his long stride to keep pace with her. They were both deep in their own thoughts, and it was only as they reached the shack that Lucy spoke, 'Should I ring again, do you think?'

He shook his head. 'No point. They've got our numbers. If there's any change they'll be in touch. And,' he added gruffly as he pushed the door open, 'Elliot was going back when he could. He'll let us know.'

Lucy looked at him quickly, but could only see his back as he led the way to a table by the window. 'I'm not sitting outside,' he said flatly as she hesitated, looking out onto the bay sheltered between curving cliffs.

'Okay,' she said, sliding onto one of the wooden chairs, urging Ben to lie under the table. 'I suppose it is a bit windy.'

'It's bloody cold,' he growled, scanning the menu on the table as he sat down.

An older woman approached, rounded and cheerful in her denim jeans and layers of jumpers. 'You're early birds,' she said brightly. 'We're not strictly open yet, but it doesn't matter. Are you ready to order? Or would you like more time?'

'I know what I'll have,' Lucy said. 'Porridge to begin with, then scrambled egg and toast please. And hot chocolate, with cream.'

Mike was staring at her, an appalled expression on his face. He realised with a start that the waitress was waiting expectantly. 'The full breakfast for me, with all the bits, and some strong coffee.'

As she made her way back to the kitchen Mike said, 'That sounds disgusting, Lucy. Hot chocolate at this hour.'

'I can't wait,' she said. 'And talking of disgusting, you're going to sit there eating black pudding.'

'Why are we talking about food?' he demanded explosively. 'We've got three people ill in hospital.'

'Four. You're forgetting Rasmussen.'

Mike snorted. 'It has to be the oysters,' he declared. 'You and I didn't eat them, the others did. Anna and Alastair were the ones who gorged themselves, and they're the most badly affected.'

The waitress placed their drinks on the table, her attention on Mike. 'We were hearing about the trouble at Pennance,' she said. 'All taken sick, we heard.'

'Not all of them,' he said shortly, as Lucy gratefully wrapped her hands around her hot glass.

'There's never been a problem with Mark Teague's oysters before,' the waitress said over her shoulder as she returned to the kitchen.

Mike grunted, but his nose twitched involuntarily as the smell of frying bacon drifted across the room. Lucy suppressed a smile as she saw Ben's black nose was doing exactly the same. 'I think you're right,' she said slowly, 'about the oysters. It can't be anything else.'

Mike poured coffee from a cafetière into his mug. He was frowning. 'Just unfortunate then, unless the cook has something against Rasmussen. But then why would she try to poison all of us?' He groaned, clutching at his head. 'I've got so used to your family involving me in crime that I've developed a suspicious mind.'

He noticed the waitress staring at him from the counter, and lowered his voice. 'Although Rasmussen's just the sort of bloke somebody would want to poison.'

'Mike!' Lucy expostulated.

He grinned at her. 'You know he is.'

She bent her head over her drink, sipping it carefully through the cream. Mike lifted his coffee, glancing round as the door opened. His hand shook, spilling the liquid on the table, as he put it down again. Lucy looked round too, quite unaware of the white moustache over her upper lip.

Mike's chair grated on the floor as he stood up, his hands braced on the table as Ben squirmed out. Inspector Elliot approached them, his face worn and tired. 'It's alright,' he said quickly, bending to stroke Ben briefly, 'there's no more news from the hospital.'

Mike took a deep breath, then sat down carefully as Elliot pulled up another chair and sank into it wearily while the collie thumped onto the floor next to Lucy with a heavy sigh.

'I thought you should see this,' the inspector said, pulling a sheet of paper out of his pocket. 'The newspapers haven't arrived yet, but this was emailed to me. The front page of one of the nationals. I gather something similar is appearing in others.'

Stretching out a hand, Mike scowled down at the large picture. His eyes widened.

'What is it?' Lucy demanded, leaning across the table. 'Mike, let me see too.'

He turned the page towards her, his fingers clenched angrily on the paper. 'Who the hell took it?' he demanded, glowering at Elliot.

Lucy's startled gaze fell on a picture of the Viking, a menacing figure on his makeshift throne, a prone figure at his feet. *Viking Defender of the Shore* screamed the headline. *Curse of the Viking* yelled the first line of the article.

Lucy's eyes swept over the words. 'It's all speculation,' she said. 'But the picture ...'

'Yes,' Elliot said. 'The picture. Does anything strike you about it?'

Mike snatched the page back and glared down at it. His brows drew together. 'Where's the sword?' he demanded.

Lucy squinted over his arm. 'Oh yes,' she said in surprise. 'I see. I suppose,' she asked hesitantly, 'it is Roger Bland's body lying there?'

The inspector nodded. 'It's Bland alright, but we don't know if he's dead. He doesn't appear to have been stabbed when this was taken. There's no sign of the sword, either in his body or under the Viking's hand.'

'Do you mean,' Mike demanded disbelievingly as the waitress approached the table with two plates, her eyes on the paper that Elliot had retrieved, 'that some maniac set up the whole thing as a photo opportunity?' He ran his hands through his tousled hair. 'No,' he answered himself as he absently picked up his knife and fork, 'that's bloody ridiculous. Why would Roger take part in such a farce?'

Elliot spoke to the waitress briefly, then turned back to them. 'It's a possibility,' he said, 'however far-fetched it sounds.' He sighed. 'We need the photographer,' he said, tapping his fingers on the table. 'But there's no indication of who it could be. We still haven't been able to get hold of Tamsyn Warne, she's our best bet at the moment. If she didn't take them herself, she's still our only point of contact. She must know who did take them.'

'That's why she's gone to ground,' Mike said thickly, chewing on a mouthful of fried bread and sausage. Lucy averted her gaze, forking scrambled egg onto her toast.

'Lucy?' Elliot asked quietly, watching her face. 'Any ideas?'

She put down her cutlery, and leaned forward to sip at her hot chocolate, her hair falling forward and concealing her expression. She looked up, wiping the cream from her lip with one hand. Elliot was waiting, and she pulled a wry face. 'I don't know for sure who the photographer is,' she said, 'but I wondered before if it might be Rosen Rasmussen, and I still think it could be.'

Across the table Mike choked and coughed, grabbing his coffee to swallow a huge mouthful. Before he was able to speak Elliot said simply, 'Why?'

'She has ambitions for a photographic career, which Tamsyn Warne seems to have encouraged. Anna says she's good, she's doing the publicity pictures for the pageant. And Rosen has a gripe with her father. He doesn't think it's a worthwhile occupation.'

'Rosen seems to have disappeared too,' Elliot said. 'We've been trying to contact her.' He was silent for a moment, thinking over what he knew. 'She was the one who told the guards around the Viking tomb that her father didn't want them there overnight. And,' he added, 'of course we need to find her to let her know her father's in hospital.'

'She's with the Warne woman,' Mike declared, frowning at the plate of kippers the waitress placed in front of Elliot. 'Find one, and you'll have them both. They're probably behind the whole scam, and got Roger into it somehow, then it all went wrong and he ended up dead.'

The inspector took a piece of kipper and ate neatly, unconcerned by Mike's impatient glowering. 'It's a theory,' Elliot said mildly, 'but there's nothing yet to prove any of it.'

Mike pushed his own empty plate away abruptly as the shack door opened again. It banged hard against the counter as a man in oilskins strode into the room, ducking his head to avoid the low door lintel.

'What's all this?' he demanded belligerently, halting beside them, arms akimbo. 'Stuffing your face while your bloody coppers spread rumours to bring down my business.'

The inspector turned round, pushing his chair back as he stood up to face the other man. 'Do you want to explain that, Mr …?'

'Teague. Mark Teague,' he said curtly. 'It's you that needs to do some explaining. What's all this about my oysters poisoning Rasmussen? That's the story going round the village.'

Elliot said, 'Eric Rasmussen and three of his lunch guests are in hospital with amnesiac shellfish poisoning, and the most likely source is the oysters they had at lunch yesterday. Oysters which we understand you provided only to him.'

'That's right,' Mark agreed. 'If you mean, I provided all of the ones he had, at least as far as I know. But if you mean I provided them only to Rasmussen, then no that isn't right.'

Lucy sat up straighter, her expression suddenly alert. 'But, Mark,' she said, 'Eric told us you gave him Pacific oysters, while the local shops get the native ones.'

Mark grinned, his teeth white against his tanned face. 'Rasmussen always thinks he knows everything,' he said. 'And he's quite right. I normally do that. Rasmussen doesn't appreciate the quality of the native oysters, so I don't waste them on him. Unfortunate if he has discerning guests, but there it is.' The humour faded from his expression as he turned back to the inspector. 'Yesterday I had no native oysters to spare, the market for them in the grand restaurants is growing and I have to meet it. So,' he bit the words out, 'everybody yesterday had Pacific oysters, not just Rasmussen.'

'Did you supply the local outlets with oysters from the same batch?' Elliot asked quickly.

Mark looked triumphant. 'You bet, and I've rung round checking. Nobody else who had them has been taken ill.' He pulled out a crumpled piece of paper. 'I've written down where they went. You can check for yourself.'

Elliot took the paper. 'Thank you, Mr Teague. We'll do that.'

Teague stood up straighter, 'And see that you scotch this story about my oysters. I haven't built up the business to see it brought down by Rasmussen. He's tried hard enough in other ways, it would be rich if he died to make sure he finished me off.'

'You don't like him,' Elliot commented.

Mark stared at him. 'No, I don't like him, and he doesn't like me. He sees environmental issues on a planetary scale, but doesn't bother with people who've got to make a living in his own area. He likes to micromanage his own environment and he got up my nose with his plans. Not just mine either, I can tell you.' He looked out of the window over the rocky head-land curving round the bay. 'He wanted a wind farm here, of all places, one of the first landfalls for migrating birds from the continent and Africa.' He smiled suddenly. 'Still, I got up his nose in return by making sure he didn't get planning permission.'

'Did he upset many people?' Elliot asked.

'You'll have to ask around,' Mark replied. 'A fair few, I reckon.'

As he turned to the door Lucy said quickly, 'Mark, we're looking for Rosen. She doesn't know her father's ill. Do you know where she might be?'

Mark swung back to look at her. 'Rosen? She's off some-where with Kevin. Birthday trip.'

'Do you know where?' Elliot asked.

Mark laughed. 'At that age they go where the fancy takes them. They'll be back when they're ready. I doubt she'll worry too much about her father. He never has about her.' He left, shutting the door hard behind him.

Elliot looked down ruefully at his plate of half-eaten kippers. 'I'd better be off too,' he said, putting some coins down beside it and getting to his feet. 'We'll need to follow up the oyster sales. I've already got the door-to-door constables asking if anyone else had eaten them, or knows anything about them. There may be other sources of contamination, not just natural ones.'

'Surely that's unlikely,' Lucy said.

'Poison,' Mike said, taking the basket of toast the waitress brought over and picking out a piece. 'You mark my words.'

'We have to be sure of our facts,' Elliot replied, opening the door. His mobile rang as he stepped outside, and he raised a hand to both of them as he reached for it. He pulled the door closed behind him as he lifted the phone to his ear.

Mike glanced at the menu, adding up their bill and putting the money on the table beside Elliot's. Lucy was watching the inspector, his back towards them as he walked across the parking area to his car. He stopped as he reached it, standing motionless for a few seconds before putting the phone back into his pocket.

'Let's go, Mike,' Lucy said urgently. 'I think Rob's waiting for us.' With a word of thanks to the waitress, who watched with interest as Mike hurriedly wrapped the remaining pieces of toast in a paper napkin, Lucy led the way outside, where Elliot still stood beside his car. 'What is it?' she asked as she reached him. 'Can you tell us?'

'Yes,' his tone was more formal. 'The search of Mr Drewe's house has found another potential source of contamination. We won't be sure until it's been checked out in the lab, but preliminary tests show traces of domoic acid.'

'Where?' Mike demanded. 'I'm sure he didn't get any oysters from the local shop.'

'In cherry brandy,' Elliot said. 'There are pieces of a broken glass in the kitchen bin, and stains on the carpet in the sitting room where the glass must have fallen.'

'Bloody hell!' Mike groaned. 'And I gave it to him.'

'You'd better explain that, Professor.'

'He told me that he generally has a tot after a meal. He didn't get any at Rasmussen's, and I guess he normally eats in the evening anyway, so he had his usual swig before bedtime, after we'd been to the pub.' Mike frowned. 'He wasn't feeling well and thought it would help. I poured it for him.'

'If the tests continue to be positive, it certainly wouldn't have made him any better,' Elliot said dryly. 'Why was the glass broken?'

Mike ran his hands through his hair, trying to remember. 'I knocked it off one of those little tables he has and trod on it,' he said at last. 'I can hardly take a step in there without falling over something. And,' he added belligerently, 'I knocked the damned bottle off the worktop in the kitchen while I was looking for salt for an emetic, and cut myself too. The place is crowded, you can barely move one thing without knocking another over.'

'I see.' Elliot was noncommittal. 'I don't imagine you had any cherry brandy yourself.'

'Too right,' Mike said. 'Disgusting stuff. I couldn't have, any way, there was only enough for Alastair. I wouldn't have deprived him.'

'Did you buy the bottle?'

Mike looked at him, astonished. 'How could I know he drank the stuff?' he demanded. 'No, I didn't buy it. He gets it from the local shop.' He frowned in thought. 'I think he said they get it in specially for him.'

'So his taste must be well known,' Lucy pointed out. 'And Alastair will probably remember all this when he recovers.'

Elliot looked at her bleakly. 'I'm afraid Mr Drewe died an hour ago.' Lucy drew in a shocked breath as Mike froze. 'And we are now treating his death as a likely case of murder.'

Hugh hesitated at the wheel of his silver-grey Audi, allowing the car to slow down as he approached Porthharrock. His brief phone call to Lucy had found her with Mike at the local police station, and he wondered whether he should join them there or go straight to Pennance. He frowned, trying to gather his wits, angry with himself for feeling so uncertain. In the driver's mirror his reflection showed how white his face was, how deep the lines of strain around his mouth.

The turning to the village was visible, and Hugh was still undecided as he braked, sending the newspaper on the seat beside him sliding onto the floor. As he glanced at it a photograph was clearly visible, the seated Viking looming over the body at his feet. Hugh's hands tightened on the steering wheel and he flicked the indicator to show he was turning left towards Eric's house. This, after all, he thought, was why he had followed in Rasmussen's footsteps and discharged himself from hospital. If only he had picked up the newspaper earlier, but he had not felt well enough until he had drunk a cup of weak tea and eaten a small amount of scrambled egg on toast. Eric must have seen this new picture as soon as the newspaper arrived and decided to confront his daughter, if it was his daughter who had taken it. Hugh had come to accept Lucy's opinion, knowing that she had an uncanny knack of spotting the unexpected. He wanted to be present when Eric spoke to Rosen.

Hugh was concentrating much harder than usual to overcome the swimming lightheadedness that made him feel unusually detached from his actions. He was driving more slowly than usual, handling his car with conscious care, as he rounded a sharp corner. Ahead of him lay a scene of devastation and he braked sharply, wrenching the wheel to one side to avoid the fire that blocked most of the lane ahead.

The car came to a stop at an angle across the verge, its front wheels tipping into the neighbouring ditch. Hugh leaped out of it, stumbling as his legs wobbled, and turned to face the leaping flames as a man staggered out of their centre, dragging a limp body behind him.

'Thank God you're here,' Eric panted through the scarf wound round his face. 'It's Tamsyn Warne. She must have come off the bike and knocked herself out. It was right on top of her, and I only just managed to shift it.' Hugh reached him, bending to grasp one of Tamsyn's leather-clad arms, wincing as he burnt his hand, and helped to pull her into safety on the grass verge, well away from the flames licking around the bike. Eric released his grip and sank down beside the woman, his head resting on his knees as he pulled the filthy scarf down and fought to get his breath. 'Is this far enough?' he gasped. 'The bike's going to explode at any moment.'

'We're out of range,' Hugh said. 'And judging from the pattern of the flames a lot of the fuel was spilled when she crashed.' He studied the fire thoughtfully for a second.

'I don't know about you,' Eric muttered, 'but I'm still as weak as a baby.' He began peeling the remnants of driving gloves off his hands, wincing and stopping as patches of skin came with them.

Hugh ignored this as he bent over Tamsyn, gingerly feeling for her wrist under the cuff of her jacket. His heart skipped as he detected a faint pulse. 'She's still alive,' he snapped. 'Have you called an ambulance?'

'No time. I'll do it now,' Eric said shakily, reaching into his jacket pocket, wincing as the material touched the raw skin of his hand. 'Sorry, I don't seem to be thinking very clearly. I came down from the house and nearly drove into the flames myself. When I braked the car skidded and hit the tree over there.' He gestured vaguely beyond the flames towards Pennance where Hugh could see the ice blue Renault skewed across the grass verge with its nose up against a spindly oak in the hedgerow. 'She can only just have come off, the flames were just flickering across the spilt petrol. She was bloody lucky they hadn't got to the engine. I got out of the car as fast as I could with my extinguisher.' He shook his head. 'But the fire was already too far gone for that, so I went in to get her.' He shut his eyes momentarily, and then opened them again to punch out the emergency code on his phone. 'I hope I was in time.'

'Her leathers have protected her body, although her hands and face are burned in places. She's lucky the fire didn't have a chance to get hold before you arrived,' Hugh said. 'Her helmet came off though, so she may have head injuries.' But, he thought, somebody didn't mean her to survive this. His sticky hands came away from a gentle exploration of the back of Tamsyn's head and he looked down at them, unsurprised to see the blood that mingled with the soot.

He glanced around. Her helmet lay some distance away, thrown clear of the flames, the strap torn off at one edge, and most of her bloodstained braids were still tightly plaited around her head, only one rope had loosened and hung frizzled against her collar. It's meant to look as though her helmet failed, but, Hugh thought, his mental processes working clearly now, I reckon somebody's ripped it off and hit her over the head to make sure the accident is fatal. And is the fire a belt and braces job, to make sure, or was her attacker caught by surprise when the leaked petrol caught fire?

He awkwardly pulled out his handkerchief and wiped his hands, leaving red and black stains on the white cotton. Behind him he heard Eric talking on his phone, succinctly explaining the situation. When he stopped Hugh said, 'There's a blanket on the back seat of my car. Get it to cover her.'

Eric stumbled to the car and Hugh frowned across at the flames that were engulfing the motorbike. He straightened up, running his eyes over it, noting that parts of the front wheel were still untouched, although flames were licking along the tyre that shimmered greasily in unexposed patches. Eric appeared at his side, clutching the thick woollen blanket and stood uncertainly. Hugh grasped it, removing it from Eric's tight hold, and laid it carefully over the journalist.

'How long will the ambulance be?' Hugh demanded, crouching down beside her and lifting her limp blistered hand to feel again for a pulse.

'They said less than ten minutes,' Eric replied. 'They're usually pretty good.' He stared down at the unconscious woman. 'She must have been on her way to see me, there were several messages from her on my answer machine.' He shook his head.

'How long had you been home?' Hugh asked, keeping his voice level.

Eric shook his head. 'I don't know.' He held up his hand, warding off the biting comment that Hugh was clearly about to make. 'Sorry, Hugh, let me think. I had a bit of a shock at the house and then this ...' his voice tailed away. With a visible effort he gathered his thoughts. 'I saw the newspaper in the ward.' He looked sharply at Hugh. 'Have you seen it too?'

'Yes,' Hugh said, his gaze on Tamsyn.

'Then you know why I left the hospital,' Eric said, sounding more like his usual self. 'I suppose that's why you're here as well.'

Hugh looked up quickly, meeting Eric's eyes. 'Of course,' he agreed.

For an instant Eric seemed startled by this. 'Well, then,' he said, 'I left at about ten and drove straight here.' He sighed. 'I hoped, of course, that Rosen would be at home.' He shook his head at Hugh's look of enquiry. 'No sign of her, so I checked my messages. Plenty from Tamsyn as I said, wanting to see me urgently, but nothing from Rosen.' He glanced down at the woman who lay so still. 'I picked up the phone when it rang, and of course it was her. I suppose somebody saw me arrive and passed the news on to her. I didn't have time to see her, and that's what I told her.' His thin lips tightened. 'I've got a lot I want to say to her, but finding Rosen is my priority right now. Tamsyn should have come up later, but I suppose she couldn't wait. Maybe I'm the next scoop she's looking for.'

He moved away, almost collapsing to sit awkwardly on a stump on the nearby verge. 'I was going down to the Teague place. I'm damned sure they know where Rosen's holed up, and I meant to find her.' His voice blurred as he put his hands up to his face.

Silence fell, broken only by the faint sound of Tamsyn's shallow breathing and the harsh calls of the gulls above. Eric lowered his hands and glanced at his watch. 'Where the hell are they?' he demanded. 'Maybe one of us should go down to the main road to direct them.'

Hugh shook his head. 'No need. They have your number. If they're lost they'll call you.'

'Yes, of course,' Eric agreed. 'Sorry, Hugh, I'm more shaken than I'd realised. The bloody great statue of Neptune over the door as near as dammit fell on my head as I was leaving. God knows what jarred it, but I suppose it must have been working loose for some time. I was bloody nearly pronged by his trident,' he essayed a weak smile, 'and now the pieces are all over the terrace.' He held out his hands, showing the slight tremor that shook them. 'It was rather unnerving.'

Hugh was not looking at him. His attention was focused on a sound in the far distance, which coalesced into a wailing siren. 'Did you warn them about the bend?' Hugh demanded abruptly.

Eric's eyes widened. 'No,' he admitted. 'One of us had better get down there, hadn't we?'

'Go on then,' Hugh commanded curtly. 'I don't want to leave her.'

Eric hesitated, but got shakily to his feet. 'I'm not sure …' he began, but Hugh had turned his attention back to Tamsyn. Eric walked uncertainly onto the road and began to speed up as he became steadier. By the time he reached the bend the sound of the siren was overwhelming. He was clearly just in time, for within a few seconds the ambulance crept carefully round the corner, pulling up well short of the flames.

Two paramedics rushed towards them from the back of the ambulance, holding a stretcher which they laid down on the nearby verge. Hugh recognised them with a shock as the crew who had arrived at Pennance last night. 'Still on duty?' he enquired.

'Too right. Keeping us busy then, aren't you?' one said briskly, pushing him aside to bend over Tamsyn. 'Seems you were better off than she is.' After a quick check he nodded to his colleague and they fetched the stretcher.

Another siren grew closer, and the paramedic glanced at Hugh. 'Police, I guess. We left your mate to stop them.'

'Would it hurt to wait a few more minutes before you move her?' Hugh asked quickly. 'I'd like the police to see how things are here.'

The paramedic looked at him curiously. 'Like that is it?' He exchanged a glance with his companion as a police car pulled up beside the ambulance, turning off its own siren. 'Okay, just a few minutes then.' He stepped back as a plain clothes officer approached, flanked by a uniformed constable.

'Sergeant Peters,' Hugh said with relief at the sight of the familiar rubicund face and square figure. 'I didn't expect you.'

'We were over at Portharrock when the call came in, with Miss Rossington and the professor,' Peters replied. 'This part of the county seems to be oddly unlucky right now.'

'Hmm,' Hugh said. 'Look here, Sergeant, I'm not happy about this. See, she has a head injury just here. Take a look at her helmet over there, especially the strap.'

Sergeant Peters bent over the journalist, his blunt fingered hands resting on his knees as he followed Hugh's points with shrewd eyes. 'Yes, I see,' he said. 'That's well spotted, Mr Carey.' He straightened up, nodding to the waiting paramedics, who immediately slid the stretcher into place. As they lifted Tamsyn efficiently onto it and strapped her down, Peters' eyes moved from her to Hugh. 'You don't look too good yourself. Nor did Mr Rasmussen when he stopped us.'

'That's what shellfish poisoning does for you,' Hugh commented. 'I expect you heard.'

The sergeant nodded, glancing down at the soot-blackened hands that Hugh was holding well away from his sides. 'Are you burned?' He turned to call to the paramedics.

'It's okay,' Hugh said quickly. 'Nothing that a local doctor can't deal with. Eric's probably worse than I am, he was pulling her away from the bike as I arrived. He must have a GP we can get up to the house.'

'Fine,' Peters agreed, conscious that Eric had just rejoined them as the paramedics loaded Tamsyn into the ambulance. 'I was sorry about your vicar friend.'

'Well, not exactly a friend,' Hugh said regretfully. 'I'd only recently met him, but he was a decent bloke.'

'What's this?' Eric demanded sharply.

'Of course,' Hugh said quietly, 'you probably haven't heard.' He drew a quick breath. 'I'm afraid Alastair died. Lucy told me half an hour ago. She heard it from Inspector Elliot.'

Eric stood as if rooted to the spot, staring at Hugh blankly.

He shook his head. 'No,' he said slowly, 'he can't be dead. We're alright, so why isn't he?'

'Anna is in a pretty bad way too,' Hugh pointed out, 'and she isn't out of danger yet.'

'Bloody Teague and his oysters,' Eric said softly. 'If he wanted to get back at me, why did he have to involve the others?'

Sergeant Peters was listening intently. 'This is Mark Teague, is it?' he asked. 'I understand that the inspector has spoken to him.'

'I hope he's done more than that,' Eric said curtly. 'In fact,' he glanced at the flames licking around the bike, 'if he hasn't he may have some more questions for Mark Teague. It's odd, isn't it, Tamsyn's bike hitting a patch of oil just now?' He swayed unexpectedly. 'Look, I'm sorry, but I must go home. You could probably do with lying down as well, Hugh.'

'I'm sorry,' Peters said genially, 'that won't be possible immediately.'

'Why not?' Eric demanded.

'I'm afraid your car will need to stay here while we check out the area.' Peters said. 'And we'll need to do a fingertip search of the lane.'

'What for?' Eric asked blankly.

'It's normal practice,' the sergeant said smoothly, 'when we've reason to think there's been malpractice. And of course,' he added before Eric could comment, 'we are now looking further into Mr Drewe's death too.'

Eric caught his breath. 'Alastair? Are you telling me ...' he broke off.

Peters nodded, pleased Eric had understood so quickly. 'Yes, that's right. He seems to have had more domoic acid than the oysters could have contained naturally. So I must talk to you about the lunch and how it was prepared.'

'But I've already told you this,' Eric expostulated, sitting down unsteadily on the ground.

'We need to go over it again,' the sergeant said patiently. 'I'm sure we can make you comfortable at the station.'

'If you must repeat your questioning you must,' Eric said wearily, putting his head in his hands.

'I'll just check my car,' Hugh interposed, walking across to it. He went round to the front, looking over and under the bonnet, before skirting the flames to check Eric's Renault, resting skittishly against its tree. 'No visible harm to either of them,' he said as he came back. 'I suppose we'll have to leave them here until you've finished. Can't we walk back to Pennance over the fields and talk there, Sergeant? We can pick up the footpath further down here without disturbing anything.'

Sergeant Peters pondered for a minute. 'I don't see why not,' he said heavily, turning as the sound of another siren reached them. 'Constable Kittoe can stay here and I'll come with you. But that's the fire brigade now. Just let me set the search in hand here and have a word with the fire officer.' He walked over to the uniformed constables waiting beside the verge and began to give them instructions in a level voice.

Eric watched him and once he was sure the sergeant was fully occupied he turned to Hugh, saying urgently, 'I must find Rosen. I'm beginning to feel she's in danger.' He hesitated, 'Or she's involved in something that's got out of her control. That's why I didn't wait to cross-examine Tamsyn. I've got to get hold of my daughter. These bloody Teagues, I really believe they'd do anything to drive me away.' He turned to stare through a gap in the hedge across the fields towards the sea.

SEVEN

The autumn sunlight was filling the interior of the coastal watch station, and Hugh blinked as he looked up from the scope he had been using. He made a brief note on the computer screen to record the boat making its way across the bay, before glancing at his watch. Nearly two o'clock. Time to get back to Pennance, he realised reluctantly. Still, Lucy would be there too, with the latest news on Anna. And he felt much better, the woolliness that had clouded his brain this morning had dispersed.

His mobile rang and he pulled it awkwardly out of his pocket, keen not to disturb the concentration of Philip, his fellow watcher, one of the local retired community, who had also come in to fill the gap left on Tamsyn and Alastair's watch. Hugh's scorched hands had been treated and were no longer sore, but his fingers were not as dexterous as usual as he fumbled with the answer button. The caller was Lucy, he saw with concern on the phone screen, as he at last managed to push the button. 'What is it?' he demanded. 'Anna?'

'She's fine,' Lucy said quickly. 'We're both fine. And so is Mike. Although we've heard about Tamsyn. And I hope you're not overdoing things there.'

'I'm fine too,' Hugh assured her, 'but I'll be glad to get away home as soon as we can. I really think we should call off the family visit to Pennance now.'

'Mmm,' Lucy said vaguely. 'Let's discuss it when we catch up with each other. We're just leaving the police station, but Mike's ducking a late lunch with Eric and going back to Alastair's cottage to get his things. He's moving into the pub, at Rob Elliot's suggestion.' Her voice lifted with laughter as she added, 'Mike thinks Rob wants to keep him under surveillance.' She drew a deep breath and said lightly, 'Look, Hugh, I'm going over to Polkenan with Mike. I've had an idea about Rosen that I'm going to follow up, so I may miss lunch too, especially if I have to walk back along the cliff path. Make my excuses, please, but don't tell Eric what I'm doing. I don't want to raise his hopes.'

'Lucy, what are you up to?' Hugh demanded urgently, cursing under his breath as the connection was broken. He stared out of the wide window, unaware that the small boat he had recorded was now framed scenically in the arched top of the rock cluster below the watch station. Philip glanced his way before he made a note on his own screen indicating the party of walkers that was approaching from the east. Hugh looked again at his watch. Ten minutes to go. He resettled himself at the counter, sweeping the bay in front of him with the binoculars, oblivious to the light breeze that came through the open window and feathered across his hot face.

The sound of angry voices made him lower the binoculars and look along the path, back towards Portharrock. The speakers were not yet visible, but Hugh recognised one of the voices. As he listened alertly his eyes fixed on the boat in the arch, which seemed suspended timelessly there.

The voices grew louder, the antagonism in their tones clearly audible, but the two men's appearance still startled Hugh. They emerged from the tamarisks fringing the outskirts of the village, striding past the station and on along the cliff path. Hugh's view of the framed boat was momentarily obscured by the taller of the two men, who was wrapped in an oilskin with a waterproof hat pulled low over his eyes. The shorter man barely reached his shoulder, and was forced to lengthen his own stride to keep up with his companion. So Eric had found Mark Teague, Hugh guessed, his eyes following the men's progress, although in that amount of outer wrapping he could be anyone. Eric did not seem to be having a fruitful discussion, Hugh realised, his heart sinking even further as he contemplated lunch at Penance.

In front of the station the boat had emerged from its frame and was moving on across the bay. As Hugh watched a memory stirred and he rubbed his ear absentmindedly, trying to place it. The arch, he knew it was something about the arch, when he was last at the coastal watch station. The evening when the hermit went by.

There was the wren that liked to perch just inside the gap, but no, it wasn't that, it had been dark. The full moon, yes, that was it. The full moon framed in the arch when he was sharing Alastair's last evening watch. And the man in a cloak and wide-brimmed hat, the Polkenan hermit, who had looked very like the man who had just passed. The one who had just gone by had obscured Hugh's view through the arch. And, Hugh stiffened, that night the hermit hadn't. Suddenly Hugh was alert, his thoughts focusing rapidly. Of course! He snapped his fingers, startling Philip, who glanced curiously at him before returning to his survey of the cliffs.

That's it, Hugh thought exultantly. Roger Bland was a tall man, at least the same height as Mark Teague. But the hermit who passed below here that night wasn't as tall as the oyster fisherman. And so it wasn't Roger Bland. Hugh paused, thinking over the scene. Yes, he was sure of his facts. And that, he thought triumphantly, solves the question of the timing of Bland's murder. And answers the riddle of the photograph of the Viking looming over Bland's body before he was killed. But who the devil was impersonating him? And why?

The last minutes of Hugh's shift dragged, and as soon as the door opened, admitting the next pair of observers, Hugh pulled on his thick corduroy jacket and made his farewells. He wasted no time, striding along the cliff path, almost unaware of the wind buffeting him on the exposed bluff. Rain began to splatter against his jacket, and he pulled the collar up, ferreting in one of the pockets for the cap he had forgotten to put on.

When he left the cliff path for the quarry field he was briefly sheltered from the squall by the drystone wall as he cut across the rough turf. The digger had reappeared in the quarry, perched on one of the ledges, where a number of men were still working in spite of the worsening weather. The Viking's gully, though, appeared deserted when Hugh scrambled over the stile to follow the path downwards. When he reached the stream he glanced back up the slope over the stunted willows towards the crevice, unable to see clearly enough through the driving rain to notice if there was still a police constable on watch, sheltering under the overhang.

Hugh leaped over the stream, the wind blowing the rain hard into his face as he sped up the far side of the gully. He left all traces of human life behind him as he rounded the outcrop and reached the field gate. By the time he was walking swiftly through the garden of Pennance the rain had set in heavily, dropping in heavy plops on the water staircase, where expanding circles rippled across the surface. The mosaic swirls of the patio had darkened into a uniform wet greyness as he crossed them and ran up the steps to the terrace. Reaching the corner he tripped on a rough lump of stone and fell heavily against the granite obelisk at the corner, which swayed ominously as Hugh fought to regain his balance. He levered himself upright again, catching his breath for a while as he rubbed a bruised ankle and tried it out carefully. Relieved to find it sore but working, he looked round at the obstacle he had encountered, recognising at once the trident from Neptune's statue and remembering Eric's narrow escape when it fell.

Hugh limped slowly towards the entrance courtyard, dodging the scattered pieces of stone and careful not to slide on the slippery streak of powdered debris and torn ivy leaves that littered the ground in front of the house. One of the opaque troughs that had flanked the Neptune statue projected at an angle over the roof's steel supporting bar and long ivy strands dangled down in a ragged curtain, the tips almost touching his face as he approached.

He glanced up at the front of the glass roof, wondering how such a heavy sculpture had become so unstable. Although, he thought wryly, the obelisk he had encountered wasn't very securely fastened either.

The front door opened noiselessly as Hugh followed the path between the rectangular pools, where the gentle murmur of flowing water was overwhelmed by the thundering of rain on the roof overhead. 'Come on in,' Eric called, from the gloomy unlit pavilion. 'The weather's set for another storm.'

Hugh pulled off his sodden jacket and cap, hanging them carelessly on pegs on the wall. 'Were you waiting for someone?' Hugh asked, trying not to stare at the other man, whose sunken eyes seemed to be looking out of a skull-like face, covered only with paper-thin yellowing skin.

'No,' Eric said bleakly. 'I was just passing one of the CCTV screens when I saw you outside.' He turned into the sitting area, walking past the bookcase to the front of the room, staring across the dim space at Hugh, who had stopped beside the chairs. 'I've been watching them closely, hoping I'll see Rosen coming home.' He shook his head wearily. 'But there's little likelihood of that. I've had no news of her at all. And,' he admitted in a tight voice, 'I'm afraid I'm a bit jumpy, I keep looking to see who else might be coming. Hugh, I'm beginning to wonder what's going on. Roger Bland is dead, Alastair Drewe is dead. They were my friends once. Does that leave me as the next victim in some madman's mind?' He moved restlessly before the glass wall, a dark shape turning to stare into the storm outside as the rain hurled itself against the house and a vivid warning streak of lightning flashed through the black clouds. 'But why?'

Hugh ran a hand over his damp hair, ignoring the drips that

trickled down the back of his neck. 'How did you get on with Teague?' he asked. 'I saw you go past the watch station.'

The dark figure moved slightly, turning to face Hugh. 'Of course,' Eric said. 'I'd forgotten you were there. I'm sorry, Hugh, you must be ready for a drink. Do help yourself. I've already started mine. But perhaps you'll want to wait for Lucy.'

Hugh crossed to the sideboard and carefully picked up the bottle of white wine, saying, 'She's been delayed, so there's no point waiting for her.'

'Not Anna, I hope?' Eric demanded anxiously.

'No, just some idea Lucy's got,' Hugh said vaguely, trying to still the anxiety that prickled in his mind. He turned, sipping his wine. 'And I've got one too. It was seeing you and Teague pass the station, and realising how tall he is. He must be the height of Bland, wouldn't you say?'

'What?' Eric asked blankly. 'Yes, I suppose so. Look,' he crossed to the sideboard and began ferreting in it, 'I'm sure there are olives somewhere. I'm afraid it's only going to be a scratch lunch, as Jenny hasn't come in today.'

'I expect she couldn't get through on the lane,' Hugh said, noticing that Eric's hands were in a worse state than his own, with glistening patches of raw skin. 'The police will have closed it.'

'Yes, of course,' Eric said, straightening up with a jar held precariously in one hand. 'Here we are. My wife always keeps some for emergencies.' He began to unscrew the lid. 'Damn,' he muttered. 'Who'd think it would be so difficult. Anyway, never mind.' He pushed the jar away. 'Now what about these ideas? You and Lucy seem to be full of them. I'm afraid I have a single track mind. It's served me well, but it can be limiting, I see that now.'

'Ah yes,' Hugh said, taking a few olives from the jar. 'I realised there's an issue about the height of the hermit who passed the coastal watch station on the night of Bland's death. And so about the identity of the figure.'

Eric was staring at him. 'Do you mean,' he asked slowly, 'that it wasn't Roger? But then ...' His eyes flickered sideways, over Hugh's shoulder, and widened. 'Who the hell are you?'

Hugh swung round towards the kitchen and heard a cry as the world exploded into darkness and showers of stars.

Lucy waved a hand at Mike in farewell as she continued up the winding pathway from the car park into Polkenan village, leaving him at the front of Alastair's cottage. She walked on slowly, avoiding the puddles and streams of water left by the storm, thinking hard. As she passed the turquoise church she glanced through the screening trees and caught sight of a wreath of fresh rosemary hung on the door. So the news of Alastair's death had already reached the village, she realised. The sound of a voice behind her made her glance quickly over her shoulder to see an elderly man leaning over his gate, calling to Mike.

Mike hesitated, looking hopefully after Lucy. She refused to go back to him, resolutely walking on to the village street.

'Dreadful, isn't it?' Thomas said gloomily as Mike squared his shoulders and glared at him. 'Vicar taken like that. What with his friend turning up too, and finding him gone. And your young lady going next, I expect.'

Mike scowled. 'She's only going home when they discharge her from hospital, and she's not my young lady,' he said. 'She's just a friend.'

Thomas's face wore a knowing expression. 'Friend, is it? Just as well then, because I reckon that copper's interested in her.' He smiled, exposing a bland set of dentures. 'Different from his interest in the vicar's friend. He was pleased to listen to what I had to tell him.'

'I'm sure you kept him riveted,' Mike said shortly, turning aside and striding up the pathway to Alastair's cottage, sending a fresh shower of raindrops down from the overhanging walnut branches. The faded blue door opened as he approached and his step faltered.

'Come in, Professor,' Constable Carlus invited, stepping back to allow him to enter. 'Inspector Elliot said you would be calling for your things.'

'Are you guarding the place?' Mike demanded as he walked into the living room, leaving wet footprints on the worn carpet.

Carlus shook her head, smiling. 'Not now, but the inspector sent me over to wait for you.'

'Making sure I don't pinch a few serpentine lighthouses?' Mike quipped grimly. 'Okay, let's not hang around. I've only got the one bag upstairs, you can come and watch me pack it.'

He picked his way through the crowded living room to the stairway door, where the covering curtain had been torn from its rail, and stamped up to the landing, followed more cautiously by Carlus. In the small bedroom Mike scooped up the clothes that littered the floor, many of them wetted by the rain that had come through the open window. He pushed them into the canvas holdall that he pulled from under the bed, grabbing the large book that lay open on a chair and stuffing it into the bag too, before looking around quickly to see if he had left anything out.

'Do you have things in the bathroom?' Carlus asked helpfully from the doorway.

Mike glared at her. 'I'm getting there,' he snapped. 'I have packed before, you know.'

She stepped back unruffled as he stalked past her into the bathroom and snatched up his toilet bag, adding a damp flannel and a razor to it. He clutched it in one hand as he took the towel that hung over the back of a cane chair and strode back to his room to cram them into his holdall.

Carlus watched with amusement as he struggled to close the zip over the bulging contents, quickly wiping her expression clear as Mike swung round and glared suspiciously at her. 'That'll do,' he said. 'I'll take it to the pub later after I've fetched Lucy Rossington. I can leave the bag outside until then. I'm sure the old bloke next door will keep his eye on it.'

'Miss Rossington?' Constable Carlus asked quickly. 'Is she packing up Miss Evesleigh's things? The inspector didn't tell me about that.'

Mike paused at the top of the stairs to look back at her. 'I don't know,' he said slowly. 'She was a bit vague about her plans, or I wasn't listening.' Carlus hid a grin. 'I think there was somebody she wanted to see. Still this place is small enough for me to spot her. And she won't be long, she's left the dog in the car. I just hope the brute isn't wrecking it.' He clattered down the stairs and hugged the bag to his chest as he crossed the living room, careful not to swing it against any of the furniture. He hesitated, remembering Alastair on the sofa yesterday morning, surrounded by his photograph albums. They were still there, piled in an untidy heap.

Mike dropped his bag and took a step across to the sofa, spotting the wet patch on its back where the rain had come in through the ill-fitting window. 'It's okay to move things, isn't it?' he demanded belligerently. 'These shouldn't be left to get wet if there's another storm. None of the windows are weatherproof.'

'Everything's been checked,' Carlus agreed, amused that Mike had not noticed the fine layer of powder that lay everywhere after the fingerprinting had been done. 'Put them on the table if you want.'

Mike snorted. 'Fat chance. There's no space. I'll just leave them here on the floor. They'll be okay away from the window.'

He shifted them with care and picked up his bag again, leaving the cottage without another glance. Outside he waited as Carlus pulled the front door shut, locking it with the large key she pulled from behind a flowerpot. 'Very modern policing,' he commented sarcastically. Carlus smiled, quite unruffled, and Mike went on, 'You can ask the old bloke, Thomas, I think it is, if Lucy's there, but when I left her she was heading into the village.' A wicked gleam shone in his eyes. 'I'm sure Thomas would be really pleased to talk to you.'

'I've met him,' Carlus said noncommittally. 'I don't think it will be necessary to check up, he and his wife know they can't release Miss Evesleigh's things until we say so.'

'Or until she collects them,' Mike snapped.

'Of course,' Carlus agreed. 'I hope that will be soon.'

His expression softened. 'It will be, knowing Anna. She's got this pageant thing in a couple of days and I can't see her missing it. Of course,' he dropped his bag beside the gateway as Carlus went out, 'that's probably what Lucy's here for, to carry out some errands for Anna.'

'I didn't realise Miss Evesleigh was up to thinking of things like the pageant yet,' Carlus said in surprise.

Mike shrugged. 'She'd think of her latest project on her deathbed.' He bit his lip as he heard his own words, then turned on Carlus. 'Don't let me keep you, Constable. I'm sure there are criminals out there waiting to be caught.'

She smiled appreciatively. 'Goodbye, Professor.'

Mike had only gone a couple of paces before he heard her running after him. He swung round, catching Thomas peering through his bank of fuchsias, as Carlus reached him.

'Sorry, Professor, I nearly forgot,' she said, pushing an envelope at him. 'The inspector asked me to give you this. Your colleague from Oxford gave it to him when she left this morning. She'd been hoping to give it to you herself.'

'She's left already?' Mike demanded in annoyed tones as he took the envelope. Without waiting for Carlus' nod he growled, 'I hoped she'd have the decency to discuss her findings with me.' His fingers tightened on the envelope, and he peered at it curiously. Hand delivered. Turning it over he found the back was embossed with the name of a firm of Oxford solicitors. He scowled. Some busybody complaining about a dig, I expect, he thought morosely, letting his thoughts run quickly through the ones he had in hand. His scowl deepened, and he thrust the envelope into his pocket. 'Thanks,' he growled. 'Just what I need.'

The constable went back towards the car park and Mike

swung round, ignoring Thomas's eager face, to stride towards the street. When he reached it, he hesitated, wondering which way to go. He remembered now, Lucy had suggested meeting on the beach, but he could not recall whether she had mentioned a time. He glanced at his watch. Surely the pub would still be open. He could wait there and keep an eye out for her.

He hesitated, wondering whether to fetch his bag, then caught sight of Thomas' figure lurking on the path, showing ominous signs of following him. Mike turned, walking briskly down the street, oblivious of the curious stares that followed him, and up the steep further slope, throwing a quick look around the beach as he passed. The tide was out, the sea rolling restlessly just in front of the protecting headlands, gradually beginning to creep inwards. The boats rested silent and still on the exposed pebbles that were slick with rainwater. Grey clouds were scudding across the sky and a dark line grew ominously on the horizon, presaging another storm.

There were already a few men in the bar of *The Three Tuns*, nursing tankards of the pub's own brew. Local men, their conversation broke off as they turned to stare at Mike, who ignored them as he ordered a pint of beer. Talk began again among the regulars as he reached across the counter for his drink and carried it carefully over to a table in the corner near the hearth, where a healthy fire was already blazing. He was not in the mood for casual conversation, as his grim expression clearly indicated to the other drinkers.

As he sat down the beer spilled over onto his hand. He cursed softly as he put the tankard down and wiped his hand over his trousers. Encountering the ridges of the envelope in his pocket he pulled it out, thinking morosely, I might as well get it over with. The day can't get much worse. Unless, he thought irrepressibly, I'm arrested for Bland's murder. I must still be Elliot's favourite suspect. And I suppose that leaves me in the frame for Alastair's death too.

Mike ripped open the envelope and pulled out a short letter, which enclosed another envelope. He skimmed through the brief sentences in the letter, letting it drop heedlessly into the puddle of beer on the table as he tore the second envelope open. This contained two pages of closely handwritten lines, and Mike leaned forward, elbows on the table, turning the sheets to catch the light from a nearby lamp.

As he began to read his eyes widened, then narrowed as they rapidly scanned the contents. He turned the first page, reading on, then moved onto the second sheet. As he finished he sat immobile, fingers clenched on the paper, crushing it into a crumpled ball as he stared disbelievingly ahead of him.

Suddenly galvanised, he pushed the table away, unaware of the tankard tumbling to the floor, beer spilling in spluttering arcs over the tiled floor as it clanged and clattered. Astonished stares followed him as he left, letting the heavy door bang resoundingly behind him.

Mike strode rapidly down the street, the letter still clutched in his fist. He paused by the beach, looking round impatiently for Lucy. Where the hell was she, he thought angrily. Well, he decided, I can't hang around waiting. As he stamped on up the street he pulled out his mobile and rang her number. Damn, he groaned, switched off, and I haven't got time to text. He shoved the phone back into his pocket as he turned into the path that led to Alastair's cottage and the car park. Mike hesitated, then spun on his heel and carried on up the street to the coastal path, his temper rising as he mentally ran through what he had just read. Lucy could wait. He would sort this out first. And nobody was going to have any warning of his approach.

It had only taken Lucy a short time to track down the place she was searching for. The fish shop owner was only too eager to tell her where it was. 'Occupied by a young couple,' she said with a slight wink. 'They must have come in late one night, but we never see them out. Otherwise engaged, I reckon, although of course they may use a boat. It's just as easy as coming in over the rocks.'

Lucy had waited for a while by the old fish cellar, watching the granite ridge, black against the grey sky, on the western side of the beach. Not a soul stirred while she waited, and few sounds reached her ears other than the slap of the waves as they crept upwards over the pebbles and the pattering of more rain as a light shower fell. Once she heard heavy footsteps on the street that paused by the beach. Mike, she guessed, keeping quite still in the shelter of the cellar. Well, he'll have to wait, she thought, while I do what I've come for. I'm sure he'll be happy for a bit in the pub.

Her green woollen beret was glittering with raindrops when she moved away from the cellar wall, hesitating as she heard hurried steps pounding down from the pub. She saw Mike's cursory glance sweep the beach, missing her as she waited in the cover of the building. As he stalked up the street Lucy recognised how angry he was and stood irresolute for a moment. Should she go after him, she wondered. Her chin jutted out stubbornly. No, I may be able to solve the issue right here, so whatever Mike might get up to won't matter much.

She waited a little longer, still hoping to see her quarry wandering through the village. At last she walked cautiously forward over the pebbles, slippery with rainwater, to the ridge of rocks that edged Polkenan bay. Scrambling over these she had to take more care, the layers of seaweed made the going treacherous, although there was a well-used route over to the far side. The old sail loft was tucked away, sheltered between the ridge she had crossed and another on the far side of a narrow channel of water that led out to the open sea. Tethered firmly to a ring in the rocks opposite, a small boat bobbed restlessly on the unsettled water.

Lucy considered it for a moment, then looked quickly around the ridges again, wondering if anybody was out, watching her. Shrugging, she set her jaw and turned towards the weather-boarded building crouched alone at the head of the channel, its rear completely hidden by the rocks that separated it from the village. Its lower level was a boathouse, and wooden stairs led up the outside to the small flat that had been converted from the first floor loft.

Lucy scrunched over the patch of shingle below the building and climbed the open treads of the stairs carefully, not even trying to be quiet. She tried the door above. To her disbelief it creaked open and she entered the dimly lit space with caution, her nostrils twitching at the sharp tang of cigarette smoke. A stir of movement in the far corner drew her eyes past the basket chairs and pine table to the sofa beyond, where a familiar black-clad figure sprawled over the cushions. 'Rosen,' she exclaimed with relief. 'I hoped you'd be here.'

The door behind her was suddenly pushed shut and Lucy turned round quickly. Kevin Teague was pressed against the wooden panels, his sharp-featured face angry as he stared at her. 'How did you know we were here?' he demanded, his soft local burr almost hidden by the roughness of his voice.

'I guessed,' Lucy said calmly, walking over to one of the chairs and sitting down, noting the ashtray full of cigarette stubs on the table, next to a couple of black and white photographs. 'I thought at first Rosen had just decided to stay away from home when the Viking photographs were published.' She glanced at the pictures on the table, half expecting to see more of the scene in the crevice, but they were of Roger Bland as the hermit. Lucy's eyes lifted to consider Rosen, her jet-black hair now lying flat and unkempt, her face surprisingly young without its usual white make-up. The girl sat up and leaned forward to stare at her as Lucy continued, 'It must have been quite handy when this all coincided with Eric forgetting your birthday. It muddied the waters a bit. But you've had quite a coup with them. Have you seen them in print?'

Rosen shook her head. 'No, we haven't been out since we got here. I asked ...'

'Rosen,' Kevin cut in quickly, picking up the smouldering

cigarette he had dropped on the table, 'be careful. We already talked too much to her at the pub. And how did she know where to find us?' He drew heavily on the cigarette, glaring at Lucy.

'I just put together lots of small things I'd heard or been told,' Lucy said. 'If you haven't been getting any news I don't expect you've heard about Alastair.'

'Yes, we have,' Kevin said immediately, 'and there's no way those oysters were contaminated. Mark's too careful. And nobody else was taken ill. Only Rasmussen's lot.'

'I meant,' Lucy said, noting that some information had obviously come in to the sail loft, 'that Alastair died this morning.'

Kevin sucked in a harsh breath, but Rosen sat immobile, staring blankly at Lucy.

'And, of course,' Lucy went on conversationally, 'Anna is still in a bad way, but Tamsyn is the latest casualty. That's why I thought I'd better come.'

'Tamsyn?' Rosen repeated quickly, her voice rising. 'What's happened to her? She's not dead too?'

'Not yet,' Lucy said bleakly, 'but she was badly injured on the lane outside Pennance. She somehow came off her bike, which caught fire.'

Rosen put a hand up to her face, covering her mouth. She stared over Lucy's shoulder out of the small window beside the door, not really seeing the rain that had started to fall more heavily now, streaking the glass and obscuring the view.

'How do we know this is all true?' Kevin said abruptly, grinding out his cigarette stub.

'Why should I lie?' Lucy asked. 'I think Rosen has a right to know what's happening.'

'Why Rosen particularly?' he demanded, moving forward threateningly. 'What's it got to do with her?'

'Kevin, she knows,' Rosen said. 'You shouldn't have come here, Lucy. It isn't safe.'

'No, you shouldn't,' Kevin said darkly, then stiffened as

they heard shingle crunch outside. They all stood still, barely breathing as they listened. There was a moment of silence, then footsteps, soft but deliberate, were heard mounting the outer stairs.

'It's only ...' Rosen began as Lucy got to her feet.

'Shut up!' Kevin said harshly. 'We'll be more careful this time. Look out of the window, see if the boat's there.' He threw his wiry body back against the door, fumbling to turn the key in the lock just as somebody pushed hard from outside. The door shuddered but stayed closed until Kevin was suddenly flung away from it, falling heavily to the floor, as it was thrust powerfully open.

The man who entered brought a strong smell of burning with him, in spite of his dripping oilskins. Although a sou'wester obscured his face, they all knew who he was. He pushed the door shut behind him and looked round the room, ignoring Kevin who was scrambling awkwardly to his feet. 'Ah, Lucy,' he said thinly. 'I wondered if I would find you here. I thought you were bright; you've definitely got your father's brains.' He smiled without humour at her. 'You're quite wasted on this piddling work you're doing for the Wronham Trust. Botanical surveys are all very well, but somebody like you should be involved in policy making. You must let me put in a word for you, there are a number of posts that would suit you very well.'

'Thank you,' Lucy said, feeling rather stunned at the turn of the conversation, 'but really I'm very happy with what I do. It fits into my life here.'

A shade of disapproval crossed his lined face. 'That's a shame,' he said softly. 'But things may change, may already have changed, for you.'

Mike's face was scarlet as he approached the Viking's gully. He had maintained a vigorous pace as he strode along the cliff path, with the wind blowing rain in from the sea. His wet red hair was plastered to his head, the knees of his trousers muddied and torn, his hands scratched from a slip on a wet patch of granite. His appearance was so dishevelled, his attitude so aggressive as he mumbled angrily to himself, that the walkers in bright waterproofs coming towards him hesitated as they rounded the bluff and were visibly relieved to see him branch off through the field gate before they reached him.

Mike swung the gate shut and turned towards Pennance, pausing to stare disbelievingly ahead of him. He had seen thick black smoke mingling with the clouds as he had crossed the grassy peninsula that housed the Iron Age fort, but had not thought anything of it. Now, though, he could see where the flames were coming from. Pennance was clearly on fire.

He broke into a run, and burst through the gate into the garden, pounding over the bridge and up alongside the water stairway. His heavy boots slipped on the stony mosaic patio, so he slowed slightly as he ran up the steps to the terrace, almost hidden from view by the smoke.

The house was well alight, flames obscuring the glass as they leaped up to lick at the edge of the sedum roof. As Mike arrived at the front of the house the heat hit him in the face and he reeled back, almost collapsing against the obelisk on the corner that wobbled dangerously at his weight.

Constable Kittoe ran up from the knot of people that Mike could vaguely see at the gate. 'Professor,' he gasped, 'I saw it from the road. I've radioed for the fire brigade. They left here a while ago, but we hope they won't be long getting back.' He stared at the burning house. 'We don't know who's in there. We don't know if Mr Rasmussen stayed at home when Mr Carey went to the watch station, or whether he went out again too. Nobody's come by the lane from the village because it's still shut, but they could have come from above or in by the cliff path.'

'Rasmussen was lunching here and Hugh Carey was joining him. He'd certainly have come along the cliff path,' Mike said grimly. 'Have you seen anyone inside?'

'Too much smoke,' the constable said. 'Hey, come back.' He hesitated momentarily, then went after the other man as he ran round the terrace towards the glass side of the central pavilion.

Mike paused to search his pockets, finally pulling out a crumpled handkerchief and pressing it against his face. His eyes were stinging badly by the time he was leaning against the glass, tears streaming down his face as he tried to peer through the thick smoke.

'It's no good,' Kittoe said hoarsely, 'you can't see a thing. I've tried.' He grasped the other man's arm. 'Come away.'

'Wait,' Mike said, wrenching his arm free to shield his eyes as he crouched down. 'What's that?'

Kittoe bent down beside him to peer through the smoke, slightly less thick at this height. 'My God,' he croaked. 'It's a body.'

Before he had finished speaking Mike was racing back to the entrance courtyard and over the path to the front door, feeling the heat searing through the soles of his shoes. 'No good,' he grunted, falling back and staggering to a halt. 'I hoped the door mechanism would still work.' He glared around desperately, his mind working furiously as he tied the filthy handkerchief precariously around his mouth and nose. 'Come with me.'

He led the way back, gasping for breath, to the corner of the terrace, where he seized the base of the obelisk. 'Get hold of the top,' he ordered.

'Professor, we shouldn't do this,' Kittoe said breathlessly. 'The fire brigade will be here soon.'

'Not soon enough,' Mike snapped. 'Hold your end and follow me.' He moved back to the house, picking up speed, and Kittoe came after, gripping the stone grimly.

Mike ran full pelt into the door, hammering the obelisk into the panel. It burst open with a bang, the men losing their grasp on the stone as they stumbled forward.

'Aaargh,' Kittoe bellowed in agony as the edge of the obelisk fell across one of his feet.

Mike felt his way forward alone, almost blinded by the smoke as he inched into the sitting area. The heat was so intense that he felt his hair crinkling and his face scorching. His breath was coming short and hard and he knew that he could not stay in here much longer.

He fell heavily, sprawling over the body that lay across the floor. Mike scrambled quickly to his hands and knees, feeling along the motionless figure. The handkerchief dropped from his face as he grasped the shoulders and levered himself into a crouch to pull the body towards the front door.

His breath became harsher, so loud in his ears that it drowned out the crackling of the flames. His eyes blurred and he knew the effort was beyond him. He still grasped the body's shoulders, reluctant to admit failure, when somebody else banged into him.

'Here,' Kittoe grunted, pushing at his arm. 'I'll take one side.'

Mike could never have said how long it was until they reeled outside, where firemen jumped from the engine that was just pulling into the drive, rushing over to take the body from their grip. Mike fell to his knees, then to his face on the stone terrace, and was faintly aware that Kittoe had collapsed beside him.

Powerful hands lifted Mike, carrying him away from the heat and smoke to lay him down on the wet grass. His face was wiped cursorily before an oxygen mask was pressed over his mouth and he gratefully gasped in the fresh air.

When he looked up, his eyes still blurred, he recognised Inspector Elliot crouching beside him. Mike pushed the mask away and struggled to sit up. Elliot bent forward to help him as Mike gasped, 'Hugh ...'

'Yes,' Elliot said, 'alive, thanks to you.'

'And the policeman,' Mike croaked. 'Couldn't have done it alone.'

'He's in the same state as you, and has a badly damaged foot. He did well, though.'

Mike coughed and gasped as he did so, feeling his chest hurt. Elliot proffered a bottle of water that Mike took with relief, sipping at the liquid until he could ask, 'How bad is Hugh?'

'Not burned,' Elliot said, 'The flames hadn't reached him, but he's inhaled a lot of smoke. The ambulance is here for him now, and you're going in it too. One of our cars is taking Kittoe, he's not as badly affected by the smoke as you are.'

'No,' Mike said forcefully. 'Listen. We don't know if Rasmussen is in there.' He gestured towards the house, his arm feeling almost too heavy for him to move. 'Lucy may be in danger too. I'm bloody sure she's guessed where Rasmussen's daughter is and has gone looking for her.' He pulled himself away from Elliot and tried to get up, accepting the inspector's help ungratefully.

'Damned women,' Mike mumbled. 'Why don't they ever tell me anything. I should have known when she left the dog in the car.' He leaned against the inspector as he looked down at his smoke-blackened trousers. 'Hell, I hope it's still legible.' He glared at Elliot, his eyes red-rimmed in his sooty face. 'There's a letter in my pocket. Explains it all.'

Elliot reached gingerly into Mike's pocket, his fingers touching paper and pulling it out. 'Yes,' he said, carefully smoothing out the paper, 'it's damaged,' his eyes ran quickly over the grubby pages, 'but the contents are still readable.'

He looked at Mike grimly. 'So that's it,' he said. 'Right, do you know where Lucy's gone? Tell me quickly and we'll get after her.'

'Let's get to your car,' Mike said, staggering as he moved away. 'I'm coming too.'

'Bloody hell, Mike,' Elliot said angrily, stepping hastily after him. 'You need to get to hospital.'

'No way,' Mike said, leaning heavily against the police car and fumbling at the door handle. 'Get us to Polkenan, and I'll tell you everything I know as we go. I worked it out on the way here, and there's no time to lose. And get hold of Mark Teague.

He's got to tell us where to go.'

'No, not the car.' Elliot grabbed his arm. 'Tom Peters is down with the police launch at the foot of the gully. We'll go that way, and I'll alert Carlus. She's only just left the village and can get back there along the road, so we'll cover both options.'

'And she can get the dog from my car,' Mike said. 'He'll take us to Lucy if Teague doesn't.'

'Well, Rosen,' Eric said, still standing in his dripping water-proofs, blocking the door of the fish loft, 'it took me a while to remember Teague was investing in property. Anyway, you've proved your point.'

His daughter was leaning against the windowsill, a black silhouette against the grey pane streaming with rain outside. She was quite still and did not reply to her father's comment.

'I'm sorry you had to do it at my expense,' Eric continued mildly, 'but I admire your enterprise. I didn't think,' he admitted candidly, 'that you had it in you. Were you involved in this ridiculous charade right from the start?'

Rosen shook her head. 'I don't know what you mean. I only took the photos.'

'And gave them to the Warne woman,' he said dryly. 'I gather you've collaborated with her before. Well, now that I see you can after all put your mind to something I'll help you as much as I can. I suppose you know which college you want to go to, but I'll find you people to give you work. I've plenty of contacts.'

Rosen stirred. 'And what about Kevin?' she demanded belligerently. 'What are you going to offer him?'

Eric stared at her. 'He's nothing to do with me,' he said indifferently, but his eyes narrowed. 'No doubt you've talked to him about your problems.' His gaze moved to the table, where a stray spiral of smoke was winding up from the laden ashtray into the thick air, and then back to his daughter.

It was not quite a question, more a realisation. Rosen said

quickly, 'Kevin only knows that you're against me. I haven't said anything else.'

'What is there to say?' Kevin asked, looking angrily from father to daughter.

'And Tamsyn?' Rosen demanded, as Lucy shot a warning glance at Kevin, who subsided reluctantly. 'What will you do for her?'

'Ah, Tamsyn,' Eric said.

'A decent funeral, perhaps,' Rosen said bitterly. 'It sounds as though that's all she's going to need.'

Eric shot an admonitory look at Lucy. 'I'm sorry you've heard already,' he said carefully. 'It's beginning to look as though Tamsyn fell foul of an attempt that was made on my life. The statue of Neptune just happened to miss me when it fell off the courtyard roof. I suspect it was loosened until only the dangling ivy held it and when I pushed through that ...' He gestured eloquently, showering raindrops on the floor around him. 'Tamsyn may have seen who loosened it.'

Rosen sneered. 'Oh yeah?' She shook her head. 'It won't work, you know. I saw you.' The last three words were laden with bleak emphasis.

Eric was watching her closely as he pushed his gloved hands carefully into the pockets of his waterproof. 'I don't know what you think you saw,' he said, 'but I believe you may be letting your dislike of me run away with your imagination.'

'That won't work,' she said promptly. 'I saw you in the gully that night, and I know what you did. I hoped I didn't. But now,' her face twisted, growing ugly, 'now, there's Alastair and Tamsyn.'

Eric moved forward suddenly and Kevin moved equally abruptly to stand in front of Rosen. 'This is ridiculous,' Eric said, coming to a halt an arm's length away from the young man. 'Look, Rosen, come outside and we'll talk about this privately.'

'No,' Kevin said urgently, glancing over his shoulder. 'Don't go, Rosen.'

'I won't,' she said. 'Anything that he can say must be said here.'

The noise Lucy had been vaguely conscious of for a few seconds became noticeably a siren, surely a police car racing down the village street. She edged to the door, just as Eric heard it too. He turned and grasped her arm, pulling her roughly back into the room, so that she staggered and fell across the sofa.

'Oh no,' he said firmly. 'I'm sorry about this, Lucy, but perhaps it's for the best. I'm sure you wouldn't want to go on alone.' One hand on the door latch, the other in his pocket, he looked across the room. 'Come with me, Rosen. There's still time.'

'No,' she said. 'I can't.'

He stared at her, thwarted, and the hand in his pocket clenched, half emerging, a glint of glass showing through his fingers. The siren was echoed by another wailing, this time from the sea, and Rosen glanced out of the window.

'It's a police launch,' she said, turning to face Eric. 'You can't get away now.'

His hand had gone back into his pocket as he opened the door. 'I've never failed yet,' he said grimly. 'Not even with you, Rosen. I'm glad of that.' He wrenched the door open and left, running sure-footed down the steps.

There was a shout from outside in a voice she recognised. 'Mike!' Lucy exclaimed. 'What on earth …' She hurried to the door, pausing to look down on the scene below.

The police launch was edging against the rocks next to Kevin's boat, but Mike had obviously leaped ashore, sliding precariously over the seaweed-draped boulders towards the sea. He flung himself down, grasping at the rocks with both hands, and hauled himself awkwardly up to a less slippery place. There he got to his feet and went racing after Eric, who was already well over the ridge, heading away from the village. Inspector Elliot was not far behind the pair, while Sergeant Peters came running with a couple of uniformed constables to the foot of the stairs.

'Are you alright up there?' Peters called.

'Yes,' Lucy said. 'But tell them to look out. I think he's got a weapon of some kind in his pocket.'

The sergeant pulled out his radio and began to speak urgently into it as Lucy came quickly down the steps, barely noticing that the rain had stopped. 'Please,' she said to one of the other policemen, 'my husband, Hugh Carey. Eric said …' she broke off as she saw the look on the policeman's face.

'I'm sorry, Mrs Carey,' he said, looking awkwardly at her, 'there's been a fire at Pennance. He's been taken to hospital.'

'Alive?' she asked, her voice barely audible.

'Yes, alive,' he said quickly, 'but I don't know how badly he was hurt.'

Ben's cold wet nose pushed into Lucy's hand and she bent over him, hiding her face against his damp fur as he licked her. She had no time to even wonder how he had got there.

'It's my fault,' Rosen said bleakly. She and Kevin had come slowly down the stairway to stand behind Lucy on the small apron of shingle. 'It's my fault Hugh's been hurt and Tamsyn too. I should have said what I saw.'

Before Lucy could speak there was another shout from the pursuers on the rocks and they all swung round to see that Constable Carlus had come into view ahead of the string of runners, blocking Eric's route.

Eric paused fractionally, looking over his shoulder and with a great leap Mike sprang at him, knocking him down. The two men rolled over and over, each struggling to get on top of the other, until Eric's grasping hand pulled up a lump of wet salty seaweed and ground it into Mike's face. With a yell of mingled rage and pain Mike fell back, rubbing at his eyes, and Eric scrambled to his feet, a rock in his hand. He swung it viciously at Mike's head, and the archaeologist dropped to the ground.

Eric was away again, with only Carlus in his path now.

The constable did not hesitate, moving forward to meet him, but a shout from the inspector made her falter and draw back. Eric's hand was half out of his pocket, but as she moved away he stretched out his other arm, thrusting her violently to the ground.

He was running hard now, avoiding the small crowd that was gathering at the top of the village street as he made for the cliff path. Only Elliot followed closely, but Mike had scrambled to his feet, blood pouring down his face, and was staggering after them. Carlus was also standing, her own face smeared green with seaweed and her hands badly scratched.

'No,' Mike gasped as he passed her. 'We'll see to it. Get reinforcements to the crevice. I'll swear that's where the bastard is heading.'

Carlus nodded as he lurched off, and spoke quickly into her radio, cautiously adding Pennance and Porthharrock to the list of places to watch. She clambered down the rocks to the small inlet below, where Tom Peters was talking to Lucy. The two policemen were shepherding Rosen and Kevin over towards the moored fishing boats in Polkenan cove and the police car parked beside the fish cellar.

'I see he found you,' Carlus said to Lucy, stooping to pat Ben. 'I got him out of the professor's car, but he wouldn't come with me when the sergeant detoured me to the top of the village. I tied him to a tree by the church path.' She glanced at the lead, bitten through near the loop. 'The inspector said he'd know where you were. I only hope he explains to the professor about the car's smashed window.'

Out of sight of the village now, the runners, fugitive and pursuers, were strung out along the cliff path. Rasmussen had drawn away from his followers when they slowed on the slippery shale beneath the tunnel of trees that led to the open cliff side. Once here Elliot found he was unable to gain on Eric, but could generally keep him in sight.

Mike had come storming on until he was on the inspector's

heels. 'The gully,' Mike grunted. 'He's going to destroy the evidence.'

'Perhaps,' Elliot panted. 'We'll never catch up with him before he reaches the crevice, but he won't have time to do anything much. And he'll be trapped. He can't get away through Pennance or Portharrock village, the alert will have gone out about both places.'

They rounded a rocky corner and stumbled to a halt, nearly bumping into the pair of walkers blocking the path, who were looking both alarmed and annoyed. Their alarm grew as they caught sight of Mike. He swore belligerently at them, his face scarlet through the mask of soot and green seaweed slime, his hands scratched and bleeding.

'Police,' Elliot gasped, reaching for his warrant card, but the walkers had already edged back, pressing themselves against the prickly sloe bushes to create passing room.

Ahead of them the two men could clearly see the green expanse of the promontory that led down to the Iron Age fort, and there was Rasmussen, racing fleetly across the open space. Mike swore in a continuous mutter as he and Elliot began to run again, regardless of the patches of slippery rock on the path.

'Save your breath,' Elliot advised curtly as they reached the promontory.

Rasmussen was nowhere in sight as they continued along the route. 'He's there already,' Mike groaned, his foot slipping on loose shingle. He regained his balance with a struggle, but the inspector did not pause, pounding on steadily. Mike was again close behind Elliot as they rounded the bluff that hid the gully, and nearly cannoned into him as the inspector stopped abruptly.

Over his shoulder Mike saw the smoke that was already creeping out of the crevice in the rocks that sheltered the skeleton in its Viking armour.

'No,' Mike bellowed, shoving the inspector between the shoulder blades and pushing past. 'We must stop him.'

'Too late,' Elliot shouted after him. 'He must have used an accelerant.' He ran after Mike, leaping the stream just behind him, unable to quite catch up with him as the archaeologist ploughed through the wet clinging heather. He reached him just as Mike was about to plunge round the granite column into the crevice, regardless of the flames and smoke filling the narrow passage.

'For God's sake, Mike,' he grabbed his arm and swung him forcibly away, 'you've been a hero at least once today. You can't go in there now. You wouldn't stand a chance.'

'What about Rasmussen?' Mike demanded, falling back as the heat began to scorch his already sore skin. He allowed Rob Elliot to pull him back along the slope, where they both sank down, crushing the wet bracken, drawing in great breaths of air.

'We don't even know if he's in there,' Elliot said, reaching for his radio, 'or if he just started the fire and slipped on up the gully. If he has, there'll be a reception party waiting for him.'

'And if not,' Mike turned back towards the crevice as the inspector put out an urgent alert, watching the smoke spiral upwards as the flames licked around the entrance pillar, 'he's made an impressive pyre for himself.'

'Thank God it's been so wet,' the inspector said prosaically, tucking his radio away. 'Otherwise the gorse and heather would catch. As it is, the smoke must already have been spotted.' As he spoke he caught sight of people racing across the quarry field from the village, and voices from above heralded the party of policemen and firemen finding their way down from the ruins of Pennance.

'I'll bet Rasmussen's gone up with his Viking,' Mike said glumly.

EIGHT

The smell of burning was still in Mike's nostrils, even though he had got out of his soot-blackened clothes and showered at *The Three Tuns*. Rob Elliot had lent him a pair of cords and a thick jumper in shades of green that suited Mike well. They were rather long in the arms and legs so he had rolled them up, creating a comic appearance with his frizzled hair and the skinned patches on his face and hands.

The small hospital room reeked with the competing smell of disinfectant. Hugh was propped up in the bed, his partially shaven head revealing the nasty wound with its ugly stitches that stretched across its crown. His heavily bandaged hands lay on the blanket and his face had taken Mike aback, the eyebrows singed off and the skin reddened and shining.

Mike lowered himself with unusual care into the plastic chair beside the bed, uncertain what to say. It was Hugh who spoke first, hoarsely. 'Thanks,' he said, coughing a little and reaching for the glass of water beside the bed.

'Here,' Mike said awkwardly. 'I'd better do that. What with your hands bound up.' He held the glass to Hugh's mouth.

'Not only our hero, but a ministering angel too,' said a light voice from the doorway, as a pleasant familiar scent of perfume wafted into the room.

Mike started, spilling a little of the water down Hugh's chin as he looked up at the two women standing there. Lucy came forward, waving Mike away, and took a handkerchief from her pocket to dry Hugh's face. Anna was staring at Mike, taking in his appearance, a shade of amusement crossing her mobile features. 'I see you and Rob are getting more friendly,' she said. 'I hope it lasts when he sees what you've done to his clothes.'

'You're back on form then,' Mike said to Anna, his eyes studying her pale face. 'Here, sit down,' he said roughly, standing up and pushing the chair towards her. 'You look as though a puff of wind would blow you away.'

'I'm fine,' she insisted, sinking down gratefully onto the seat, 'and I want to hear all about it. I can't believe I missed all the excitement.'

Mike had taken in the violet shadows under her eyes and the lines about her mouth. He was about to expostulate when Anna went on, 'And you worked it out for yourself, too. I'm seriously impressed.'

Mike scowled. 'I expect you'd have been able to sort it out much faster than I did, if you hadn't been such a glutton over Rasmussen's oysters.'

Anna's fingers tightened in her lap. 'He didn't care, did he? We could all have died.'

'He wasn't quite that callous,' Inspector Elliot said as he came into the room. 'He didn't worry about making any of you ill, but it was Alastair Drewe he wanted out of the way, and he provided an extra dose of domoic acid to make sure he died. It was in the vicar's cherry brandy, his favourite bedtime tipple, as Rasmussen must have known.'

'Domoic acid?' Lucy queried. 'Why that?'

'It's the toxin in oysters that causes amnesiac poisoning. The kind that was found in the discarded shells at Pennance.' Elliot put down on Hugh's bed the folder he carried and went out again, returning with three more chairs. Lucy took hers to the other side of the bed, while Mike sat on one side of Anna and Elliot on the other.

The inspector was examining her. He nodded, satisfied. 'You are feeling better, aren't you?'

'Yes, I'm fine,' she said valiantly, ignoring Mike's snort. 'Rob, you've had the lab results if you know about this domoic acid. Are you going to tell us the full story?'

'That's why I'm here,' he said, stretching out his legs carefully. He had changed his usual immaculate grey suit for jeans and a jumper. 'Just don't expect me to go into full details of shellfish poisoning, it's rather complicated.' He glanced across Anna to Mike, a pained expression crossing his face as he saw his clothes. 'You were a strong possibility as fall guy, you know.'

'Too obvious,' Mike said airily.

'Perhaps,' Elliot conceded, 'but you were lucky over the cherry brandy. Rasmussen made sure there was only enough for one left in the bottle, being fairly sure you wouldn't drink it if it was offered to you.'

'Too right,' Mike muttered, his nose wrinkling. 'Alastair thought there was more than that left,' he remembered, 'so that bastard Rasmussen must have tipped some away.'

'No doubt,' Elliot agreed. 'He certainly wouldn't have wanted any left. He was confident that the vicar would have his tipple, to which he had added a little dose of domoic acid. We have just got all the results back from the lab and he'd definitely added a smidgeon to the oysters as well.'

'How do you know it wasn't there naturally?' Lucy asked.

'It was fortunate for Mark Teague that his supplies of native oysters were low, otherwise Rasmussen would have been the only person to get Pacific oysters. Rasmussen knew that Teague always sent him that kind while other customers got the better sort. But yesterday they all got the Pacific ones.'

'And nobody else was taken ill,' Mike concluded shortly.

'Not only that,' the inspector said. 'We were able to recover some of the shells from other users and they showed no trace of domoic acid. There are lots of scientific details from the lab, but what it boils down to is that it was impossible for Rasmussen's oysters to have been the only ones to be contaminated naturally.'

'Was he building Teague up for a suspect too?' Anna asked shrewdly.

'I think he was the first choice,' Elliot said. 'There'd been bad blood between them. Everybody knew that. But that was only feasible if Rasmussen was the intended victim. Teague had no reason to dispose of the vicar. Nor had he any known interest in Roger Bland, so his usefulness as a prime suspect had waned in Rasmussen's mind.'

'And then Mike came along,' Anna said, 'and Rasmussen quickly figured out he'd be an ideal alternative candidate if foul play was suspected.'

The muscles in Mike's cheeks worked as he ground his teeth, glaring at her.

Elliot nodded. 'Of course. He couldn't have been better. The archaeological links with the Viking, the tie with Roger Bland, the connection with Alastair Drewe. You were too good to miss,' he told Mike blandly.

'Tell it in order,' Hugh croaked.

'Very well,' the inspector said. He drew a deep breath and looked round at the others. 'As Mike knows now, the story started over twenty years ago with three young students. They had perhaps little in common except their youth and a fondness for amateur dramatics, but one year they went together to stay on a lonely farm in Norway owned by one of Eric Rasmussen's cousins. It sounds,' Elliot said wryly, 'as though Rasmussen was quite different then, with a pronounced fondness for practical jokes. This inclination was roused by an accidental find on the far reaches of the farm.'

'Accidental be damned,' Mike burst out. 'Roger Bland would have been looking for just what he found.'

'Perhaps,' the inspector conceded. 'Then let's say the Viking burial site they found was unknown and unrecorded, and a marvellous discovery according to Bland's account in his letter.'

Mike grunted. 'It was pretty much what he reassembled for us, minus all the surrounding artefacts.' He groaned, burying his face in his hands. 'I still can't believe it.'

'Bland and Alastair Drewe expected that they would report the site, but Rasmussen pre-empted them, removing the armour from the warrior without their knowledge. Once it was done, he persuaded them to let him play a joke at a local Viking festival, where he suddenly appeared in a miraculous cloud of purple smoke, a striking figure with wild hair under his helmet, his mail shirt glinting in the light of the fire at the centre of the celebrations. Before any of the stunned participants could act, the apparition vanished. But the local reporter kept his wits and got a photograph, such a good one that it made the national press.'

Elliot leaned forward, picking up his folder and taking out a yellowed scrap of newspaper that he passed round. 'Bland enclosed it with the letter he sent to Mike.' As Anna examined it curiously the inspector went on, 'The interest it aroused put paid to any idea of replacing the armour where they had found it and pretending it was the ghost of the Viking who had appeared at the festival. Rasmussen wanted to do that, but Bland knew experts would realise the site had been tampered with. The mail shirt had been damaged ...'

Mike groaned, trying to run his fingers through his shrivelled curls.

Elliot cast him a sympathetic glance. 'And when Rasmussen removed it the skeleton became disarticulated. Bland knew it couldn't be put back together without showing traces of their activities. The students staying on the farm were bound to be suspected as the culprits. That would certainly put paid to Bland's hopes for a career in archaeology. And Alastair Drewe had never been comfortable with the whole plan, his religious scruples troubling him about desecrating the burial site.'

'He'd probably have felt the same about an archaeological

dig,' Hugh said with difficulty.

'No doubt,' Elliot agreed, 'but perhaps the scientific element would have soothed his conscience. This had happened purely to indulge Rasmussen's sense of humour and urge to fool people.'

Mike's hands clenched on his thighs as he muttered under his breath. Anna leaned across him to pass the cutting to Hugh, laying it on the sheet in front of him.

'After they returned I gather each of the three students went their own way, perhaps consciously avoiding the others. Rasmussen, the principal in the act, was the only one who went on with his life in the way he'd planned. Roger Bland's career in archaeology became a damp squib, never reaching the heights that had been predicted as his attitude became more and more eccentric. Alastair Drewe had been expected to reach the senior levels of the Church of England, but after a severe crisis of conscience he moved down here to the extreme end of the country to tend a rural parish, where he lived in relative obscurity.'

'Did they feel guilty over this?' Anna asked, puzzled, gesturing at the cutting that Lucy had picked up. 'Surely it wouldn't have mattered so much.'

Elliot glanced at her. 'Bland made it clear in his letter that they both dreaded having the incident made public. Perhaps it had grown out of proportion in their minds, perhaps they thought that Rasmussen would find it amusing one day to expose them.'

'Was he blackmailing them?' Lucy asked quietly, returning the cutting to the inspector.

'I don't think so,' he said as he tucked it back into the folder. 'There's no evidence or any kind of indication that he was.'

'Why did they come to this area if Rasmussen lived here?' Anna asked. 'Surely they must have known?'

Elliot shook his head. 'Rasmussen wasn't here when Alastair Drewe first came to Polkenan. The vicar had been here on holiday with Roger Bland in their earlier student days, and when the living came up at a crucial time perhaps he remembered happier days and hoped to regain something of them.' He spread out his hands. 'Who knows? I doubt that he did either. But Bland still came down on holiday, sometimes to stay with the vicar, sometimes to camp somewhere else.'

'And then Rasmussen came,' Mike said heavily. 'Did he know they were here?'

'Who knows?' Elliot repeated. 'They'd lost touch with him, and there's no real reason why he should have followed their careers.'

'But you think he did know,' Anna said, watching him.

'Yes,' the inspector admitted. 'I think he did. Certainly that Alastair Drewe was vicar at Polkenan and that Roger Bland visited him. I don't know if he was aware that Bland became the autumn eccentric at the huer's hut, but I believe not.' His grey eyes swept round the others in the room, all watching him with interest. 'I think it amused him to know that he was making them nervous about his intentions. But I can't prove that. Almost certainly, too, Bland's increasing sensitivity about Rasmussen exacerbated his growing eccentricity. He adopted that amazing costume and began to stay in the hut for longer periods. The locals knew him and tolerated his visits, perhaps,' he shot a look at Mike, 'thinking his habits natural for an academic.'

Mike grunted, drumming his fingers on his legs. 'Get on with it,' he said. 'Anna will probably keel over again if you take all day.'

'I'm alright,' Anna protested. Her pale cheeks had acquired a faint flush and her blue eyes were sparkling with interest, so Mike swallowed the retort he had been about to make.

'Well, you've got all three of them here in the area,' Lucy intervened. 'They must have co-existed for years, whatever the tensions. What triggered Roger Bland into action?'

'Two things, according to his letter,' Elliot said. 'The first was the knowledge that he was terminally ill with cancer, the second was the rumour of Rasmussen's impending knighthood. Bland felt Rasmussen's act, and their own acquiescence in it, had damaged both himself and Alastair Drewe, but left Rasmussen's reputation untarnished. Bland was determined to redress the balance.'

'Had he kept the Viking armour all that time?' Anna asked.

'No. They returned it to the original site and wearer, concealing the entrance and waiting for somebody else to make the great discovery one day. That never happened, so Bland went back for it when he'd made his plans. He was a keen sailor and often went over to Norway in his own boat. He made his last trip this summer and brought back the armour.'

'And the skeleton?' Anna was horrified.

Elliot smiled at her. 'No, he didn't do that. He found one here.'

Her eyes widened. 'Where would he find a skeleton? Oh,' she relaxed, 'a medical one, I suppose.'

'I'm afraid not,' Elliot said, enjoying the expressions crossing her mobile features. 'A few of the old churchyards along the coast are being eroded by the sea, and occasionally a body or skeleton is exposed. Bland removed one of these and dressed it up in its finery. Perhaps,' he added, 'with Drewe's sensitivities in mind, Bland has given us the location so the skeleton can be identified and re-interred.'

'Did he have his boat here?' Lucy asked. 'Is that how he transported the Viking?'

'Yes.' Elliot regarded her with respect. 'He kept the boat moored below the huer's hut, well out of sight. The villagers knew about it, of course, but there was no reason why it should ever have been mentioned. Bland simply sailed his boat round to the little bay below the crevice and transported the skeleton and the armour when the cliff path was clear.'

'And now it's all gone up in flames,' Lucy said. 'I suppose that's what Roger Bland had planned originally, when he brought in all that dried bracken. I'm so sorry, Mike.'

Annoyance and relief warred visibly on Mike's face as he said abruptly, 'No, it didn't. Elliot had Lynette Mellors supervise its removal. No one thought to tell me. Still,' he conceded reluctantly, 'as it turns out it's just as well they did move it. At least we've got everything safe.'

'So Bland set the scene for Rasmussen or somebody else to find,' Hugh said hoarsely. 'What happened then?'

'Once news of the discovery filtered through Bland went out early for his regular evening walk on Monday and detoured up to Pennance to call on Rasmussen.'

'Rasmussen must have known what it was in the crevice before he saw Bland,' Mike said abruptly. 'He came down with us at lunch time and saw the set-up then.'

'Oh yes, he knew straight away,' Elliot agreed, 'but he didn't know that Roger Bland was in the area. He wasn't really interested in other people and had probably never even noticed the eccentric in his cloak and broad-brimmed hat. I think he suspected Alastair Drewe was behind it all, and made his plans accordingly.'

Mike snorted. 'It would never in a million years have been Drewe.'

'Did Eric always plan to kill Alastair?' Lucy asked sombrely.

'We can't know when his thoughts took him that far,' Elliot said, 'perhaps not until after Bland arrived on the scene. Bland wasn't going to stay quiet for anything now, so he had to go, which really, in Rasmussen's mind, meant that the vicar had to as well. He'd be only too likely to work out what had happened, and he was already a man with a troubled conscience.'

'So Eric Rasmussen must have got a horrid shock when Roger Bland appeared at his house,' Anna commented thoughtfully.

'Especially when he heard what Bland had to say,' Elliot said. 'Bland was intent on nothing less than full exposure at a time when it would matter most to Rasmussen.'

'Rasmussen drugged him?' Hugh asked with difficulty.

'Yes. Sleeping tablets, presumably some of his second wife's supply, in wine. One of the village women, Jenny, the one who prepared the lunch yesterday, told us there were pills of all kinds lying around before Mrs Rasmussen killed herself. Jenny thought Rasmussen cleared them all away after her death.'

'Roger expected Rasmussen to kill him,' Mike declared. 'That's why he left the bloody letter for me. He'd written it before we met down here, it was addressed to the college. If,' he growled, 'Lynette Mellors had delivered it sooner, we might have avoided Drewe's death.'

'She couldn't know that it was important,' Elliot pointed out. 'And if she hadn't brought it down we wouldn't know anything about it until your post was forwarded or you returned to Oxford.'

'And Bland may have thought he'd die naturally, given his state of health,' Anna said. 'That might be why he wrote to you.'

Mike subsided, scowling, as Lucy asked, 'How did Eric get Roger Bland down to the crevice?'

'He probably walked down with him, waiting for Bland to pass out,' Elliot said, crossing his long legs carefully. 'Rasmussen timed his arrival there for after the guards had left, knowing full well that there wouldn't be anybody on duty later.'

'So he did tell Rosen to put off the evening shift,' Lucy commented.

'She's very definite about it,' the inspector said. 'And it makes sense. Rasmussen asked her to pass on the message with no ulterior motive. But when the need arose he took advantage of the unguarded crevice. He hoped that if he denied giving the instruction, it would put us off his scent. He hadn't,' Elliot added wryly, 'given any thought to Rosen's intentions.'

'I suppose she took the chance to get her photos?' Mike demanded.

'Of course,' Elliot replied. He ignored Mike's scowl and continued, 'Anyway, Rasmussen got Bland to the crevice and laid him out at the feet of the Viking, having taken off Bland's cloak and hat for his own temporary use. If Rasmussen didn't already know about Bland the hermit's evening walks, I'm pretty sure that Bland will have told him during his visit, perhaps dwelling on the times he'd passed Pennance or watched Rasmussen on the cliffs.'

Elliot heaved a sigh. 'So the walk fitted with Rasmussen's plans to have Bland seen elsewhere. He set off from the crevice, wearing Bland's distinctive outfit into Porthharrock and back, lingering in strategic spots to make sure he was noticed. But he passed the coastal watch station and failed to acknowledge the watchers. Bland always did, as very often one of them would be Alastair Drewe. Hugh,' the inspector nodded towards him, 'couldn't know that was what usually happened, although Alastair must have noticed the omission. Perhaps he just thought Bland was preoccupied. But Hugh did eventually realise that the hermit he saw that night wasn't as tall as Roger Bland.'

Hugh nodded. 'It narrowed the field,' he said painfully. 'Both Alastair Drewe and Mark Teague were as tall or taller than Bland.'

'So you went up to accuse Eric,' Lucy said crossly. 'Really, Hugh, you're always saying I rush into trouble.'

'It wasn't quite like that,' he said, sipping again at the glass of water Lucy offered him. 'I was suspicious, yes, but it still could have been somebody else we didn't know about.' Mike snorted. 'Anyway,' Hugh said, 'as soon as I mentioned the subject Rasmussen must have gone into action. He was already jumpy because of the photos that were appearing in the paper, and was probably beginning to feel there was a conspiracy.' Hugh lifted one hand towards his damaged head, then let it fall heavily back onto the sheet. 'He must have used the serpentine column on the sideboard. I didn't notice a thing, just felt the blow and saw stars. I suppose,' he said heavily, 'he was getting into the habit of killing. How is Tamsyn?'

'You were quite right, she didn't get that blow on the back

of her head by coming off the bike. She was hit once she was on the ground, but she's going to survive. She's already had her say,' Elliot said non-committally. 'But she's lucky you turned up when you did. She said her bike went from under her, and she doesn't remember beyond that.'

The inspector inclined his head towards Hugh. 'Judging from the marks on the tree that you spotted by Rasmussen's car, he used the old and simple trick of a rope that was raised as Tamsyn approached. He spread a patch of oil too in the same area. But the petrol tank burst when the bike hit the ground, leaving that wider slick across the road that caught light. He hadn't expected that, and it probably made him pause to rethink his plan.' His eyes were still on Hugh. 'The fire officers say the fire at Pennance was set with some sort of accelerant, they suspect some concoction of Rasmussen's. If you hadn't turned up in the lane he might have used something similar there to help things along, and the newspaper world would have had one less journalist.'

'Why did he want to kill her?' Anna asked.

'She has a fine nose for a story,' Elliot said with reluctant admiration. 'She called round early at the vicarage in Polkenan after the poisoning at Pennance, hoping to catch Mike and get some printable comments.' Mike snorted. 'She knew the door was rarely locked so she wasn't surprised to find it open. She went in, in case, she told us, Mike hadn't heard her knocking. While she was calling for him in the cottage she happened to notice the photograph albums on the sofa and happened to see a photograph of three young students, whom she recognised.' He glanced at Mike. 'It was lucky she did try to get hold of you and saw the picture. Rasmussen must have removed the album when he went to the cottage shortly afterwards, because we haven't found it among the pile you moved to a drier spot.'

'When was Rasmussen there?' Mike demanded.

'Well,' Elliot's face relaxed into a rare grin, 'your neighbourhood watch saw him twice, although he didn't know who he was until we showed him Rasmussen's photograph. Late on the evening of the poisoning, when you and the vicar were out at the pub, and early this morning, probably between leaving hospital and returning to Pennance, before the news of Drewe's death reached us.'

'Thomas was lurking behind the fuchsia hedge all the time, was he?' Mike demanded. 'I've a damned good mind to buy him a pint.'

'You do owe him,' the inspector agreed. 'Rasmussen presumably came the first time to poison the cherry brandy, and afterwards he came to replace the bottle, carefully smashing it and using it to replace the pieces of the one you broke. He didn't realise the paper-wrapped parcel below the bottle pieces contained the shards of Drewe's glass. Maybe the chaos in the vicar's kitchen unsettled his organised mind, or he thought the washed glass by the sink was used for the cherry brandy.' He lifted a shoulder in a slight shrug. 'That was probably when he took the album. The photograph in the newspaper was a bonus for him in one way, it offered a cast-iron reason for discharging himself from hospital.'

Elliot smiled suddenly. 'Thomas wasn't able to catch up with Rasmussen on either occasion, perhaps fortunately, or he may well have had a sudden accident too. He says that he only caught a glimpse of Rasmussen at the cottage each time, but he's prepared to swear to it.'

'How do you know what Rasmussen did with the bottle?' Mike demanded, leaning forward.

'A small detail,' Elliot said. 'You cut your hand on the bottle when it broke. There were no traces of blood on the pieces of glass we found in Drewe's bin. And no traces of domoic acid either. But there were distinct signs of it in the fragments of broken glass, and faint marks of it in the cherry brandy stains on the carpet, enough to test. That's where the domoic acid was found. It matched the traces from the oysters.'

'You did have a smashing time,' Anna murmured to

Mike. 'Lucky, though, otherwise you'd have really been in the spotlight.'

He ignored her, sitting back in his chair as Hugh said resignedly, 'I suppose Tamsyn naturally had to ask Rasmussen about the photograph she'd found.'

'Naturally,' the inspector agreed. 'And perhaps she was already suspicious of him, maybe because of Rosen's extreme reaction to the death of Roger Bland.'

'Did Rosen see Eric kill him?' Lucy asked in horror.

'No. She went along to the crevice at about half-past six, knowing there would be no guards there by then. She was just in time to see what she thought was the hermit leaving the place.'

'Surely Bland's body was there when she sneaked in to take her photographs?' Mike demanded.

'Yes. She was taken aback, but that young woman keeps a cool head,' Elliot said appreciatively. 'She didn't know that she was seeing Roger Bland, the real hermit, because she had never seen him out of his costume. She thought there was some kind of joke being set up, possibly aimed at you, so she took a couple of quick photos and got out of the place before there could be any reaction to the camera flash. She couldn't, of course, have known that Bland wasn't able to react. And she couldn't have realised that the sword had been moved.'

'Where was it?' Mike demanded.

'Lying beside Bland, hidden by his body,' Elliot replied. 'Ready for use.'

'What a nerve she has,' Anna declared admiringly.

'Yes,' Elliot said. 'She certainly has. And you owe her too, Mike. Her curiosity got the better of her, especially after you all left the pub so hastily. She got young Teague to take her home. He went on to see what was happening at the watch station, while she slipped down to the crevice. She didn't go far, just enough to see that Bland still lay at the foot of the Viking. She was determined to know what was going on without being seen, so she went up the far side of the gully and lay flat on the ground among the gorse bushes on the edge, watching the entrance to the crevice. Just in time too, because the fake hermit was pelting down the path towards it. He went in, and less than a minute later she saw Eric emerge and hide behind a bush beyond the column. Mike was already pounding noisily down the slope. She saw him disappear into the crevice too, while Eric came out from behind the bush and pelted up the gully towards his house.'

'Did she suspect her father then?' Hugh croaked.

'She still didn't know what was happening at that stage,' Elliot said. 'Remember, she didn't recognise the body on the floor of the crevice. And at that time she had no reason to suspect that the hermit she'd seen leaving and returning to the crevice was actually her father. Her biggest fear was that Eric had been in the cave all the time and had seen her take the photos. She knew he'd once had a reputation for practical joking and thought she was seeing some bizarre example of it.'

'When did she realise what had happened?' Anna asked bleakly.

'As soon as she knew who had been killed. She soon guessed that her father must have killed Bland,' Elliot said. 'She printed out photos she'd taken of Bland as the hermit and had them with her at the fish loft. I think she was trying to convince herself she was wrong, but she must have known she wasn't. After all, she knew Rasmussen had told her to cancel the guards, whatever he said afterwards.'

His mouth tightened briefly. 'She didn't go into hiding on her birthday just because the first photograph was published, but because the killer would guess he might have been seen. Mark Teague knew about the Viking photographs too, and thought that was why his nephew wanted to hide her away in his fish loft flat. Mark undoubtedly wanted to score off Rasmussen, and knew he'd be mad about the photos and even madder about his daughter sheltering with the Teagues, but I think he has a soft spot for the pair of youngsters as well.'

'What will Rosen do?' Anna asked. 'She can't go home, can she?'

'Even if it weren't a crime scene, Pennance won't be habitable. And I doubt she'd want to live there anyway. She's staying with the Teagues for the present.' He smiled at Anna. 'Don't worry about her. She's tough, she'll survive and get her own way too.'

'That's women for you,' Mike growled.

'But we needed you this time, Mike,' Anna consoled him. 'We wouldn't have managed without you.'

He eyed her suspiciously, then relaxed, his chest swelling as he said as casually as he could, 'I always knew you would one day.' He could not help adding, 'Given the habit you and Lucy have of getting into trouble I knew it wouldn't be long before I was helping you out of it.'

'We always like to give you an opportunity to shine,' Anna said sweetly. 'We wouldn't want you to feel too useless.'

Hugh winced as he muffled a laugh. Mike scowled.

MARY TANT'S Rossington series

The Rossington Inheritance

Lucy Rossington has put a promising career on hold, so that she can keep the family home going for her young brother Will – not an easy task, when home is an Elizabethan manor that the family have lived in for generations.

When the taint of avarice and deceit from the past seems to stain the present, it becomes essential to know who she can trust, not only for her own happiness, but also for the safety of her family and friends. Will she find out in time?

2007 ISBN 978–1–903152–21–8

Death at the Priory

Lucy Rossington doesn't need any more trouble just now. She's got plenty of that already at the family manor in an idyllic West Country valley.

So it's really the last straw for her when odd incidents plague the priory excavations, under the controversial leadership of the mercurial Mike Shannon. Does the death of an archaeologist mean more than a temporary disturbance? Is Lucy imagining evil where none exists? She is soon to know.

2008 ISBN 978–1–903152–17–1

Friends... and a Foe

Life looks promising for Lucy Rossington and her family – there is no way they could guess that in just a few days their happiness might be shattered for ever..

Old friends rejoin the family circle – one of them brings in their wake a secret that somebody would kill to keep. How could the Rossingtons know that this secret will cost them dearly?

2009 ISBN 978–1–903152–22–5

Players and Betrayers

The play's the thing. Or is it?

It certainly is for Anna Evesleigh, with her first summer production at Rossington Manor. She needs to prove to herself – and irascible archaeologist Mike Shannon? – that she can succeed with this.

But Mike's attention is elsewhere, and there is somebody else who has a watchful eye on Anna. For behind the scene another hand is gathering a hidden cast to play a drama of deceit and betrayal.

By the time Lucy picks up the threads of this latest mystery the shadow of that master hand lays heavily over her family and friends, and inevitably she finds herself in danger

2010 ISBN 978–1–903152–26–3

COMING SOON

The sixth novel in the Rossington series will be available
in Spring 2012. Watch the Threshold Press website for
further details closer to publication: www.threshold-
press.co.uk

ISBN 978–1–903152–30–0

Order these books directly from your local bookshop
or in case of difficulty direct from the publishers at
www.threshold-press.co.uk or phone 01635–230272.